This edition published in 2020 by Farrago,
an imprint of Duckworth Books Ltd
1 Golden Court, Richmond TW9 1EU, United Kingdom

www.farragobooks.com

ISBN: 978-1-78842-187-4

Printed and bound in Great Britain by Clays Ltd, Elcograf S.p.A.

THE ICE MAID'S TAIL

The No. 2 **FELINE** Detective Agency

MANDY MORTON

farrago

This book is dedicated to the tireless work of the animal rescue centres across the country, and to the lovely people who open their hearts to adopt the strays and the unwanted.

Chapter One

Winter had been kind to the town's inhabitants. Admittedly, there had been some harsh storms in November and the rain had been relentless in December, but by Christmas a weak but determined sun was mocking the festive season, and only the images of snow on Christmas cards gave any hint of winter. Undeterred, the feline population brought in Christmas trees, covered windows in fake snow, and celebrated in style with days of roaring fires and feasting until the New Year, when resolutions had to be made and work resumed. January brought frosts and some very cold nights, but nothing could have prepared the townsfolk for the February blizzards; an Arctic winter finally arrived, throwing lives into chaos, closing schools and businesses, and producing a general air of panic about food and fuel shortages. Roads were blocked, and pavements too dangerous to walk on without fear of broken limbs or worse.

Hettie Bagshot had never subscribed to any sort of convention. Her flourishing detective business was run on what she called an 'ad hoc' basis: if she and her friend and sidekick, Tilly, needed money for rent, they would answer the telephone which they kept in the sideboard in their small bedsit at the back of the Butters' bakery; if their coffers were full from past cases, they would both become quite deaf to anything that signalled a communication from the outside world. Now, as Tilly stared out in wonder at the latest overnight fall of snow, she realised with concern that, even though they lived in a bustling high street, they were actually cut off from everything – whether they wanted to be or not.

'Thank goodness we did the shopping yesterday,' she said, filling the kettle for their morning tea. 'There's no hope of going anywhere today.'

Hettie struggled into a sitting position in her armchair and pulled her dressing gown around her. She blinked at the extreme light flooding in through the window, which overlooked the Butters' backyard. Shading her eyes with her paw, she offered her first comments of the day. 'Well, the first thing they need to do is sack that weather cat on the local TV news. He stands in front of his map, waving his stick around and chucking in the odd technical word like isobars, jet streams, wind chills, and what was that new one he was enthralling us with last night? Noctilucent cloud! Whatever happened to "it's going to bloody snow"?'

'I'm not sure they're allowed to swear on TV before nine o'clock,' responded Tilly, as she stirred an extra sugar lump into Hettie's tea, hoping that it might improve her mood. 'I love it when he talks about icy bars. It makes me think of lollies on hot summer days.'

Hettie was about to clarify the weather term when an urgent thundering on their door put paid to their meteorological discussion. The dulcet tones of one of their landladies rang out loud and clear. 'Wake up you two! Me and sister have a rescue mission on this morning, and we need all paws on deck.'

Tilly skipped to the door and pulled it open to see Betty and Beryl Butter standing in the back hall in matching galoshes, swathed in plastic macs over their winter coats. The two white cats were waving saucepans about in a rather warlike manner.

'No time to waste,' said Betty. 'Get yourselves dressed for snow shovelling. Poor old Bruiser will be stuck in his shed and we need to get him out of there before the next load of snow comes. It's too cold for him in that garden and his door opens outwards, so he'll be trapped in there and freezing to death.'

Bruiser was an old friend of Hettie's and an integral part of The No. 2 Feline Detective Agency, as he drove Miss Scarlet, their motorbike and sidecar. He had been a wandering cat, but now, in his older years, he had settled in a purpose-built shed at the bottom of the Butter sisters' garden, lending a paw to any odd jobs they needed doing and acting as back-up muscle to Hettie and Tilly's investigations.

At the thought of Bruiser being in any sort of danger, Hettie sprang from her armchair and she and Tilly set about the bottom drawer of their filing cabinet, which they used as a wardrobe. Dragging a hotchpotch of multi-coloured thick socks and jumpers out, they pulled the clothes on over their pyjamas, finishing the outlandish look off with a pair of wellingtons each, purchased from Tilly's friend Jessie's charity shop earlier in the week.

They joined the Butters and the four cats discussed their campaign to free Bruiser from his snowbound shed. 'The first thing we'll have to do is get out the back door,' said Beryl, giving the handle an aggressive tug. The door gave way but the snowdrift that had gathered outside fell into the hallway in a miniature avalanche. Betty received the brunt of it, and her sizeable form collapsed in a shower of snow and ice. It took every ounce of strength that Hettie, Tilly and Beryl had to haul the cat to her feet, then they ladled the snow back into the yard with four of Betty's best non-stick saucepans.

'Well, you can see what sort of a job we've got on here,' said Beryl. 'Times like this, I wish we had a shorter garden, sister. It's going to take some time to dig our way to Bruiser's shed.'

Hettie agreed, but felt that breakfast would help to keep their spirits up. 'Maybe we'd get on quicker if we had a hot drink and something to eat?' she suggested.

Betty looked from Hettie to Tilly, realising that they'd been dragged from their beds without so much as a cup of tea. 'I'll tell you what – you two and sister make a start on the shovelling and I'll fix us all a nice hot breakfast,' she said. 'We're not opening the bakery up today, as no one can get through to us. We've got plenty of baps from yesterday, so I'll fill them with a nice bit of bacon, and how about mugs of hot chocolate all round, like they have in those Swiss chalets on the TV?'

Hettie's heart leapt at the thought of a hot breakfast, and she led the party out of the back door, ladling as she went and followed by Beryl and eventually Tilly, who benefitted from letting the others go in front of her. The snow was very deep and the drifts were high above Hettie's head, and to make matters worse it was freezing. There was nothing familiar about the backyard, just giant ice sculptures where the coal stack and dustbins normally stood, buried now in several feet of snow and ice.

The mittens that the three cats wore were soon frozen to their paws. They made progress, but had barely reached the fence that separated the yard from the garden when the wind picked up with a deafening whistle, blowing much of the snow they'd cleared back onto the path. It was to great relief that Betty's voice was heard above the noise, signalling that hot food and drink was waiting for them. Hettie, Beryl and Tilly slid back into the bakery, where Betty had set up a temporary breakfast bar next to the warmth of the bread ovens.

As promised, there were bacon baps and hot chocolate, but Betty had added a tray of flapjacks, hoping that the sweet addition would give them all an energy boost to help them with their task. 'I can't feel my paws,' said Tilly, pulling her mittens off with teeth that were chattering at the same time, 'and my wellingtons are full of melted snow.'

'You need to put plastic bags over your mittens to stop the wet getting in,' said Beryl, trying to be helpful. 'That's why sister and me have got our macs on over our good wool coats – to stop the wet. Takes a whole day to dry out a good wool coat, doesn't it, sister?'

Betty nodded enthusiastically as she chewed on her bacon bap, and Tilly – now free of her sodden mittens – warmed her frozen paws on a mug of hot chocolate. Outside, the wind became a blizzard and once again the sky deposited another load of snow onto the Butters' garden. Fears for Bruiser's safety grew.

When breakfast was over and the final dregs of hot chocolate had been drained from their mugs, the four cats tackled the snow with a new resolve. Inching forward as the blizzard blew around them, they got beyond the yard and made good progress across the garden. Heads down against the icy blast, they soon became part of the snowy landscape themselves, advancing towards Bruiser's shed like four giant snow monsters.

As quickly as it had begun, the wind suddenly died and the blinding blizzard became a gentle swirl of giant snowflakes. Hettie – who had led the expedition – was first to arrive at the shed. Although there were no visible signs of windows or doors, she knew she was in the right place in relation to the tall birch trees that bordered the plot and offered the only familiar landmarks to the snowbound garden. Bruiser's home was a giant structure of snow and ice. Now that the storm had abated, the four cats stared ahead of them in silence and great sadness. There were no obvious signs of escape from the icy tomb, and all that was left to them was to complete their mission with heavy hearts and frozen paws.

'Come on,' said Hettie, attacking the snow with her saucepan. 'There's no way that Bruiser could have survived a night in there. We need to prepare ourselves for the worst, but we have to get him out for decency's sake.'

The Butter sisters joined her to hack away at the wall of ice and snow. Tilly stood back and watched, paralysed with cold, her whiskers frozen and hot tears turning to ice as they tumbled from her eyes. She loved Bruiser like the big brother she'd never had. From the moment he'd turned up in the Butters' yard one winter's morning, she'd felt comfortable with him; he'd been their protector, a safe pair of paws when things got rough and totally loyal to her and Hettie, saving them from harm during their more extreme detective work. In short, Bruiser was Tilly's hero, and now, as she watched his shed being reclaimed from the snow, it was more than she could bear.

Hettie abandoned her saucepan and began to dig in a desperate frenzy with her paws until she struck wood. Betty and Beryl continued to ladle the snow away on either side of her, and eventually the door to the shed was revealed. The sisters stood back with Tilly as Hettie gave the latch an almighty tug, and the door gave way. Her heart thundered in her chest as she stood on the threshold, not wanting to be the first to discover her old friend's body. The shed was dark, as the window had been blocked by the snow, but Hettie could just make out Bruiser's old armchair. She moved forward into the gloom, preparing herself for the inevitable.

Betty, Beryl and Tilly stood in silence, waiting for Hettie's anguished cry; it came loud and clear, but not exactly in the way they had expected. 'I don't bloody believe it!' she shouted from inside the shed, following the remark with a row of even more creative expletives. She appeared at the door, waving a piece of paper in the frosty air and looking furious and relieved at the same time. 'He's gone to stay with Poppa,' she said, stepping out into the snow. 'He pinned this note to his armchair: "Too cold, gone to stay with Poppa, have taken Miss Scarlet. Bx" I'll give him too bloody cold when I catch up with him.'

Hettie was too cross to notice the rather outlandish ice dance developing in front of her as Betty, Beryl and Tilly clapped their frozen paws together and stamped their feet in sheer joy at the news. 'Time for a slap up lunch to celebrate, I think!' shouted Betty, a little louder than was necessary. 'Let's get back in the warm before we all catch our deaths.'

The thought of lunch defused Hettie's anger, and after shutting the shed door, the four cats shuffled their way back to the bakery and out of the snow.

Chapter Two

Hettie and Tilly were never going to starve while living in the Butters' old storeroom at the bakery. The sisters had offered the lodgings for a small rent to Hettie when she was down on her luck, and had thrown in daily luncheon vouchers to be exchanged for their pies and cakes. The arrangement had continued in blissful harmony and pastry ever since. When Tilly moved in to share Hettie's bedsit, the Butters had welcomed her with open arms and had supported the new detective venture with great enthusiasm and encouragement. Now that the business was prosperous, Hettie and Tilly could easily afford somewhere bigger, but their little back room next to the bread ovens was home and the only home that either cat had known with any permanence. They had everything they needed: a small coal fire to keep them warm; a large sideboard, which Tilly treated as a storage chest for life's necessities; a three drawer filing cabinet for clothes; an unused typewriter and some very random paperwork; a desk that doubled as a table; and a small sink and kitchen area, big enough for a pop-up toaster and kettle, with cupboards above for groceries. There were luxuries, of course: a TV and video recorder; a very comfortable armchair for Hettie; and a growing library of crime fiction books which were very much Tilly's domain. Since the demise of Turner Page's library van, Tilly had taken to buying her shockers from Jessie's charity shop in Cheapcuts Lane, where she and Hettie also bought most of their clothes.

'I'm soaked to the skin,' said Tilly, abandoning two wet cardigans, a T-shirt and a pair of pyjamas. 'My paws and ears feel like they're on fire, and they're all tingly.'

'That's because you're standing too close to the fire. You should let yourself thaw out gradually. Just pretend you're a fish finger or a chicken drumstick.' Hettie delivered her helpful suggestion and left her own wet clothes in a heap by the door. 'We'd better find some dry stuff to wear before we go upstairs for lunch. I wonder what we're having?'

Tilly pulled herself away from the fire and burrowed into the filing cabinet, emerging with an assortment of daywear. 'I think I'm going to put my winceyettes on first and stick a cardie over the top. It'll save me having to get undressed for bed later.'

Hettie laughed at her friend as she paraded about in a pair of warm, fluffy pyjamas which were slightly too big for her. She chose a warm jumper and a pair of second best business slacks for herself, and, after banking up their fire, they skipped up the stairs to the Butters' flat above the bakery to find Beryl laying the table for lunch.

'Sit yourselves down,' she said. 'Sister's dishing up, so I hope you've got your eating trousers on.'

Hettie had no time to reply as Betty pushed a hostess trolley through from the kitchen, laden with covered dishes which Beryl loaded onto the table. Betty returned to the kitchen and brought out a monster of a pie which she placed in front of her sister, ready for serving. Beryl wasted no time in cutting into the pastry, releasing first the glorious aroma of steak and kidney, then an avalanche of rich gravy which tumbled out onto the plates as Beryl wielded her serving spoon.

Betty lifted the lids on the dishes, giving a rundown of the options. 'We've got buttered mash, buttered swede mash, mushy peas and buttered carrots, and a jug of extra gravy for them that's inclined, so help yourselves and tuck in. There's a surfeit of everything now that the weather's closed the shop, so we'll all have to grow fat till things thaw out.'

Hettie considered Betty's words as she heaped some buttered mash onto her plate. There was clearly very little room to manoeuvre as far as Betty and Beryl's waistlines were concerned, but she couldn't think of a better place on earth to grow fat than in sight of a Butters' pie with extra gravy.

Tilly attacked her pie with both paws, demolishing the pastry first, then the steak, and finally the kidney, before turning to the swede and potato mash, which she spooned into her gravy, adding mushy peas for decoration before scraping, sucking and eventually licking every hint of dinner from the plate. She cleaned the escaped residue from her face and ears, paying particular attention to her whiskers.

'I hope you've left room for pudding,' said Betty, gathering up the empty plates. 'I've got one of my apple dumplings boiling away in a muslin bag out there. As soon as sister has made her custard, we'll be ready to dish up. Perfect for tucking under your ribs on a bitterly cold day like this one.'

Hettie and Tilly offered no argument, but sat waiting patiently as the Butter sisters busied themselves in their kitchen. Eventually they emerged with the giant pudding, robbed of its muslin, and a huge jug of custard. Tilly clapped her paws at the sight of Betty's masterpiece, and Hettie gasped with sheer delight as Beryl cut into the suet and the sweet, sugary apples filled the room with the unmistakable aroma of a late summer orchard.

The four cats settled to their puddings, saying very little until their bowls were almost empty. It was Hettie who came up for air first. 'I hope Bruiser and Poppa are OK,' she said. 'I wonder what effect the snow is having on Poppa's narrowboat? I wouldn't want to be anywhere near the river on a day like today.'

Poppa Phene had been a friend of Hettie's since her music days, when she had had her own band and travelled up and down the country with Poppa as her roadie and constant companion. Like Hettie, Poppa had settled in the town when their gigging days were over, and he now ran a lucrative plumbing business from his narrowboat, as well as adding an extra pair of paws to Hettie's detective business as and when required.

'Those boys will be fine,' said Betty. 'Narrowboats are lovely and cosy in the winter with their log burners, and knowing Poppa he'll have plenty of supplies stowed away until the thaw, so they won't go hungry.'

Beryl nodded in agreement and carried the subject a little further. 'When we were kittens, we had an uncle who worked a barge on the canals in Lancashire, and we used to spend our winter holidays with him. Most of those boats carried coal and wood, but Uncle Potts, as we called him, carried decorative china, tea services and lovely vases, all packed in straw – the sort of things that Clarice Clip and Josiah Woodworm used to make. We had some lovely winter holidays, tucked up snug in our little bunks, reading our Enid Blighter books.'

'Why did he transport crockery?' Hettie asked.

Betty picked up the subject from her sister. 'Well, some of those potteries in the north were getting fed up with the breakages, transporting by road over the lumps and bumps of the Pennines, so Uncle Potts got the job as his barge was much more gentle. It was the old way of doing things, really. It's all died out now, of course. Canals are mostly for pleasure boats these days.'

'And what happened to Uncle Potts?' asked Tilly, keen to have a proper ending to the story.

'He took up with a cat who did barge art,' said Beryl, adopting a rather dismissive tone. 'Drusilla Smudge, her name was. She called it barge art, but really all she did was paint up old tin jugs and cans and sell them at extortionate prices. She convinced him to turn his barge into a gallery of her works on the river. They had one of those launch parties, where they stick red dots on stuff they've sold and everyone wears a cravat. It was quite some party, by all accounts. They went to bed happy that night, leaving one of the gas burners on their compact cooker on by mistake. According to the first cats on the scene, you could hear the explosion for miles around. All that was left was a few bits of her barge art, bobbing up and down in the water.'

'And bang went our cosy winters on his boat,' added Betty, as she collected up the empty pudding bowls.

Hettie rose from the table, so full she could hardly move. The Butters' lunch had made up for the morning's exertions, and she wandered over to the window overlooking the high street to see if the weather had improved. The street was unrecognisable, and there was no distinction between the pavement and the road. She stared across at Lavender Stamp's post office, which had been closed for several days due to the weather. The snow was piled high against the door and window, and even the postbox was completely obscured by the drifts.

Lavender was possibly the most unpopular cat in the town. Her unpleasant manner and autocratic behaviour won her no friends, and the fact that she disliked other cats as much as they disliked her offered no room for redemption of any kind. She loved keeping her customers waiting, finding great comfort in humiliating any cat who crossed her, and thoroughly enjoyed the power of having the only post office in town. The Butter sisters had befriended her, putting her nastiness down to a thwarted love affair with Laxton Spratt when she was much younger, but it was an uneasy relationship, offered more out of sympathy than friendship.

Hettie glanced up at the windows above the post office. 'Lavender's curtains are still closed. Isn't that a bit odd at this time of day?'

'Perhaps she's trying to keep the cold out and the heat in,' Tilly said, joining Hettie at the window with Betty and Beryl.

'Come to think of it, those curtains have been shut tight for a couple of days,' said Betty, moving to the telephone and dialling Lavender's number. 'It's ringing, so at least the phone lines aren't down, but she's not picking up.'

Betty replaced the receiver and tried again, but there was still no answer. 'Maybe she's gone away, sister,' suggested Beryl, giving the tablecloth a cursory shake and putting it in the sideboard drawer.

Betty shook her head. 'I can't see her leaving the post office in all this bad weather – she keeps money and stamps on the premises. I think we need to see if she's all right.'

As the four cats stared down into the high street, assessing what to do next, Tilly detected the unmistakeable sound of Miss Scarlet, their motorbike and sidecar. Eventually it slid to a halt outside the bakery, with Bruiser and Poppa on board. 'Ooh look!' she cried, clapping her paws excitedly, 'they've turned Miss Scarlet into a sledge and there are chains on the tyres.'

'Well I never!' said Betty in admiration. 'Those boys can turn their paws to anything and they've got here just in time. We may need to mount a rescue operation.'

The thought of having to rescue Lavender Stamp from any situation filled Hettie with very little enthusiasm, but she was keen to look closer at Miss Scarlet's winter makeover. The four cats tumbled down the stairs and through to the shop part of the bakery, where Beryl pulled open the door to greet Bruiser and Poppa, who had just clambered off the motorbike. Miss Scarlet had been turned into a snowmobile, with makeshift runners under her sidecar for a smoother ride across the snow. As Tilly had correctly observed, the wheels were clad in snow chains ready to break up the ice and prevent any unwanted sliding on the perilous surface.

Hettie was impressed at the ingenuity and said so before rushing back into the bakery out of the cold, bringing a flurry of snow with her.

'Come in, you two. You're just in time for a little job that needs doing,' said Betty, anxious to shut the door against the icy blast.

Both Poppa and Bruiser were clad in leathers that were caked in snow, and they wasted no time in shaking it off all over the bakery floor. Beryl mopped around them as her sister explained the situation. Hettie and Tilly looked on with mild amusement, too full from their lunch to do anything else.

'So you want us to go over there and see if she's all right?' said Poppa. 'I think we'll have to go round the back. There's no chance of getting in by the post office door, not with them drifts.'

Bruiser nodded in agreement before adding his own thoughts. 'She got me ta carry 'er shoppin' round once. There's a small backyard that leads into 'er kitchen, but she 'ad a high wall with a locked gate, I seem ta remember. Could be a bit tricky in this weather.'

'Would a big slice of steak and kidney pie followed by apple suet pudding and custard help you to get over her wall?' asked Betty. 'We could have it waiting for you when you got back.'

Tilly giggled as Bruiser and Poppa scampered out of the bakery. With the inducement of two of the Butter sisters' signature dishes on offer, there was nothing they wouldn't do – even if it meant rescuing Lavender Stamp.

Chapter Three

Bruiser and Poppa were gone for some time. The Butters returned to their flat to wash up after lunch, and Hettie and Tilly went back to their room for an afternoon nap. The snow had begun to fall again as they settled themselves in their blankets beside the fire, and neither cat gave a second thought to what may or may not be happening across the road at the post office until Poppa woke them by knocking on their door. Tilly rose to let him in, and he was followed into their room by a worried looking delegation consisting of Betty, Beryl and Bruiser.

Hettie sat up in her chair, rubbing her eyes, and was about to offer one of her best temper tantrums for being disturbed when Betty spoke. 'Looks like Lavender's in trouble. We think she might have had a fall or something.'

'She's definitely in there somewhere,' said Poppa. 'We looked through her kitchen window, and there's pots in the sink and the washing up water is all iced up, like she's got no heating on. We hammered on the door but there's no sign of her. The upstairs curtains are closed, but there's a small window open in her bathroom. We need a very small cat to get through it.'

Suddenly, five pairs of eyes turned towards Tilly. There was no doubt that she was the smallest cat in the room, but she also knew that Lavender Stamp's bathroom was upstairs; as far as she was concerned, that meant she couldn't possibly help and she said so. 'I can't do heights of any sort, not since the Blarney Stone!'

Bruiser, Poppa and the Butters looked on, confused by Tilly's reasoning, which was never straightforward. It was Hettie who felt obliged to explain. 'We had a bit of an incident during one of our surveillance jobs last year in Ireland. We'd successfully tracked down Brendan O'Flummery, who'd been importing Guinness-flavoured catnip, and reunited him with his old mother. Before we came home, Tilly decided that she wanted to lick the Blarney Stone for luck. We queued up with all the other cats, climbed all the steps up to the stone, and just when it was Tilly's turn to lick it she had a panic attack. There was no turning back, because there was a queue behind us, so she had to be lowered down in an emergency bucket, blowing into a brown paper bag to sort her breathing out.'

Tilly began to lick her paws nervously at the very mention of the Blarney incident, but Beryl wouldn't be put off. 'Well, the best way to fix that is to face your demons, as our mother used to say – didn't she, sister?'

Betty nodded enthusiastically. 'Demon' sounded exactly the right word as far as Lavender Stamp was concerned, but Tilly needed more convincing. 'I just can't,' she said, getting more and more upset.

'What if we promise a cream horn every day for a week?' offered Beryl.

'And you can borrow our Agatha Crispy boxed set of Miss Marble videos,' chimed in her sister.

Tilly thought for a moment and pictured herself settling down by the fire with a cream horn and a favourite Agatha Crispy film. Eventually she caved in, receiving a cheer from the assembled company for her bravery before she'd even put a paw on the ladder.

Hettie and Tilly sought out as many layers of dry clothes as they could find. Their room already resembled Widow Twankey's laundry, with a string of clothes drying across the fireplace from their morning's work. The Butters buttoned up their good wool coats, adding their macs, and the six cats assembled outside the bakery like a set of overweight Russian dolls. Poppa and Bruiser led the way to Lavender Stamp's back door, clearing a path as they went, but the snow was relentless and covered their tracks as fast as they made them. The ladder that Bruiser had found by the side of Lavender's shed was propped against the wall at the back of the post office, and Tilly began to hyperventilate at the very sight of it. As a precaution, Beryl had brought one of the bakery's paper bags with her, and she coaxed Tilly into taking some deep breaths and blowing into it.

Hettie was now a little uncertain of the task that lay ahead. The rungs of the ladder were covered in snow and the climb to the open bathroom window looked far too dangerous for Tilly to cope with. 'I think we should abandon this plan!' she shouted as the wind took her words away. 'Even if Tilly makes it up the ladder, I'm not sure she'll fit through that window. It's just too dangerous!'

Tilly was a mild-mannered cat, even-tempered and the perfect foil for Hettie's volatile nature, but there were moments when she could be braver than any cat Hettie had ever known, and this was one of them. In one brisk movement she took up the challenge. Shaking off her top coat to give herself more freedom for the climb, she shinned up the rungs with her eyes tightly shut against the blinding snow.

Bruiser and Poppa clung to the ladder as Tilly reached the bathroom window. Not daring at any stage to look down, she reached inside for the catch, pulled the window fully open and heaved herself over the sill, falling into Lavender Stamp's bath with a thud. There was silence down below in the yard as the five cats waited for news of her safe landing. Hettie's heart was pounding in her ears, and she was convinced that at any moment now she would be revisiting her lunch, but the sickness passed as soon as Tilly's head popped out of the window. Triumphantly, she gave the claws up to stage one of the rescue mission.

As her friends waited in the snow, Tilly looked round the bathroom. Like Lavender Stamp, it was very plain: beige lino on the floor; plain white tiles from skirting board to ceiling; and no home comforts except a hand-knitted rug on the floor, badly fitted around a pedestal basin. Hanging on the back of the door was a dowdy wool dressing gown in grey, with matching slippers pushed over by the bath. Tilly shivered and moved to the radiator, hoping for some warmth for her frozen paws, but it was stone cold. The flight up the ladder had left no time to discuss what she should do if she was successful in gaining entry, and she suddenly realised that there might be something horrific waiting on the other side of the bathroom door. Was Lavender lying dead with a broken neck at the bottom of her stairs? Had there been a break-in, ending in her murder? Or was she sitting in her parlour, going through her accounts and just not answering her phone? That, perhaps, was the most frightening prospect of all. Tilly felt that she'd been brave enough for one day and decided to let her friends have a turn. She carefully opened the bathroom door and crept out onto the landing, stopping to listen for any sound, but all she could hear was the clamour of the snowstorm rising and falling outside. There were two more doors on the landing and they were both closed; she decided to ignore them and make her way downstairs, careful not to make any noise in case Lavender should mistake her for a burglar and attack. Getting her bearings, she noted the door that must be the entrance to the post office, and then, in the lower hallway, two more doors, both closed. Looking for the kitchen, she struck lucky first time, and her heart leapt at the sight of her snow-covered friends staring in at her from the backyard through the kitchen window. She rushed for the back door, turned the lock and shot back three bolts, climbing on a chair to free the final one. Hettie, in her keenness to be out of the cold and reunited with her friend, was first over the threshold, knocking Tilly off the chair and into a pile of tea towels which were waiting to be washed on the kitchen floor. On closer inspection, they were soaking wet, and had in fact been bunched up under the leaking radiator.

'It's like Shroud and Trestle's freezer in here!' said Betty, blowing some heat onto her paws.

'Well, as you've chosen to compare the temperature to our local undertakers, let's just hope that Lavender isn't laid out in her parlour awaiting collection, sister,' responded Beryl. 'Come on – let's see what's happened here.'

The Butters pushed forward into the hall, leaving Poppa and Bruiser to investigate the radiator. Betty and Beryl had spent the occasional fractious evening with the postmistress and were familiar with the layout of the house. Hettie and Tilly followed them into Lavender's parlour, which, on first sight, looked like the back room of Madame Tussauds. There were two armchairs, pointing in the direction of an empty, unused fireplace; one of them was vacant and the other held a cat-sized hand-knitted male doll, dressed like a character from an eighteenth-century romantic novel. There was another knitted cat leaning against a Welsh dresser, dressed as a post cat and looking like he'd dropped in for a chat. Hettie had seen Lavender's work before, as she often put her creations up for sale in the post office, but it was her need for a knitted companion that rang alarm bells in Hettie's head. The dolls seemed to be very much part of the furniture, the preferred companions to any living, breathing cat who dared to cross Lavender's path.

Beryl looked the knitted cats up and down and tutted. 'Poor Lavender. She's never recovered from Laxton Spratt. Toyed with her affections then hooked off, he did, but not before he'd given her fleas. She hasn't been close to another proper cat since.'

Hettie wanted to add that Laxton Spratt had had a very narrow escape, but she decided to press on with the rescue – if indeed there *was* anyone to rescue.

Beryl moved to the foot of the stairs and called out Lavender's name, listening for any response. She repeated the call several times as she led the party upstairs, pausing at the door she thought was to Lavender's bedroom. Knocking gently, she waited to be invited in but there was no reply. She called again, this time turning the handle and pushing the door open. The door gave way slightly then resisted any further pressure, as if something had been put up against it from the other side.

Beryl looked back, focusing on Tilly. 'I think this is another job for a small cat,' she said. 'See if you can squeeze your way in through this gap.'

Tilly shrank back. The thought of forcing her way into Lavender Stamp's bedroom was just too much, and she was aware that she could be facing a dead body on the other side of the door. Beryl could see that a further bribe was needed. 'How about one of sister's fresh cream trifles with chocolate curls all to yourself?' she offered.

Tilly emerged from behind Hettie but needed more convincing. 'Will that trifle have chocolate sponge in it as well?' she asked.

'It will indeed,' said Betty, keen to move things on.

'All right, then. I'll go in, but if she's dead I'll need more than a week of cream horns.'

The Butters nodded in unison and Tilly approached the bedroom door. Pushing as hard as she could, she finally managed to squeeze through the gap, only to be confronted by a suffocating wall of stocking stitch. She pushed and the knitting pushed back, squashing her against the door. She clawed at it, trying to fight her way further into the room, but the mountain of wool just wouldn't give way. It filled the space from floor to ceiling and there was nothing Tilly could do but try to escape back onto the landing. Eventually she managed to squeeze herself through the gap in the door, and found Hettie and the Butters waiting patiently for news.

'Well, what did you see?' demanded Hettie as Tilly tried to recover from her ordeal.

'I was attacked by a giant wall of knitting,' she gulped.

'Of course you were,' said Hettie playing along with what she thought was one of Tilly's jokes, 'but besides the knitting what did you see?'

'Just knitting!' Tilly cried, stamping her foot in frustration. 'That's what's blocking the door – a wall of orange, green and brown knitting!'

Poppa and Bruiser joined them on the landing and quickly assessed that some muscle was needed to free the door. Poppa leapt down the stairs and returned with an assortment of knives and scissors from Lavender's kitchen. 'If it's as bad as Tilly says, we'll need to cut our way in.'

Bruiser nodded and put his shoulder to the door, forcing a gap wide enough for Poppa to squeeze through wielding a large, sharp kitchen knife. He slashed away for several minutes at the knitting until there was enough room for Bruiser to join him, and the two cats made slow progress through the thicket of knit-one-pearl-one. It was some time before the foot of Lavender Stamp's bed was reached, and at this point Poppa and Bruiser withdrew for decency's sake to allow the female cats to take over.

By now the room was in shreds, with assorted colours of wool everywhere. The final hurdle was to explore the bed and establish whether there was any sign of life. Hettie stepped forward and stared at the solid mass of knitting. The foot of a bed was just visible, but there was more cutting to be done. She picked up the knife that Poppa had abandoned and began to slice gently through the remains of the obstacle as Tilly cleared away the discarded threads. The Butter sisters looked on, their paws in their mouths, waiting for the moment when Lavender's body would be revealed.

When the moment arrived, it was a peaceful sight. The bespectacled postmistress was sitting upright in a bright yellow cocoon of wool, her face the only thing peeping out of her igloo shroud. No one spoke until Betty broke the silence. 'Oh my, what a state to find her in – and all that wool wasted.'

'She looks almost nice now she's dead,' added Tilly.

Hettie stepped forward for a closer look at the corpse, then stepped back again very quickly. 'Do you want the bad news?' she asked. Tilly nodded, thinking that matters couldn't be much worse. 'Her whiskers are very slightly twitching. I think she's breathing.'

Betty and Beryl moved closer as Lavender Stamp opened first one eye and then the other, peering at her visitors in bewilderment.

'Thank goodness you're still with us,' said Beryl. 'You gave us such a fright. We had to break in to rescue you.'

Lavender's eyes filled with tears and she began to sob uncontrollably, and the giant ball of wool that encompassed her rose and fell with each sob. Eventually she was able to offer a stilted explanation. 'My heating broke, and I had no food and nothing to keep me warm. I took to my bed and just knitted and knitted to stop the cold getting in. Then I ran out of wool and tried to get up, but there was too much knitting. I think I must have passed out. I really don't remember.'

The sobs returned and Hettie decided that she and Tilly had had enough of Lavender Stamp and her knitting for one day. It was only a matter of time before she returned to her belligerent self, which would not be a pretty sight. The effects of the Butters' lunch had worn off and all Hettie was looking for now was a nice supper and a pipe or two of catnip. They excused themselves, leaving the Butters to deal with the fallout, and joined Poppa and Bruiser in Lavender's kitchen, where Poppa had dealt with the leaking radiator and fired up the boiler. The four cats let themselves out into the snow, and Hettie and Tilly returned to their room after waving Poppa and Bruiser off on Miss Scarlet. They'd decided to take up the Butters' kind offer of pie and pudding for another day, choosing instead to have a boys' night in with a fry-up in front of Poppa's wood burner.

Hettie and Tilly settled to a roaring fire and several rounds of sardines on toast, satisfied that Lavender

Chapter Four

Hettie had grudgingly given in to the installation of a telephone in the early days of her detective business, on the understanding that Tilly would answer all the calls and keep the telephone smothered in cushions in the staff sideboard when it wasn't in use. The addition of an answerphone had brought great joy to Tilly, as she loved leaving messages on it when she was away from home, delighting in playing them back on her return and revelling in the magic of hearing her own voice, much to Hettie's annoyance. The messages she left herself were of no great importance, more a passing of the time of day or a rundown of the shops she was visiting and what she'd bought in them. Hettie's phobia about telephones was based on the idea that anything loud and intrusive was morally wrong – and anyway, she preferred not to speak to cats she didn't know. This attitude was quite unhelpful if you were trying to run a business, but with Tilly as head of communications, Hettie was willing to suffer the occasional ringing in her ears.

The telephone in the sideboard that morning had been ringing for some time before Tilly shook off her blanket to answer it. Hettie refused to respond at all until Tilly shook her fully awake and forced the receiver into her paw. 'It's Fluff Wither-Fork from Wither-Fork Hall,' she said, as Hettie struggled to a sitting position in her armchair. 'She wants to speak to you on an urgent matter.'

Fighting back the tirade of abuse that was forming in her head, Hettie responded. 'Miss Wither-Fork, how lovely to hear from you. How can we help?'

Tilly marvelled at her friend's welcoming tone as she went into business mode to speak to the town's landowning aristocat. She filled the kettle and put two slices of bread into the toaster, knowing that Hettie would need a milky tea after fielding such an important call. They liked Fluff Wither-Fork and had worked for her before on a rather nasty murder case, which had ended in another lucrative triumph for The No. 2 Feline Detective Agency. Fluff had propped up her family seat for many years, taking on the problems of a crumbling Jacobean mansion house and substantial surrounding parkland; she provided employment for many of her sitting tenants, a duty passed on to her through ancient family covenants that she could neither break nor really afford.

As with most of Fluff's conversations, it was short and very much to the point and Hettie replaced the receiver before the kettle had boiled. 'Bloody kittens!' she exclaimed, 'and in this weather!'

Tilly was already intrigued but knew that the tea would have to come first. She filled two mugs, resting one on the arm of Hettie's chair, and Hettie sipped her drink thoughtfully, giving Tilly the time she needed to toast the bread and cover it in a liberal spread of butter and Marmite. The two cats disposed of their breakfast in record time, licking any traces of Marmite from their paws before Hettie was ready to share Fluff's conversation.

Tilly waited expectantly for her to begin. 'Well, it seems that Fluff has set up some sort of orphanage in the old Folly by Wither-Fork Woods. A couple of cats called Anthea and Preston Munch run it, evidently, and some of the kittens have gone missing, so she wants us to find them. They were out playing in the snow yesterday afternoon and haven't been seen since.'

'That's terrible,' Tilly said.

'I know. It's certainly not the weather to go out in.' Hettie added another shovel of coal to the fire.

'No, I meant it's terrible that they've gone missing.'

'In my opinion, one or two fewer kittens in the world has got to be a good thing,' Hettie replied, settling into her subject. 'You'd think Fluff Wither-Fork would have enough to deal with without taking in more mouths to feed on her estate, and kittens are the worst sort of cat! Ruining the furniture, bouncing off the walls, screeching and squealing all over the place, fussy eaters, out of control. What a nightmare!'

'But we were all kittens once,' countered Tilly.

'That's precisely the point – why make the same mistake twice? Anyway, I think we'll have to take the case on but I've no idea how we'll get there. Bruiser's gone to Poppa's with Miss Scarlet and there won't be any other transport in this weather. Even if Clippy Lean's bus could negotiate the high street, it would never get up Wither-Fork Hill. That old wreck breaks down at the slightest excuse.'

'What's a folly?' asked Tilly, keen for more details on their new assignment.

'It's one of those silly buildings that cats with more money than sense stick up to look at from the big house. They're usually completely useless. That's why they call them follies, I suppose.'

'I thought folly meant a mistake,' Tilly said, warming to the subject.

'That's exactly it. A bloody big mistake, especially if you fill the thing with a load of unwanted kittens and Anthea and Preston Munch – whoever they are.'

Tilly stared out of the window into the backyard as she put the kettle on again, hoping that another milky tea might improve Hettie's mood. 'I think there's been even more snow overnight,' she said. 'If those kittens have been out all night, they've probably frozen to death.'

'My thoughts entirely,' said Hettie, 'so not much point in hurrying out to Wither-Fork Hall on foot – we'd never get there in these temperatures. We'll just have to wait until Bruiser turns up on Miss Scarlet and see what's to be done then. In the meantime, I think we should have another round of toast, this time with some of that salmon paste you got us from Malkin and Sprinkle.'

Tilly was about to put the bread in the toaster when there was a polite knock at their door. Cursing under her breath, Hettie pulled her dressing gown around her, cross that yet another interruption to her morning was about to present itself. It was Bruiser, returned from his boys' night out on Poppa's narrowboat and looking cold and in need of a hot drink. 'I thought I'd better see if we 'ad any more rescues ta do,' he said, crossing to the fire to defrost his paws. 'It's wicked out there. Everythin's frozen solid, roads are like ice rinks and the town's deserted. Elsie Haddock lurched out in front of us as we drove up the high street. She says 'er fish fryer's frozen solid in 'er front shop. Poppa's seein' what 'e can do for 'er. We was goin' to 'ave a slap-up breakfast at Bloomers, but Molly's 'ad to close up 'er café 'cos she's got no deliveries. All she's got is tinned stuff and a few bits in 'er freezer.'

'I can offer you toast and salmon spread,' said Tilly, much to the annoyance of Hettie, who felt she was first in the queue.

Bruiser was about to accept her kind offer when yet another knock came at the door. Tilly answered it and the Butter sisters marched in with Poppa, fresh from Elsie Haddock's fish fryers.

'It's like Piccalilli Circus today,' grumbled Hettie, mostly to herself.

'Sister and I have decided to impose a state of emergency,' announced Beryl. 'Lavender Stamp is holed up in our box room, claiming that she's having a "crisis of confidence", whatever that means, and our friends up and down the high street are in dire need of supplies, so sister and me are making up food bags and we hoped you might like to deliver them for us.'

Hettie opened her mouth to point out that they had just been hired to search for some kittens when Betty Butter took over what had become an urgent call to arms. 'We've got plenty of pies, cakes and bread ready-baked, and it's all sitting doing nothing. There's no point in opening the shop when no one can get to us in this weather, so we've got to get to them. I'm making the bags up and sister's putting the list of deliveries together, so look sharp – we need all the help we can get.'

There was no time for argument. Having delivered their rescue plan, the formidable Butter sisters bustled out, leaving Hettie, Tilly, Bruiser and Poppa in a state of flux. 'Well, that's told us,' said Hettie, wishing she'd got dressed before her room filled with visitors.

'I suppose we could do the deliveries on our way to Wither-Fork Hall.'

'Why do you want to go to Wither-Fork on a day like this?' asked Poppa.

'Kittens!' shouted Tilly as she rummaged through the bottom drawer of the filing cabinet, looking for her extra warm business cardigan. 'Anthea and Preston Munch have lost some in the snow, and Fluff Wither-Fork has hired us to look for them.'

'Who on earth are Anthea and Preston Munch?' sniggered Poppa.

'That's them missionaries who got thrown outta St Kipper's fer upstagin' the vicar with their happy clappy stuff, isn't it?' Bruiser said. 'All over the *Daily Snout*'s front page it was, a while back now. I think they'd just come back from Africa after spreadin' the word. Paper said they'd met with hostile resistance from the natives due to a mix up over the Old and New Testaments. Somethin' to do with Abraham takin' five loaves and two fishes up a mountain.'

Hettie, Tilly and Poppa stared at Bruiser in amazement. He rarely showed interest in anything that wasn't a motorbike bible, but clearly the Munches' failed overseas mission had resonated with him sufficiently to store it in his memory.

'Well, that's all we need,' grumbled Hettie. 'A pair of born-again crisp packets and a litter of lost kittens!'

'I think you mean born-again Christians,' said Tilly, giggling at Hettie's irreverence.

'No I don't, and with a name like Munch I think my description is perfect.'

Hettie's ambivalence to any sort of religion was part of who she was. Nothing had ever convinced her that any cat walking the earth should possess a divine right to indoctrinate others into believing that there was a better life waiting if you stuck to the rules of a God who allowed so much misery and destruction. She regarded the Bible as a glorious book of stories, but had never felt the slightest urge to live her life by them. Tilly, however, was willing to hedge her bets and did her best to steer Hettie away from the possibility of damnation whenever she could, but she knew in her heart that if Anthea and Preston Munch were purveyors of the so-called good book there would be problems ahead for the case.

After several rounds of salmon paste on toast and milky tea, Poppa and Bruiser went out to check on Miss Scarlet, giving Hettie and Tilly time to get dressed and present themselves in the Butters' bakery for further orders. The bags of food were ready with names pinned to them, including four labelled 'No. 2 FDA', the shortened version of Hettie's detective business. Betty opened the shop door so that Hettie and Tilly could load them into the sidecar. It was a bit of a squash, as Poppa had insisted on joining them for the kitten hunt at Wither-Fork Hall. He rode pillion with Bruiser, and Hettie and Tilly crammed themselves into the sidecar with the Butters' rescue bags.

Betty and Beryl waved them off and Miss Scarlet slid down the icy high street, stopping first at Molly Bloom's café to deliver her food bag. Molly was delighted with the Butters' generosity, and with Poppa who delivered it. The two cats had come to an understanding over the past few months, and had been spending more and more time together.

Next came Hilda Dabbit, who ran the dry-cleaners, and Bruiser did the honours this time. Hilda was so grateful that she offered to dry-clean one of his fancy waistcoats for free next time he passed by. Bruiser had never had anything dry-cleaned in his long life, and most of his clothes were allowed to disintegrate with wear, but he appreciated the offer.

Elsie Haddock's fish and chip shop was next on the list and it was Poppa's turn to be benevolent. Elsie was thrilled with her food bag, as she'd made herself heartily sick of fish since the snow arrived, and a Butters' steak and kidney pie was just what she was looking for. Now that Poppa had fixed her fryer, she looked forward to adding some chips to her meal and promised Poppa a free fish supper when the weather improved.

With three food bags delivered, things were becoming a little less crowded in the sidecar. Hettie agreed to deliver the next bags to Meridian Hambone, the oldest cat in the town and proprietor of the high street's hardware store. Betty had labelled two bags for Hambone's, as Meridian lived with her son, Lazarus, who ran the motorbike and scrap business from the backyard. Lazarus also procured a number of almost white goods to sell in his mother's shop from time to time on a no-questions-asked basis.

The snow had begun to fall again and Hettie shivered at the door to Meridian's store. It took some time for the ancient cat to descend from her flat above and make her way through the jumble of paraffin cans, garden tools, paint tins and unsold Christmas decorations which littered the shop in no particular order. When the door finally opened, Hettie was greeted with an ecstatic toothless grin as Meridian gratefully clawed the food bags out of her paws, shutting the door quickly to keep the heat in and leaving Hettie to shiver her way back to Miss Scarlet without the slightest word of thanks.

Poppa arrived back at the same time, having delivered a food bag to Dorcas Ink, the town's printer. Dorcas's printing works was down a rough track at the back of Elsie Haddock's, and Poppa had had a difficult job getting through the snowdrifts. Dorcas had been surviving on Jammy Dodgers since the snow struck and had been thrilled to receive the Butter sisters' cake and pastry lifeline.

With almost all the deliveries completed, it was time for the four cats to make their way to Wither-Fork Hall. Except for their own, there was one bag left, addressed to Tilly's friend Jessie who ran a charity shop in Cheapcuts Lane, and they decided to drop it off later on their way home.

The snow was blinding now, and Bruiser was grateful that there was no other traffic about as Miss Scarlet slid perilously across the ice from one side of the road to the other. Having absolute trust in Bruiser's driving, Tilly was exhilarated by the ride. 'Ooh! It's much more exciting than rides at the fair,' she screamed above the roar of the engine. 'It's just like being in one of those two-cat blobsleighs on the television.'

'Bob!' corrected Hettie, causing Tilly to duck her head down in case they were going to hit something.

By the time they reached the bottom of Wither-Fork Hill, the snow was thicker than ever. The snow chains that Bruiser and Poppa had attached to Miss Scarlet's tyres were frozen solid and Bruiser, who was rarely defeated, shook his head. 'We're goin' ta 'ave ta leg it from 'ere. There's no way she's goin' ta make it up that hill.'

Clutching their lunch bags, the friends abandoned Miss Scarlet and set off up Wither-Fork Hill. The sharp incline that defeated many a motorist on sunny days had become a glaciated mountain to climb. With drifts three cats high on either side, and the blizzard hitting them head-on, progress was slow. Bruiser led the way with Poppa, gallantly shielding Hettie and Tilly from the worst of the icy blast. By the time they reached the summit, they resembled four animated snow cats and were most grateful to see the gatehouse to Wither-Fork Hall, where Fluff now lived, choosing the comfort of the small turreted cottage instead of the large draughty rooms of the main house.

'Good gracious, what a sight!' said Fluff, throwing the door open to her snow-covered visitors. 'I really am most grateful that you've even attempted to get to me in this shocking weather. Blackberry! Help our guests out of their coats and put them to dry in the kitchen, will you?'

A pretty black and white cat appeared in the hallway with a nod of recognition to Fluff's newly arrived visitors. Blackberry Tibbs was a talented artist who created life-size models of cats for TV, films and carnivals, but she had also become Fluff Wither-Fork's maid-of-all-work in a companionable sort of way. The position gave her plenty of time to be creative, and a free roof over her head in a small bedsitter at Wither-Fork Hall. She had been one of Fluff's resident allotment holders, but her cooking skills and sunny disposition had made a great impression on her landlady and now she was very much part of Fluff's inner circle.

Blackberry staggered through to the kitchen under the weight of the coats and food bags, and Fluff opened the door to her parlour, where there was a blazing fire. 'Sit yourselves down and get warm. You're just in time for lunch. I'll go and get Blackberry to lay some extra places in the dining room.'

Now that her nostrils had thawed out, Hettie was suddenly aware of the smell of roast chicken that filled the room. It was some time since she and Tilly had visited the gatehouse, and then it had been under very sad circumstances, but there was no trace of sadness now. Fluff had made the place her own: warm, cosy and with just the right amount of inherited treasures dotted about the room. Highly polished silver candlesticks glinted from the mantelpiece; a delicate crystal chandelier hung from the ceiling; leather-bound books lined the bookcases; and an assortment of highly decorated Chinese vases was stunningly eye-catching.

The climb up Wither-Fork Hill had been exhausting. Hettie sank into Fluff's brocade sofa, happy to spend the rest of her life in such warm comfort, but when Fluff returned from the kitchen to announce that Blackberry was ready to serve lunch, she was first in the stampede through to the dining room, hotly followed by Poppa, Bruiser and eventually Tilly, who had nodded off on a small velvet footstool by the fire.

Chapter Five

The dining room was equally inviting, a far cry from the barn of the Great Hall at the big house. No sooner were they seated than Blackberry arrived from the kitchen with the first plates of food, which she put down in front of Hettie and Tilly, returning quickly with two more for Bruiser and Poppa and bringing Fluff's in last on the principle of guests first. 'Shall I stay to clear away, Miss?'

'No thank you, Blackberry. This all looks lovely. You'd better make tracks for the Hall and get the suppers underway. I'll come across shortly with Miss Bagshot and her team.'

Blackberry almost curtsied and left the dining room. Fluff turned back to her guests, who sat politely waiting to start. 'We're under siege from my allotment tenants at the moment,' she said, lifting her knife and fork. 'After the first night of snow, I invited them into the Great Hall at the House. I just couldn't have them freezing to death in their old sheds and chalets. Bonny Grubb resisted, of course. I'll never quite understand why gypsy cats are so keen on sleeping in caravans. She soon changed her tune when I threw in three meals a day and a massive fire in the baronial grate. Thank goodness it's only temporary. Poor Blackberry has been run ragged by their demands. I've set them all on peeling the old wallpaper off the walls, just to give them something to do. Fascinating, really – they've revealed some fresco work underneath, which will be a nice talking point for the visitors in the summer.'

Hettie had been right about the chicken, and the addition of creamy mashed potatoes flooded with gravy was heaven after the climb up Wither-Fork Hill. Except for Fluff's gentle banter about her tenants and the impact of the weather, Hettie, Tilly, Bruiser and Poppa made no attempt at conversation until their plates were cleaned, resisting the urge to lick the final traces of gravy from them for the sake of good manners.

Leaning back in her chair and thoroughly satisfied with her lunch, Hettie felt that she should broach the subject of the missing kittens, as Fluff seemed to have forgotten why they were there. 'I assume the kittens are still missing?' she asked.

Fluff slowly shook her head. 'Missing, presumed dead, I fear. There was hope until this damned blizzard kicked off again, but it was minus twenty out there last night. The only hope is that they've found some shelter in the woods, but they should have turned up by now. I'm afraid you'll be looking for bodies – not ideal,

I know, but one has to make some attempt to find them and give them a decent burial. The Munches are distraught. Anthea has had to be sedated and Preston spends most of his time on his knees in the snow, praying to a higher authority for their safe return.'

'What happened exactly?' asked Hettie.

'Well, as far as I can gather from Preston, Anthea let the kittens out after her Bible instruction class yesterday lunchtime. She said they were distracted by the snow. They played quite nicely, building snow cats and tobogganing on old tea trays until she called them in for tea, and that's when she discovered that three of the female kittens were missing. We heard the screeching from Anthea over at the Hall while I was inspecting one of the frescos, so we all bundled ourselves up and joined the search. The cold defeated us in the end. The Mulch sisters had to go in first, as Dahlia decided she had frostbite. Rooster Chit sent Desiree and young Blight in and stayed out with Preston for most of the night, and Apple Chutney and Blackberry were up at first light this morning, but there was just no sign of them.'

Hettie felt at this point that she needed some background on the orphanage and the Munches. 'What made you decide to open an orphanage at the Folly?' she asked.

'It was down to Anthea and Preston, really. They're a sweet couple – well meaning if a little too Godly for my taste, but I was impressed by their concerns over the alarming amount of abandoned kittens in our area. They're the sort of cats who set out to save the world, whether it needs to be saved or not. Preston approached me at our Christmas Fair here at the Hall and asked if they could set up some sheds on the allotment to give the kittens a home. He told me they'd just returned from Africa as missionaries and were looking for a place to set up an orphanage of sorts. I felt that the allotments weren't entirely suitable, so I offered them the old Folly by the woods. Preston did a marvellous job of converting it, and the Munches and ten orphaned kittens moved in at the beginning of January. They've been no trouble at all, and the little kittens are so well behaved. Anthea has a way with them: she marches them everywhere, just like a mother and her ducklings. I feel for her, I really do, and Preston is such a thoughtful cat – he does everything for Anthea as she's always so busy with the kittens. I'm surprised they don't have any of their own, but one doesn't like to pry. Anyway, you must come across and meet them. I'll get your coats from the kitchen and we'll set out for the Hall.'

'Blimey,' said Poppa, after Fluff had left the dining room. 'No happy ending with this case, I don't reckon. It's a shame for it to happen to such kind cats. I wonder if they'll keep the orphanage after this?'

'Well, they've still got seven kittens,' said Tilly brightly, as Fluff returned under a mountain of coats and food bags.

Hettie, now full of chicken and mashed potato, left the bags by Fluff's hat stand in the hall to collect later. Fluff Wither-Fork strode out into the deep snow and the four cats followed on across the parkland to Wither-Fork Hall. Tilly gave up halfway, as she was the shortest in the company and the snow was up to her shoulders; Bruiser picked her up and swung her onto his back, where she clung on gratefully until they reached the huge oak door to the Jacobean mansion.

Hettie and Tilly were no strangers to Wither-Fork Hall. The last time they were called in, the house had been in a real state of disrepair with buckets placed strategically throughout the rooms in service to the vast number of missing slates on the roof. Fluff had had some luck when one of her tenants left her a sizeable legacy in recognition of her kindness, and she had put the money to good use, making some urgent repairs and opening the Hall to visitors throughout the summer and autumn months. Her allotment tenants had been encouraged to 'muck in', as she called it, lending a paw when and wherever it was needed in exchange for their own parcels of land on the Wither-Fork allotments. The arrangement had worked well, and the house was gradually being restored to its original splendour.

On entering the Great Hall it was clear to Hettie that the most recent part of the restoration was definitely a work in progress. At one end, the baronial inglenook stone fireplace was ablaze, with cat-sized logs throwing out a furnace of heat across the flagstone floor. Around the walls were planks of makeshift scaffolding, giving a platform to several cats who were scraping away at the walls, some with their claws and others with paint scrapers. At the other end, a number of camp beds were piled with blankets and a long trestle table set out with bowls, plates and spoons. Fluff had clearly made her residents comfortable during the severe cold snap. Hettie recognised several of the cats from the allotments, and offered a wave of recognition.

Fluff moved to the giant French windows that looked out across the gardens and her fountain walk. The statues of playful cherub cats now looked more like grotesque ice sculptures, frozen in time, than their joyful summer selves. In the distance stood the Folly, a round, four-tiered miniature castle, complete with castellated battlements and a flagpole which – in better weather – flew the Wither-Fork coat of arms.

'I'm sorry it's such a trudge over to the Folly,' said Fluff, pulling open the French windows and letting a blast of icy air into the hall. 'Would you like me to come and do the introductions to the Munches?'

Hettie shook her head. 'I don't think we need any introductions after what you've told us. I feel we know them already.'

The hint of sarcasm in Hettie's voice seemed not to have registered with Fluff. She retreated towards the fireplace to admire the newly revealed fresco, leaving Hettie, Tilly, Bruiser and Poppa to strike out for the

Chapter Six

The door to the Folly was open as they approached, and Hettie could hear voices as she drew closer. Not wishing to intrude, she paused on the threshold and listened. 'Now my dear, there's no point in keeping up with this crying and wringing of your paws – you'll make yourself ill. We must trust in the Lord that He may deliver us from this situation and move on, or we shall be lost in despair. We still have our boys to consider, so we must continue on our righteous path.'

Hettie waited for a response to the male cat's voice, but all that came was a pitiful sobbing which she assumed to be coming from Anthea Munch. She decided that now would be a good time to announce herself and tapped on the open door.

Preston Munch appeared and stared out at Hettie, then beyond her to Tilly, Poppa and Bruiser. 'Can I help you?' he asked, treating the delegation with suspicion.

'Well, I hope we may be able to help you,' replied Hettie. 'Miss Wither-Fork has sent for us in connection with your missing kittens. We are The No.

2 Feline Detective Agency, I'm Hettie Bagshot, and my assistants are Tilly, Poppa and Bruiser.'

Preston Munch was about to respond when Anthea appeared in the doorway, red and puffy eyed, her ginger fur matted and streaked with tears. 'Have you news?' she cried. 'Please tell me you've found them. Blessed be the fur on their innocent little heads.' Anthea sank to the floor and began to hug Hettie's legs; she was clearly hysterical.

'I'm afraid there's no news at the moment, good or bad,' said Hettie, struggling to free herself gently from Anthea's clutches.

Preston came to her rescue, lifting the distressed cat to her feet. 'Please forgive Anthea. She is greatly troubled at present and not at all herself. Come in out of the cold and warm yourselves. Anthea was about to make some hot chocolate, weren't you my dear?' Anthea nodded her head, allowing a fresh set of tears to splash onto her white starched apron.

Bruiser and Poppa remained outside, not wishing to involve themselves in Hettie's first meeting with the Munches. They decided that a scout around the area might be helpful, especially as it was doubtful that the missing kittens had survived. Bruiser was keen to save Hettie and Tilly from making a gruesome find; if there were bodies to be recovered, he felt as their protector that it was his job.

Hettie and Tilly followed Preston into a rather quaint, circular room, a little stark in its decoration. Grey stone walls with leaded light slits rather than windows gave very little light once the door was closed. There was a range with several pots bubbling away on top and a kettle forcing a plume of steam up into a wooden clothes dryer, laden with rows of identical kitten socks, smocks, bibs and bonnets. The scene was a domestic one, but not exactly homely. Tilly took in the details, deciding that it was too clean and tidy; there was nothing out of place, and for a building that housed a multitude of kittens, it was also much too quiet.

'Please sit yourselves down,' said Preston, pointing his paw in the direction of a highly polished bench seat.

Hettie and Tilly did as they were asked, watching as Anthea laid out a tray of small mugs and proceeded to spoon a measured heap of cocoa powder into each before adding hot milk and stirring until the powder had dissolved. There was no conversation as everyone focused in silence on the making of the drinks. Even Preston watched Anthea's every move, as if he were being taught a new skill. The scene reminded Hettie of one of those difficult films, where no one spoke and you were supposed to know what was happening from the brooding atmosphere, as cats played out their roles using everyday activities to emphasise a non-existent plot. Starting to feel a little annoyed and needing to move things on, she decided to break the silence. 'Perhaps you could tell me a little about the missing kittens?' she suggested, addressing Preston.

'One moment,' he said, clasping his paws together and turning to the mugs of chocolate. 'Blessed be the drink that passes our lips and quenches our earthly thirst.'

Anthea bowed her head and repeated Preston's words before passing a mug of cocoa each to Hettie and Tilly. Preston helped himself, and Anthea took the rest of the drinks over to a narrow flight of stone steps, disappearing up them into the room above.

'You must excuse my dear Anthea,' said Preston. 'She lives on her nerves at the best of times, but losing three kittens is more than she can bear. Camay, Windolene and Comfort have left a big hole in her heart. She loved those girls as if they were her own.'

Hettie tried hard to disguise her merriment at the three lost kittens being named after cleaning products, and Tilly buried her head in her notebook, jotting down anything that might be helpful. 'I understand that the kittens were out playing in the snow yesterday when they went missing – can you tell me exactly what happened?'

'I was out in the woods, gathering some logs for the fires. I could hear the kittens squealing with delight as they played in the snow. We only allow them to make a noise like that if they're outside. We like them to be seen and not heard indoors; it's important for them to understand that silence opens a channel to our dear Lord.'

Hettie fidgeted and sipped her cocoa. She was becoming very tired of Preston Munch's attitude, and realised that they were getting nowhere fast. 'Could you tell me *exactly* what happened yesterday?' she repeated, this time with a little more conviction.

'Well, I'm not sure I can tell you anything more. My dear Anthea went to fetch the kittens in for tea and there were only seven of them. We raised the alarm at the Hall and Miss Wither-Fork formed a search party, but they found nothing.'

'It would help if you could describe the lost kittens, and anything about them that might be useful for us to know,' said Hettie.

Preston pondered over the question before answering. 'Well, Camay and Comfort are ginger short-hairs and Windolene is grey with stripes, she's a little older than the other two. We don't identify with vanity here, and our orphans are all dressed the same in blue smocks for indoors and red cloaks when they go out. The girls also wear bonnets, as Anthea is keen on starching them.'

Hettie did her best to avoid a vision of Anthea starching kittens, and carried on with her questions. 'Did you ask the other kittens about the disappearance?'

Preston nodded. 'Yes, I did. Brillo and Duster said that the girls ran off after Jaycloth threatened to bury them in the snow. He was only joking, of course, and they came back eventually and built a snow cat with Daz and Omo before they disappeared.'

Tilly was now scribbling happily in her notebook, marvelling at the addition of yet more cleaning products to her list of kittens. Hettie was beginning to feel like the whole situation was a very bad joke. 'The kittens seem to have some very odd names,' she said. 'Is there a particular reason for that?'

'Anthea names the orphans,' Preston replied, draining his cocoa mug. 'She's fond of cleaning, and cleanliness is next to godli…'

'Yes, yes,' cut in Hettie, trying to avoid more of Preston's religious fervour. 'Are the remaining kittens all male?'

'Yes, but girl cats tend to stick together, don't they? More secretive than boy cats. I suppose they were playing some sort of game, and they wandered off and got lost. After all this time, out in the freezing weather, we must fear the worst.'

Hettie thought for a moment before continuing. 'Out of the three kittens, was one of them what you'd describe as the leader?'

'Definitely Windolene. She's a born leader – a little high-spirited, perhaps, but she knows her scriptures. Camay follows her everywhere, and Comfort is a greedy little kitten, a bit overweight and prone to blasphemy at times.'

Hettie immediately had a liking for Comfort: it was good to know that at least one of the orphans questioned Preston's ideology. Anthea appeared at the bottom of the stairs with an empty tray, and Preston stood to take it from her. 'I think you should show the detectives the schoolroom, my dear. I'm sure they'd like to meet the boys.'

Anthea nodded, and invited Hettie and Tilly to follow her up the stairs. Preston trailed behind and lingered in the doorway as Anthea embarked on her guided tour. When they entered the room, seven kittens stood to attention at their desks. Hettie stared at the little faces, noting that they were all dressed in the same blue smocks, their only individuality coming from the length and colour of their fur. 'Please welcome our visitors in the usual way,' said Anthea to her class.

'Blessed be the fur,' they intoned together before Anthea gave them leave to sit and return to their work.

The desks were laid out with paper and pencils, and the kittens continued to copy the writing from a large blackboard in front of them. Except for the scratching of pencil on paper, not a sound came from them. Tilly was reminded of a scene from one of Mr Dickens's novels but she couldn't remember which one; she did, however, recall that there was a schoolmaster in it called Wackford Squeers, a name she particularly liked the sound of.

The schoolroom, like the kitchen, was basic, but it benefitted from a small fire and larger windows that made it a little more cheerful. To one side of the blackboard stood a colourful globe – a tool, no doubt, for Anthea's geography lessons. The walls were adorned with scenes from the Bible: Moses amongst the bull rushes; the stable scene from the nativity; Noah's ark; and an horrific depiction of the crucifixion which dominated the room, detailing gratuitously the impact of nails hammered into paws. Tilly shuddered as she took a closer look, feeling sorry for the tiny kittens who spent their days in the same room as such a brutal image.

Hettie stared at the blackboard, wondering what the kittens were so diligently copying from it. It was no real surprise to discover that it was the ten commandments, with key words like 'shall not' heavily underlined in chalk.

'Would you like to see the dormitory?' Anthea whispered, pointing her paw in the direction of another set of stone steps.

Hettie was about to say no, but thought better of it as she reminded herself that there may be clues to the missing kittens. After what she'd seen so far, she could easily believe that Windolene, Camay and Comfort had made a bid for freedom away from the Munches' strict regime. 'Yes, that would be lovely.'

The three cats climbed the narrow stone staircase up to the third floor of the Folly, leaving Preston Munch in the schoolroom. The dormitory, like the rest of the rooms, was neat and tidy. The kittens' little beds were arranged in a circle to follow the line of the wall, with a long trestle table and chairs in the central space, all laid up with spoons and bowls.

'Our little ones eat and sleep here,' Anthea said proudly, casting her paw around the room to take in the neatly made beds, with their crisp white sheets peeping out from ten identical plain blue eiderdowns.

Each bed had a small cupboard next to it with a miniature Bible placed on top, and at the head of each bed hung a crucifix – a protection or a threat.

Anthea moved to one of the cupboards to reposition the Bible so that the angle was exactly the same as the others. While she was there, she picked a tiny crumb from the surface and placed it carefully in her apron pocket. Her behaviour was making Hettie nervous. There was so much she needed to discuss with Tilly, but there were some obvious questions to address before they left the Folly. 'Which beds belonged to the missing kittens?' she asked.

'Those three over there,' Anthea replied, and her tears began to fall again. 'I can't bear to see their empty beds when I come to read the bedtime parable,' she sobbed. 'I just think of them lost in the snow, when they're all so small. I fear that God has forsaken us like he did in Africa.'

'My dear, you're upsetting yourself all over again,' said Preston, appearing at the top of the stairs and coming to Hettie and Tilly's rescue. 'Let the detectives do their work. It's time you prepared tea for the kittens. Off with you to the kitchen, and do try to cheer up a bit.' He stood to one side to allow Anthea onto the stairs, and gave her paw a comforting squeeze as she passed. 'I'm not sure that Anthea is entirely cut out to run an orphanage,' he said, shaking his head. 'She has a heart of gold and is the sweetest cat you could ever meet, but I think I put too much on her shoulders sometimes. One day, all our kittens will be gone out into the world to make their own way, following God's path, and I'm not sure how she'll cope without them.'

'You could get some more,' said Tilly brightly, feeling the need to cheer Preston up. 'There are plenty of kittens who need homes.'

'I suppose you're right,' sighed Preston. 'If you've finished up here, I must return to the schoolroom.'

'You go ahead,' said Hettie. 'I'd like to spend a few minutes looking around if that's OK?'

'Of course. Come down when you've finished.' Preston disappeared down the flight of stairs and Hettie waited until she was certain he was out of earshot.

'I think it's pretty clear that those kittens have run away, and I think in his heart Preston knows they have. He's just going through the motions for Anthea's sake, and she's a bit of a nutcase anyway. Did you see her putting that crumb in her pocket? Why didn't she just sweep it onto the floor like any sane cat would? And why aren't they out searching? Life seems to be ticking away as normal here. Even if the kittens are lying frozen to death somewhere, you'd still want to find them, wouldn't you?'

Tilly looked thoughtful as Hettie bent down to look under the beds that Anthea had pointed to. As she expected, there wasn't so much as a speck of dust to be found, and there were no personal effects inside the bedside cupboards, just identical comb and brush sets and several neatly ironed smocks, all in uniform blue.

Tilly opened one of the boy kitten's cupboards and found exactly the same items. 'If I were an orphan, I think I might run away, too,' she said, closing the cupboard door. 'Preston and Anthea are quite nice, but they *are* a bit strange and strict. Kittens should be allowed to play and discover the world in their own way. It's warm and safe here, but it's far too clean.'

Hettie laughed at Tilly's honest assessment of the situation. 'Come on – let's get out of here before they start getting the communion wafers out. Poor old Bruiser and Poppa are out in the snow and we'll be losing the light soon.'

'I prefer pink myself,' said Tilly, heading for the stairs.

'Pink what?' asked Hettie, following her down.

'Wafers,' replied Tilly.

Chapter Seven

Hettie and Tilly were relieved to be out in the snow again, as they'd found the Folly and its occupants oppressive. The Munches were obviously kind-hearted cats, but wrapping up their benevolence in a shroud of Christian doctrine took the shine off things a little. Then there was their concern over the cleaning obsession that Anthea had allowed to leak into the kitten's lives; naming them after her favourite subject was a burden they would have to carry into adulthood.

'Watcha!' said Poppa, crunching his way across the snow with Bruiser from the edge of Wither-Fork Woods. 'Any news on the kittens?'

'Nothing really,' said Hettie, putting her mittens on. 'It's a strange set-up, really – all very well meaning, but I can see why the kittens might have wanted to escape Anthea and Preston's clutches. A little bit claustrophobic, to be honest. How did you get on?'

Poppa shook his head. 'Nothing much to report. We had a good look round the area – lots of tracks in the woods, which must be from the search party, but out here in the open everything's been covered by a fresh fall of snow. Even the snow cats that the kittens built are buried up to their necks. If the missing kittens are out here somewhere, they've either found some shelter or they've frozen to death, and there's no hope of finding bodies until this lot has thawed.'

No sooner had Poppa acknowledged the snow than the wind began to blow, howling across the landscape and collecting everything in its path, reshaping the drifts and blinding the four cats as they tried hard to anchor themselves to the icy ground. Bruiser struggled forward and hoisted Tilly onto his back. Hettie reached for Poppa's paw, and slowly but surely they headed towards Wither-Fork Hall. Fluff – who'd been watching for them – flung open her French windows and the four friends stumbled over the threshold. 'Any luck?' she asked anxiously. 'What did you make of the orphanage?'

'Very odd, to be honest,' said Hettie, kicking the snow off her boots. 'I think the kittens may well have run away.'

'Why do you say that?' Fluff looked concerned. 'You don't think they've been ill-treated, do you?'

'No, not really.' Hettie paused, searching for the right words. 'It's just that Anthea and Preston do seem to run a very tight ship, which might be quite daunting for some kittens. There doesn't seem to be much room for fun in their curriculum.'

'Mm, they struck me as being a bit serious, I have to admit. But why would the kittens choose the worst weather we've had for years to make a run for it? That really doesn't make any sense, and where would they run *to*?'

Fluff Wither-Fork's questions were all valid and Hettie wished she had some answers, but with yet another blizzard raging outside and the light beginning to fail, there was nothing to do but wait. 'I think we must hope for better weather tomorrow and get as many cats out searching as we can,' she said, trying to assert herself and sound like she had a plan. 'We need to search all the outbuildings on the estate in case they're sheltering somewhere, and there are probably plenty of hiding places in the woods to explore as well.'

Fluff could see the sense in waiting for the weather to improve and agreed to put a search party at Hettie's disposal for the following day. 'It's funny that you should mention Wither-Fork Woods,' she said as an afterthought. 'If you'll excuse me, there's something in the old nursery that I must fetch for you to see. Warm yourselves by the fire, and you may still be in time for tea. Blackberry will sort you out.'

Having shed their outdoor clothes, they moved towards the fire, feeling its welcome heat long before they reached it. Bonny Grubb, the estate's gypsy cat, was waving a toasting fork in the air as they approached. Hettie and Bruiser had known Bonny for years, and she had proved a real asset to Fluff since taking on the role of storyteller, offering the occasional crystal ball gazing session to visitors to the house and gardens. Like most of her ancestors, who'd travelled the highways and byways of England in their carts and caravans, Bonny was a born teller of tales – tall or otherwise. After one cruel winter too many, she had unhitched her caravan from her old horse and taken up a permanent position on Fluff's allotments, where she grew vegetables and brewed moonshine, much to the delight of her allotment neighbours.

'Sit yerselves down and get warm,' she said, cramming a large muffin onto the end of her toasting fork and forcing it almost into the fire. 'The next four muffins is yours, and there's Blackberry's chocolate buns and hot tea as well, so tuck in. No sense in starvin', is there?'

Bonny thrust the toasted muffin at Hettie, who pulled it from the fork, burning her paws, before tossing it to Tilly, who buttered it and passed it on to Bruiser. Bonny repeated the process until all four friends had enjoyed a hot muffin, washed down by a mug of tea.

It was a jolly gathering in the Great Hall as yet another snowstorm raged outside. Hettie was content to stay put and enjoy the fire and the chatter of Fluff Wither-Fork's allotment tenants. She even found herself musing over what Blackberry might have in mind for supper, but reality struck when Bruiser pointed out that Miss Scarlet, whom they'd abandoned at the bottom of Wither-Fork Hill, would need rescuing before it got dark.

Fluff returned several minutes later with a book. 'Here it is,' she said, pushing the slim volume into Hettie's paws. '*The Ice Maid's Tail*, one of my favourite books from my kitten days. I used to insist that my nanny read this to me every winter. Strangely enough, it was written by a nanny here at Wither-Fork many years ago. Her name was Albertine Chop, and the story goes that she delighted in frightening the young Wither-Forks in her charge by telling them horror stories. She developed a talent for it, and wrote her own book before being hanged for murdering one of the Wither-Fork kittens in a saucepan of scalding strawberry jam – although I believe there were other incidents laid at her door before she became unstuck, so to speak. She was a bit of a witch, by all accounts, but I have to say she told a wonderful story if this book's anything to go by, and some say it's a prophecy. It's probably a bit far-fetched, but it *does* deal with disappearing kittens and it's set here on the estate – in Wither-Fork Woods during a long, cold winter. You may find it interesting.'

'Is that there old Albertine Chop's book, Miss?' asked Bonny, abandoning her toasting fork to take a closer look.

'Yes, Bonny – have you heard of her?'

Bonny nodded. 'No good can come of meddlin' with the likes of her, Miss. The stuff of nightmares, she is.'

'*Was*, Bonny, *was*,' Fluff corrected. 'She's been dead for a very long time.'

'Some wrong'uns never die, Miss. They say she haunts the woods round here. Some won't even speak her name for fear of bringin' her back.'

Fluff was getting slightly irritated with her gypsy tenant's lurid tales. 'Bringing her back from *where*, exactly, Bonny?'

'From the Winter Lands, Miss, like it says in the book you got there.'

'But I thought you couldn't read, Bonny. How do you know what the book says?'

'I knows that story off by heart, Miss. My old Granny Grubb, who knew her letters, used to read it to me on cold nights when I was tucked up warm in her van. She told me that Albertine Chop was known to the gypsies in these parts, them that lived in the woods.'

'What do you mean by "known"?' asked Fluff. 'Are you saying that she was of the Romany persuasion?'

'Not exactly, Miss, but some say she was sweet on one of them who helped her with the murderin' of them kittens,' mumbled Bonny, helping herself to another of Blackberry's buns.

Tilly was intrigued by the conversation and took the book from Hettie for a closer look. 'I'm not sure Albertine Chop knew *her* letters very well,' she said.

'Look – she can't even spell "tale" properly. It's the wrong sort.'

'No, I'm afraid it's the right sort,' said Fluff. 'You'll have to read it to understand. The tail is one of the... well, one of the more macabre aspects of the story.'

'They chops 'em off,' chimed in Bonny, offering a cackle worthy of freezing the blood. 'You can't be one of them Ice Maids unless you 'ave your tail docked. I s'pose it's on account of the frostbite, see.'

The conversation was becoming more surreal as time went on, and as Bruiser had pointed out, Miss Scarlet needed rescuing and they still had Jessie's food parcel to deliver on their way home. Tilly had taken charge of Albertine Chop's book, now keen to read it for herself.

Pulling on their wet coats, scarves and mittens, Hettie, Tilly, Poppa and Bruiser set out across the snowy parkland with Fluff. Dropping her off at the gatehouse Lodge and collecting their food bags, they promised to return in the morning to lead the search party in the vain hope of finding Windolene, Camay and Comfort alive.

Now that the wind had died down, the descent of Wither-Fork Hill was almost fun. Bruiser was the first to lose his footing and slid to the bottom of the hill in a powdery cascade of fresh snow. Tilly went the same way, taking Hettie with her, and Poppa – who had been given the food bags to carry – was the only cat left standing, having picked his way carefully down the slope. Miss Scarlet took some digging out, but, with four pairs of paws and a good-humoured snowball fight in the middle of their efforts, they were soon sliding along the roads towards Jessie's charity shop in Cheapcuts Lane to make their final delivery of the day.

Jessie was shovelling snow away from her shop doorway when they skidded to a halt in front of her. 'Whatever has brought the entire staff of The No. 2 Feline Detective Agency out on a day like today?' she asked, looking delighted to see them. 'I was beginning to think I was the only survivor of an Arctic winter. I haven't seen a soul for two days. Come in and have a cup of tea.'

Hettie was first through the shop door, followed by Poppa and Bruiser, but Tilly lingered outside to take in Jessie's latest window display. Jessie's charity shop was a real asset to the town: she prided herself on selling good quality cast-offs, as well as a certain amount of warehouse leftovers and a range of not-quite-designer wear. There was something to suit every cat's pocket, and Hettie and Tilly looked no further than her clothes rails whenever they needed a new outfit. Tilly in particular had procured all her best cardigans from Jessie's box of hand knits, and often kept shop for her friend when she was away on business.

Tilly stared at the latest themed display. It was a snow scene to go with the weather, and showed several cat dummies dressed in padded ski suits; there was even a snow cat made out of cotton wool in the centre of the window, wearing a top hat and a long, multi-coloured scarf, but it was the ski suits that Tilly was taken with.

'Come in out of the cold!' Jessie called from the doorway. 'You can look at the stuff in the window from inside. I'm putting the kettle on and there's some shortbread in the tin with your name on it.'

Tilly bustled in from the snow and climbed up into the window for a closer inspection of the display. 'These ski suits are lovely,' she said, running her paw up and down an ice blue one. 'They look so warm and cosy. Do you think I could try one on?'

'Of course you can,' said Jessie, 'but I think the ones in the window would swamp you. I've got a nice blue outfit here that would be perfect for you.'

She pulled the padded suit out from behind her counter and Tilly pounced on it, abandoning her wet things. 'Oooh! This is lovely and warm,' she cried, posing in front of a full-length mirror. 'I feel like one of those cats on *Ski Sunday*.'

Even Hettie had to agree that her friend looked ready to brave another day in the snow. 'I don't suppose you have one in my size?' she said, eyeing up the red one in the window. 'This one looks like it might fit.'

'Go for it while I make the tea,' said Jessie, leaving Hettie, Poppa and Bruiser to lift the dummy out of the window and undress it. By the time she had returned with tea and shortbread, Hettie had struggled into the red snow suit, Bruiser had found himself a set of bright yellow waterproofs, and Poppa had chosen a black padded jacket and a striped, knitted bobble hat. Jessie was thrilled to see that her friends had all found treasure in her shop, and the five cats drank their tea and munched on the contents of her biscuit tin in happy contentment.

'I almost forgot,' said Hettie through a mouthful of buttery shortbread. 'The Butters have sent you a food parcel.'

Bruiser leapt up and out of the shop, returning with a slightly damp food bag from Miss Scarlet's sidecar. 'What a lovely surprise,' Jessie said, emptying the contents onto her counter. 'Pies, cakes, sausage rolls and even some crisps! And just in time, as I'm down to my last tin of sardines and the bread ran out yesterday. Your landladies are saints.'

Hettie had to agree, and seeing the savouries tumble out of the food bag onto Jessie's counter reminded her that they hadn't touched their own packed lunches thanks to the hospitality at Wither-Fork Hall. It put her mind at rest to know that they were now 'all found' for supper.

'So come on then – what have you four been up to? Or are you just delivering emergency food parcels around the town?' Jessie asked as she collected up the empty mugs.

'Well, we did have several deliveries to do, but we've been called in by Fluff Wither-Fork up at the Hall

77

to look for some missing kittens,' Hettie explained. 'They're orphans, being looked after by Anthea and Preston Munch in the old Folly.'

'Oh my goodness! Not *the* Anthea and Preston Munch, the failed missionaries?' cried Jessie, putting her paws up to her face in mock horror. 'Why would anyone trust *them* with orphaned kittens?'

'Why not?' asked Tilly, keen to get Jessie's opinion of the Munches.

'I heard they tried to bring a load of kittens back from Africa, which would have been fine if the kittens had needed rescuing, but as far as I can tell they were just rounding them up from villages without bothering to ask if they had homes or not. They were rumbled just as they were leaving, and all the kittens were returned to their families. I don't believe they're at it again up at Wither-Fork Hall!'

'Are you saying they're kit-nappers?' said Hettie, more than a little concerned at Jessie's revelation.

'I'm not sure I'd put it that strongly, but some cats need to be needed, don't they, and from some of the conversations I've had with my customers, it seems that Anthea and Preston Munch like creating a crisis so they can solve it – and all in the name of Jesus, which doesn't go down very well round here, where most of us are non-believers.'

Hettie nodded in agreement, more convinced than ever now that Windolene, Camay and Comfort had made a run for it and were most probably holed up somewhere on the Wither-Fork estate, fending for themselves without the help of Anthea, Preston or even Jesus. The four cats settled up for their bargain clothes, and Jessie waved them off as Miss Scarlet slid from one side of the road to the other. The temperature was dropping dramatically, and in spite of the fresh fall of snow the road had become a solid sheet of ice.

On reaching the bakery, Poppa decided to spend the night with Bruiser in his shed as they would need an early start the following morning. The two cats had dusted off an old paraffin stove and lit it, making the shed much more hospitable. Betty and Beryl invited them all to a hot supper, which delighted Bruiser and Poppa as they'd missed out the day before. Hettie and Tilly declined, keen to avoid an evening with Lavender Stamp, who was still resident in the Butter sisters' box room, recovering from her self-inflicted knitting trauma.

Their room was cold when they got back to it. Tilly raked the fire, finding a few glowing embers which she added some dry sticks and newspaper to. With the help of some encouraging puffing and blowing, she eventually managed to tempt some small flames to lick the chimney breast, adding coal until she achieved a real blaze. Hettie busied herself in laying out their supper in front of the fire, choosing a pie, a packet of crisps and a sausage roll for each of them from the Butters' bags. She switched on the TV in time to see the weather cat pointing his paw at yet more snow on his chart before the TV itself gave up, offering nothing but wavy lines and intermittent bursts of speech. 'Bloody marvellous!' she said. 'I suppose the aerial is frozen solid up on the roof. No television for us tonight.'

'We could have a story instead,' suggested Tilly.

'What sort of story?' asked Hettie, filling her catnip pipe for later.

'I could read us *The Ice Maid's Tail* if you like? Fluff said we might find it interesting.'

Hettie wasn't convinced. She was too concerned about Anthea and Preston Munch to enjoy a fairy story penned by a murderous witch, but she had to agree that it would probably be more interesting than the Premier League feline football that was due to be broadcast on TV all evening had their set been working, featuring a clash between Tottering Hot Paws and Nottingham Forest – although the snow had probably put paid to that as well.

Reluctantly, the two cats struggled out of their new snowsuits, replacing them with their pyjamas and dressing gowns. Having hung their wet coats on the picture rail to dry the two cats settled in front of the fire to eat their supper. The pies were good, and Tilly added a glass of fiery ginger beer each from a bottle she kept in the staff sideboard. They ate their crisps and decided to leave the sausage rolls until later.

Full and warm, Hettie lit her catnip pipe and Tilly reached for the book that Fluff Wither-Fork had given them. '*The Ice Maid's Tail* by Albertine Chop,' she began.

"'Long, long ago, before anyone could be bothered to remember, there dwelt a community of ice cats. They lived in ice caves and tunnels below the ground in Wither-Fork Woods, and were rarely seen in daylight. They hunted the woods after dark, pouncing on anything nice enough to eat and dragging their victims back to their holes in the ice to boil them alive. Nothing was wasted. Rabbit, stoat and weasel skins were dried and used to make hats, mittens and bedcovers, and their bones propped up the endless tunnels which led to the ice caves where the families lived.

"These were the days of the Winter Lands, a time when the sun appeared for one day each year, melting the ice and flooding the tunnels. The day of the sun was dreaded by all the ice cats, as many of them were drowned in the icy water that filled their caves. As the water froze again, their bodies were entombed in the ice like ghostly sculptures, staring out at the survivors and reminding them that the sun would return to claim more victims.

"The ice cats were ruled over by a magnificent queen, who lived in the Halls of Glass, an ice palace where Wither-Fork Hall now stands. The palace was below the ground, and the Ice Queen chose her servants carefully as she trusted no one. To become an Ice Maid was a very high honour, and the Queen insisted on docking their tails in a special ceremony where they swore to serve her. After they had been removed, the tails were frosted and hung in the Queen's cave of jewels and sparkly things with her other treasured possessions, all guarded by a giant male Snow Cat, whose only mission in life was to protect the Queen from harm. She led a solitary life, with only her Ice Maids for company. They fed, bathed and dressed her, and brushed her beautiful long white fur until it shone. They sang to her and read to her and danced for her, and she loved them as if they were her own kittens – but she grew tired and old, and one of her Ice Maids turned against her and gave her a deadly poison in a cake she'd baked.

"The Queen took many days to die, and her Ice Maids watched her writhe in agony. On the day she finally died, the sun returned and stayed for longer than expected. The tunnels and ice caves flooded, drowning all the ice cats, and the water reached even as far as the Halls of Glass. The Queen's body was swept away with all of her Ice Maids but one – the cat who had murdered her Queen.

"When the Ice Maid realised she was the only cat to survive, she waited for the waters to freeze again and crept through the tunnels as the eyes of the many dead cats stared at her from their frozen tombs. She found the Ice Queen and all her Ice Maids frozen together in the cave of jewels and sparkly things, and she wept for what she had done.

"She cried for three days and three nights in the frozen chamber. Without food, her strength failed her and her life began to slip away. She lay curled up on the icy floor of the cave, waiting for death to punish her for her wickedness.""

'Is there much more of it?' asked Hettie, as Tilly turned the page. 'It's not what I'd call riveting, and why are they all living in those conditions anyway? Ice caves, tunnels, Halls of Glass – it's absolute nonsense.'

'Don't you want to know what happened to her?' said Tilly, rather indignantly.

'I'd prefer a sausage roll and a cup of milky tea, but I suppose we should get to the end of the story.'

Hettie added more coal to the fire. Tilly was tempted to abandon the book and put the kettle on, but there were only a few pages left so she decided to push on with the story, while Hettie settled to another pipe of catnip in the hope that it might improve the grand finale.

'"The Ice Maid had almost breathed her very last breath when she heard a thundering of paws down one of the tunnels,"' Tilly continued. '"She raised her head to see the giant Snow Cat appear in the cave, and as he stared at the dead Queen and her frozen Ice Maids, his eyes filled with tears which fell in icicles to the floor. He had deserted his Queen to save himself from the flood, and now he hung his head in sorrow at what he'd done.

"The Ice Maid lifted her head and caught the Snow Cat's eye. He stared at her, then slowly moved towards her, sniffing the frozen air to pick up her scent. He prowled around her, nudging her with his nose, and she lay still, waiting for him to pounce and hoping that her misery would soon be over. He lifted one of his giant webbed paws and brought it down on her back. She cried out in terror, and he shrank away from her, for he was as frightened as she was.

"In time, the Snow Cat returned to the Ice Maid and lay down by her side to show that he meant her no harm. He could see that she was weak and dying of hunger, and he knew that he had to save her. She fell into a deep sleep, and he lifted her up on his shoulder and carried her through the tunnels and up into the snowy woods. He laid her down and built a fire, and left her wrapped in his cloak as he stalked the woods for food. He returned with a rabbit, which he skinned and roasted on the fire.

"The Ice Maid woke to the smell of roasting meat, and soon the two cats were comfortable with each other and shared the rabbit and licked the bones clean. As night fell in the woods, they sat together and shared their sorrows. She told him how she had poisoned the Ice Queen, and he told her how he had run away like a coward when the floods came. They agreed that they had both been wicked and would mend their ways.

"The snow swirled around them as they slept that night, and in the first light of the morning something very strange happened. The sun rose like a giant red ball in the sky and the Winter Lands were no more. The snow melted away as if it never had been, the trees in the woods sprouted fresh green leaves, the fields filled with buttercups and daisies, and from the woodland floor came legions of bluebells, forcing their way through the tangle of tree roots.

"The Snow Cat lifted the Ice Maid high into the air, showing her to the sun, and they danced with the sheer joy of being alive. Paw in paw, they skipped through the fields as if seeing the world for the first time, their sins forgotten as their new life began.

"In time, Hugo Nightspark – for that was the Snow Cat's name – built a grand house for his Ice Maid, above the ground where Wither-Fork Hall stands today. She became his Queen, and bore him many kittens. The boys became brave warriors, hunters and gypsies; the girls served their parents until they were old enough to have kittens of their own.

"The tunnels, ice caves and the Halls of Glass were long forgotten, and, through the centuries, the Nightsparks became the Wither-Forks and the sun continued to shine on them, but below ground the Ice Queen and her Maids waited in their frozen tombs for the return of the snows. On cold winter nights, when the snow is thick on the ground, they do say that the Ice Queen haunts the woods and snatches kittens to turn them into Ice Maids, docking their tails and imprisoning them in the Halls of Glass, never to see the sun again. And it is said that the Ice Queen will take her revenge on the descendants of the Nightsparks, when the Winter Lands return and cover the earth in snow and ice once again."'

Hettie waited a moment to make sure that Tilly had finished the story before offering her critique; when it came, it was short and to the point. 'What utter tosh!' she said, hauling herself out of her chair to put the kettle on.

Tilly – who loved a good story – felt somewhat crushed by her friend's attitude and wasted no time in defending Albertine Chop's foray into folklore. 'Well, I thought it was quite a *good* story. It's probably a bit far-fetched, but it's better than some of those Brothers Grump stories I read when I was a kitten. It's lovely to have so much snow, and the ice tombs were a bit scary.'

'I'm more interested in Albertine Chop herself,' said Hettie. 'She obviously had a vivid imagination, but it would be useful to know what turned her into a murdering nanny. Maybe she was really the Ice Queen in the story? I can see what Fluff Wither-Fork was getting at about the lost kittens, but I don't think we're ready to believe that they've been snatched by some mythical cat dressed as an ancient ice lolly who's charging around Wither-Fork Woods docking tails and changing kittens into Ice Maids.'

Tilly giggled and had to agree that Albertine's story had very little to do with their present case. A much more tangible solution had to be found for the disappearance of Windolene, Camay and Comfort. She prepared the milky tea and the two cats sat by the fire, both deep in thought. It was Hettie who broke the silence after swallowing the final piece of her sausage roll. 'I wonder where Albertine Chop got the story from? It sounds like one of those old folk legends I used to sing about when I had the band.'

Tilly brushed some pastry off her fur and picked up Albertine's book again. The title page included a dedication, which she read out. '"This story was told to me by Jenkin Cowdiddle, a direct descendant of Hugo Nightspark and King of the Gypsy Cats." There you are – that explains it. It wasn't her story – she just wrote it down, and Bonny was right about the gypsy connection.'

Hettie shook her head. 'Well, you couldn't make a name like Jenkin Cowdiddle up, that's for sure, and Albertine Chop's not much better. I think we should get some sleep. I get the feeling that there's a long day ahead of us tomorrow, with or without the Ice Queen's help.'

Chapter Eight

Tilly woke early, and even swathed in her blankets she was cold. The fire had dwindled virtually to nothing, and their room was like ice. She counted to ten and hauled herself out of her covers, her teeth chattering away to themselves as she filled the kettle and eyed up her new snowsuit. The thought of taking her pyjamas off to get dressed was completely unacceptable in such temperatures, but the comfort of the snowsuit beckoned. She pounced on it as if it were a spider and wriggled into the padded warmth, instantly feeling the heat and wondering why she hadn't discovered the joy of snow wear before. The extra layer made her a little more clumsy than usual as she moved about the room, bouncing off the furniture and coaxing the fire back to life, making the tea and putting two slices of bread in the toaster – but the comfort of her new outfit far outweighed the morning chores that always seemed to be hers while Hettie slept on.

She lingered by the window, wondering if the snow would ever give way to spring. Her sleep had been filled with images of the Ice Queen, surrounded by giant snow cats and strange-looking gypsies. It had left her fearful of a winter that lasted for ever, and, as yet more snow fell onto the Butters' backyard, she found it hard to contemplate a life without spring, summer and autumn.

'Is it still coming down?' asked Hettie, stretching under her blanket.

Tilly jumped, not having realised that Hettie was awake. 'Yes, and even bigger flakes than yesterday if that's possible,' she said. 'If those poor little kittens are still out in this, they'll be ice sculptures by now, or buried so deep that we'll never find them.'

'Well, I see you're dressed for action, whatever the outcome,' Hettie observed, as Tilly delivered a mug of milky tea to the arm of her chair.

'I just love my snowsuit, and I think I'll wear it all the time until things warm up a bit.' Tilly bounced off the staff sideboard, spilling some of her tea onto the hearth rug. 'It's a bit tricky in a small room, though. I feel like one of those Michelin cats on the tyre adverts, but at least it doesn't hurt when I bump into things.'

'Probably a good idea to keep the best china in the cupboard, then – if we had any,' said Hettie, as Tilly struggled to sit down on her blankets.

The two cats enjoyed their breakfast in quiet contentment before Bruiser broke the silence by hammering on the door to announce that Miss Scarlet was ready and waiting to take them to Wither-Fork

Hall. Hettie scrambled into her own snowsuit, adding a pair of thick socks and wellingtons to the look that Tilly had already adopted, and they made their way out into the high street, where Poppa was waiting.

The snow was still falling, but the sky also boasted a hint of wintry sun, which Tilly was relieved to see as it brought hope of a thaw. Miss Scarlet slid across the icy roads and once again was brought to a halt at the bottom of Wither-Fork Hill. The four cats completed the journey on foot, arriving at the Hall in time for a round of bacon rolls and frothy coffee. Fluff had called all her tenants together so that Hettie could address them, which took Hettie a little by surprise as she had never organised a search party before and had no idea where to begin.

'I've looked out an old map of the estate,' said Fluff. 'It's got all the outbuildings marked and some of the old tunnels as well – not exactly *The Ice Maid's Tail*, but it's true that my ancestors seemed to like burrowing underground for some reason.'

Hettie pounced on the map. 'That's really helpful,' she said. 'I think Tilly and I will study this while Poppa and Bruiser brief the search party.'

Passing the buck was something that Hettie was rather good at, and Poppa and Bruiser responded by calling the assembled cats to order and splitting them up into two small groups to await instructions.

Hettie stared at the map, trying to get her bearings. The names of the various buildings on the estate were in Old English and hard to understand. 'I'm not sure where Wither-Fork Hall ends and the parkland begins,' she said. 'I can just make out the woods, but what are all these wavy lines everywhere?'

'Ah, those are the ancient tunnels,' said Fluff, taking charge of the map again. 'If we start from the Hall here, we can see that the tunnels lead out in every direction. The Great Hall, where we're standing at the moment, is the oldest building on the estate; everything else has been added on over time, and the outbuildings all seem to have been connected to the main house by tunnels as and when they were built. The church, as you know, has a crypt like a rabbit warren, with underground passageways stretching out as far as the woods. I used to play down there when I was a kitten, but it started giving me nightmares so my father had the crypt locked and now we only open it for family interments.'

Hettie couldn't help but remember the case they'd worked on before at Wither-Fork Hall, and the emotional cost to Fluff herself. She had admired her then for her resilience, and did so even more now that she had taken on her crumbling ancestral home and turned it into a place of historical beauty. The estate was a major source of employment for some of the town's homeless misfits, who now found shelter there.

Tilly loved a document of any kind, especially if it held secrets from long ago, and her thoughts kept returning to *The Ice Maid's Tail* as she stared at the web of tunnels that Fluff had pointed out. 'Can you still use those tunnels?' she asked.

Fluff shook her head. 'I would think that most of them crumbled to nothing years ago. There might be some left that serviced the Hall, like this one leading to the old icehouse from the kitchens, but they haven't been used in years.' She traced the tunnel on the map with one of her claws, bringing it to rest on a circular building.

'Icehouse?' said Tilly. 'What's an icehouse?'

Fluff warmed to the subject, always happy to discuss her history. 'It was exactly what it says, and an icehouse was a vital part of preserving food in the olden days. In winter, whenever the lake by the woods froze, the cats at the Hall would cut out giant blocks of ice and store them in the icehouse in layers, with straw in between to insulate them. The tighter the ice was packed, the longer it lasted – up to two years, I believe. The kitchen maid cats had the job of chipping away at the ice to keep the food cool in the kitchens. Wonderful idea, but I have to say whoever invented the fridge gets my vote every time. It's no wonder we had to have so many staff – everything took so much time and effort in those days.'

Tilly was fascinated, and had quite forgotten that they were there to look for the missing kittens, but the bacon rolls had all been eaten and it was clearly time for Hettie to take control, as Poppa and Bruiser were waiting for instructions.

Much to Tilly's delight, it was decided that she and Hettie would remain at the Hall to search the attics and the buildings close to Wither-Fork. Poppa agreed to lead his team out to the woods around the Folly, and Bruiser took several cats out to search some of the old farm buildings on the edge of the estate.

The cats left behind in the Hall returned to the job of uncovering the wall painting, and Tilly could see that progress had been made overnight. The scene that was gradually revealed as layers and layers of old wallpaper were removed seemed to be an illustration straight out of Albertine Chop's book: the central figure was a cat seated on a throne, surrounded by smaller cats dressed in bonnets and red cloaks. 'That must be the Ice Queen,' said Tilly, waving her paw at the mural. 'And those must be the Ice Maids.'

Fluff stared as if it was the first time she had seen the painting. 'You're absolutely right,' she said, moving in for a closer look. 'I've been so distracted by the missing kittens that I've hardly noticed what was happening on the walls, which reminds me – I've got an art historian coming this morning to take a look at it. Artemesia Klimp, she's called. You may have heard of her – she writes a column in the *Sunday Snout* and is a painter herself. She works in gouache, I'm told.'

Hettie found herself resisting the temptation to laugh out loud, but Tilly waded in as only Tilly could. 'Isn't that a bit messy? And if she's putting meat in it, wouldn't it go off?'

Fluff looked bewildered for a moment, then suddenly laughed. 'Oh, my dear, I said gouache, not goulash. It's a thick sort of paint.'

Tilly was relieved to learn that good food wasn't being wasted on Artemesia Klimp's efforts, and was now keen to take a look at Wither-Fork Hall's attics. 'Shall we start our search?' she suggested.

Fluff responded by calling Bonny Grubb down from the scaffold, where she'd just clawed off a sizeable piece of gilded wallpaper to reveal a male cat holding up a cat's tail in his paw in a triumphant manner. 'That there must be Hugo Nightspark, Miss, like in Albertine Chop's story. 'E's one of them giant snow cats, like old Jenkin Cowdiddle.'

Fluff was impressed with the new figure that Bonny had exposed in the painting, but – with Artemesia Klimp due at any minute – she had no time for one of her stories. 'Yes, Bonny, well done, but now I'd like you to show Hettie and Tilly up to the attics so that they may start their search. Blackberry tells me that lunch will be served at one o'clock, so you'd better get a move on.'

The thought of another of Blackberry Tibbs's meals put a spring in Hettie's step, and she and Tilly followed Bonny out of the main hall to explore some of the hidden histories of the Jacobean mansion.

Chapter Nine

The Wither-Fork attic rooms were freezing cold and dark. Electricity was obviously a luxury not afforded to the servants in days gone by, and the tiny windows set in the roof gave very little hope of natural light; what there was had been almost lost in the build-up of snow. Hettie and Tilly were pleased to have the comfort of their snowsuits, and Bonny pulled her shawl around her as they moved from one attic room to another.

Initially, there was very little to see. A few boxes of unwanted kitchen items sat abandoned on the dusty bare floorboards in one of the rooms; another room adjoining it had a tower of old, broken furniture piled high in one corner and some rather ornate picture frames, devoid of their original images and waiting for faces or landscapes to reclaim them.

Hettie stared round at the emptiness, satisfied that the missing kittens would have found no comfort in hiding in these abandoned rooms. 'I think we're wasting our time up here,' she said, brushing the cobwebs from her snowsuit. 'If the kittens have hidden themselves in the house, they would surely have chosen somewhere warm and close to food. An old pantry near the kitchens would be more likely.'

Bonny agreed, especially as the prolonged cold had crept under her shawl and begun to seep into her bones, but Tilly felt she had been robbed of a golden opportunity to 'step over the rope', as she put it. Tilly loved looking through old things; it was a rare treat to go where no other cat had been for years, and the missing kittens had given her an opportunity to do just that, even though she secretly agreed with Hettie that the last place they should be looking was in freezing cold attics.

'If we could just finish up here, we could do the kitchens after lunch and maybe explore the tunnels?' she suggested brightly as she opened another door, leaving Hettie and Bonny to follow on reluctantly. The new room was much bigger than the first two and had obviously been set up as a nursery in days gone by: there were two small beds, a cot and a multitude of very old-fashioned toys; dolls in various states of undress, some with limbs and ears missing, others with holes where eyes and whiskers used to be; and there was a dolls' house, vaguely resembling Wither-Fork Hall. Tilly crossed the room and pulled the front open to stare in at the miniature toy cats who were going about their business in perfect room settings, patiently waiting for the next kitten to come along and orchestrate their lives. There were day rooms, a large kitchen, bedrooms and a whole nursery suite at the very top of the house, full of tiny replicas of everyday things, and Tilly couldn't resist the world before her.

'This is so lovely,' she said. 'I could play with it for hours. Just look at the tiny tea set in the nursery and that stacked tea! They've got sandwiches, cakes and sausage rolls, and there's a bookshelf full of little books.' She reached in to pull one of the books from the shelf, inadvertently rearranging the room setting with her large paw. 'Oh bugger! I'll have to put all this back to normal now,' she muttered, more to herself than to Hettie and Bonny.

Hettie left Tilly playing with the dolls' house to take a closer look at the full-size nursery. There was a small room adjoining it which drew her attention. It obviously belonged to an adult cat, as the bed was much larger than the others and there were books in piles on the floor that could never be described as suitable for kittens. The subject matter included torture, black magic and witchcraft, and there was nothing more recent than the turn of the old century. Notably, there were several copies of *The Ice Maid's Tail* covered in a coating of thick dust, the last proof of Albertine Chop's existence.

Bonny shivered as Hettie flicked through some of the pages. 'No good'll come of bein' in these old rooms. I can feel her now, watchin' us. She's still 'ere, spinnin' 'er evil.'

Hettie looked up as Bonny backed towards the door for dramatic effect. 'Who's still here, Bonny?'

'Albertine Chop, that's who. This old nursery was closed up after her 'angin', and from then on the Wither-Fork kittens was raised downstairs in the main house – them that was left, that is.'

'So how come you know so much about it? And for that matter, who was Jenkin Cowdiddle? And I thought Albertine Chop only murdered one kitten by boiling it in strawberry jam?'

'Well, I knows a bit more than I was lettin' on yesterdee, when Miss Wither-Fork gave you that book. My old granny had the story from her old nan Rumble, see.'

Tilly had finished putting the miniature world to rights and joined Hettie and Bonny in time for the story. She and Hettie perched themselves on the edge of what might once have been Albertine Chop's old bed, and Bonny settled herself in an old rocking chair, pulling a blanket she'd found around her, ready to recount a story that had been passed down by the gypsies who wintered in Wither-Fork Woods longer ago than any cat could remember.

'My great Granny Rumble was married into the Cowdiddle family. Some of them was good and some was very bad,' Bonny began. 'Granny Rumble married a bad'un name of Jenkin Cowdiddle. Jenkin was deecended from the royal gypsies that went back all the way to the fourteen 'undreds. Now, in Granny

Rumble's time, Jenkin appointed 'imself King of the Gypsies, and 'cause he was a strong, fightin' cat, no one argued. 'E took 'imself many wives and fathered many kittens, but they was all boy cats, and, as Granny Rumble and 'is other wives grew old, there were no female cats to carry things on, so one long cold winter while they was camped in Wither-Fork Woods, 'e took up with Albertine Chop, the old nursery maid at the big 'ouse. 'E charmed 'er into doin' all sorts for 'im, includin' stealin' and the like. She was a bad'un, too, and liked to tease and torture the young Wither-Fork kittens. They say she used to stick pins in 'em and pull their whiskers out one by one. Anyway, Jenkin 'ad 'is eye on the little girl kittens that she looked after, and one cold day, when the snow was deep on the ground, 'e told 'er to bring 'em to the edge of the woods to meet 'im. She did as she was told and 'e snatched them kittens away and they was never seen again. As the weeks passed, the Wither-Forks gave up lookin' for their kittens, and in the spring the gypsies moved on. Before they left, Jenkin Cowdiddle told Albertine the story of *The Ice Maid's Tail* and she wrote it down and made it into her book. I think she believed that the missing kittens had been turned into Ice Maids like it says in the story, and that Jenkin Cowdiddle had passed 'em on to the Ice Queen. What Albertine didn't know was that one of the boy kittens at Wither-Fork saw 'er handin' 'is sisters over to Jenkin. 'E'd kept that secret all winter 'cause 'e didn't care much for 'is sisters, until Albertine beat him with a soup ladle one day. Then 'e said 'e was goin' to tell on 'er, so she drowned 'im in a pan of strawberry jam and the cook caught 'er red-pawed. They took 'er to the icehouse and kept 'er there till she froze up. As the summer came on, she thawed out but she was still alive, so they took 'er to the Magic Tree in the middle of the woods and 'anged 'er from the 'ighest branch, leavin' 'er to dangle for 'er crime. That's why she haunts them woods.'

Bonny appeared to have come to the end of her story, and Hettie was about to offer a few choice words on the subject when Bonny raised her paw to silence her. 'I don't ever dare to tell this next bit, in case Miss Wither-Fork turns me away, but my Granny Grubb told me that she was one of the missin' kittens from Wither-Fork, stolen away by Jenkin Cowdiddle. She said she ran away after 'e'd docked 'er tail. She got picked up at one of them hirin' fairs and put into service, where she took up with Buster Grubb, a tinker who used to call on the 'ouse she was placed in. She 'ad a good life with 'im till 'e took bad one winter and died, leavin' 'er to raise my ma on 'er own – but she always said we was royalty descended from the King of the Gypsies and the Wither-Forks.'

Hettie sighed deeply before raising several inconsistencies in Bonny's story. 'If your Granny Grubb was one of the missing Wither-Fork kittens, how can Granny Rumble be her granny and your great-granny?'

'Well, that's easy,' replied Bonny. 'Us gypsies 'ave blood grannies and old grannies. Old grannies are usually the wisest, as they've lived longest, so when my Granny Grubb was stolen away by Jenkin Cowdiddle, she was given to Granny Rumble, who looked after 'er before the ceremony and taught 'er the ways of the gypsies.'

'What ceremony?' asked Tilly.

'The tail dockin', just like in Albertine's book.'

Hettie shook her head. 'I think we're getting a bit mixed up here with two stories. There's the Jenkin Cowdiddle abduction of the Wither-Fork kittens, and *The Ice Maid's Tail*, which is clearly a mythical legend, probably made up by Jenkin to keep cats out of Wither-Fork Woods. We know there were tunnels on the estate, and we know there were long winters in Jenkin and Albertine's time, so it's a very small leap for a gypsy cat to make up a story incorporating ice queens and giant snow cats. The big question is – what has all this got to do with Camay, Comfort and Windolene? I'm beginning to suspect that my first hunch was right, that they have quite simply run away from the rather strict regime set up by Preston and Anthea Munch at the Folly.'

It was Bonny's turn to shake her head. ''Istory always repeats, you mark my words. There's old magic in them snowflakes swirling round out there, and them kittens is in grave danger. I feels that in me old bones.'

Hettie shrugged off Bonny's warning but was intrigued by something else the gypsy cat had mentioned. 'You say that Albertine Chop was frozen, thawed out, and then hanged from a Magic Tree in the woods. Is this Magic Tree still there?'

Bonny nodded. 'Oh yes, but it's not my place to tell. You'll 'ave to share a pipe with old Bombazine Bright if you want to know more about the Magic Tree.'

'Bombazine Bright!' spluttered Hettie. 'Who on earth is Bombazine Bright?'

'She's a witch in charge of the Magic Tree. Lives in Wither-Fork Woods in an old stone cottage, but she's not one for visitors unless they got somethin' nice for 'er. She likes catnip and moonshine, and a nice cream cake on occasions, if 'er temper's calm.'

Tilly liked the sound of Bombazine Bright, and while Hettie held her head in her paws at Bonny's latest pearl of information, Tilly had her own question. 'Do you think Bombazine might know about the missing kittens?'

'She does seem to know most things,' said Bonny. 'Trick is gettin' 'er to tell you. She's a cat of few words and talks mostly in riddles, but I could take you there if that might 'elp with your 'vestigations.'

Tilly was about to respond when the noise of a dinner gong came from deep inside Wither-Fork Hall. Hettie got to her feet immediately, knowing that it was the signal for one of Blackberry Tibbs's lunches.

'Come on, I think we've had enough tales for now. I'm starving.'

Hettie bustled out of the nursery, leaving Bonny and Tilly to follow. Tilly paused at the dolls' house to treat herself to another look before catching up with Bonny. She opened the front, and there, to her horror, was the nursery in complete disarray: beds turned upside down; books thrown about; and the tiny kitten dolls broken and scattered everywhere, as if there had been some sort of massacre. She looked down at the small kitchen, and there on the kitchen range was a pan full of red liquid. She dipped her claw in and tasted the sweet, sticky substance. It was unmistakably strawberry jam.

Chapter Ten

The Great Hall was in chaos as Hettie, Tilly and Bonny entered. Bruiser and Poppa had arrived back with their search parties, cold, wet and hungry. Blackberry Tibbs was wielding a ladle at the head of the trestle table, and cats queued to have their bowls filled with her delicious beef stew, each bowl crowned with a special cheese dumpling. There was a mad scramble for places to sit, and in the middle of it all Artemesia Klimp had just arrived, wearing what appeared to be a pair of tennis racquets strapped to her feet.

Hettie and Bonny joined the dinner queue, but Tilly hung back. She was upset at what she'd seen in the dolls' house, but wanted to wait until she could get Hettie on her own to tell her about it. The more she thought about it, the more she doubted what she'd seen, and her first instinct was to return to the attic in the hope that everything had magically been restored to some sort of calm normality, but she was too frightened of what she might find. She joined the queue with very little enthusiasm, and waved away the cheese dumpling when it was offered, before joining Hettie and Bonny on a bench by the fireplace to eat her stew – but she was soon distracted from her troubled thoughts by a gala performance starring the newly arrived Artemesia Klimp and Fluff Wither-Fork.

'My dear Miss Wither-Fork, never has there been such a ghastly day to venture out. I almost turned back at the railway station, but I just knew that it would be worth it,' the critic said, making an attempt to release herself from the sawn-off tennis racquets that had served her so well as snowshoes. She was a very thin cat; long legged, short-haired, and – once she'd discarded her outdoor coat – dressed in a garment resembling a multi-coloured wigwam. Once the tennis racquets had been jettisoned, she floated rather than walked across the hall, her voice booming out above the lunchtime chatter as she gazed up at the partially revealed wall painting. 'Fresco, fresco, magnifico!' she cried, clapping her paws together. 'Such faded glory, in the style of Blotto of Assisi. The plaster has been exquisitely mixed with the paint and the image executed to perfection. My dear Miss Wither-Fork, you have a masterpiece on your paws! But one needs to ask – what is it that the artist is trying to say?'

Fluff opened her mouth to respond, but Artemesia danced away from her, using the space in the Great Hall to accommodate some form of forced ballet that had clearly been inspired by the mural. She came to a halt at the head of the dinner queue and swept a bowlful of stew off the trestle table, dancing it across to a chair by the French windows, where she sat and ate it. Fluff and the rest of the diners looked on in bewilderment as Artemesia Klimp finished her stew and proceeded to lick the bowl clean, before resuming her position in front of the painting.

'There is conflict in the work,' she continued. 'Several artists have had a paw in its creation, and the figures are quite primitive. The cat seated on the throne is painted to a much smaller scale than the male cat here, who dominates the work. I would say that the artists who created this were more used to farming than fresco work, as none of them could draw, but it's the sheer size and audacity that makes it so magnificent. If I had to date it, I would say it was quite old – after Blotto and before Banksy – but one can never be sure these days, when we can all get our paws on ready-mixed bags of plaster of Paris. The world's our fresco, as one might say.'

Fluff Wither-Fork was beginning to doubt the critic's credentials. She had started well, but seemed to be moving away from the point a little. 'Do you think the painting has any value?' Fluff asked, conscious that she'd already agreed to pay the critic twenty pounds for her opinion.

'Well, who can say?' Artemesia replied, floating towards the trestle table again, where Blackberry was now serving large portions of bread and extra butter pudding. Again the critic presented herself at the front of the queue, but this time she was thwarted, as Blackberry – seeing the injustice – picked up her tray of pudding and took it to the back of the queue, allowing the cats to help themselves as she passed. Artemesia stared blankly after her, trying to process the fact that she'd actually been refused something that she wanted, which was a situation she simply wasn't used to.

Feeling spiteful because of the lack of pudding, she turned back to Fluff. 'To sum up, Miss Wither-Fork, I would say that unless you enjoy staring at rather crudely executed artworks, you might think about painting or wallpapering over it. It's a nice space you have here, and there are plenty of walls for the celebration of other, shall we say, more contemporary artists. I have myself recently finished a series of gouache landscapes featuring different aspects of the biscuit factory on the edge of the town – industrial noir, if you like. They would look very well on these walls.'

Fluff realised that she was getting nowhere with the critic. Avoiding her sales pitch, she suggested that Artemesia might leave in plenty of time to catch her train. Artemesia Klimp looked a little crestfallen as she strapped her tennis racquets reluctantly back onto her feet; with twenty pounds in her pocket, she swept out of Wither-Fork Hall, leaving everyone hoping that she just might encounter an extra large snowdrift on her way home.

When the lunch things had been cleared away, Hettie, Tilly, Bruiser and Poppa settled at the trestle table to exchange notes on the morning's investigations and decide what should happen next. Bruiser's search party had drawn a blank in the old derelict farm buildings on the edge of the estate. Poppa's team had almost struck lucky as they followed a set of small paw prints into the woods, only to discover that they belonged to Jaycloth, one of Anthea and Preston Munch's orphans, who was out collecting wood for the fires at the Folly.

'I'm surprised they're letting any of those kittens out with three still missing,' observed Hettie.

'Well, we marched him back to the Folly, but he seemed a bit upset as it was his "task for the day", or so he said. He probably thought he'd be in trouble if he returned without any wood. I felt sorry for him, really. He told me he'd taken a fancy to Windolene, and that's why God had taken her away. He said he wanted to be her special friend, but she'd just laughed at him, and now he was sad because she'd gone.'

'Young love in the middle of all this chaos. It sounds like Windolene is – or was – a bit of a tease. I think we need to pay another visit to the Munches. They seem quite unconcerned about the missing kittens. I would have expected Preston to be out looking, but it sounds like it's business as usual at the Folly. As for Anthea, I suspect she's always been a nervous wreck, with or without her missing orphans.' Hettie thought for a moment, then added, 'Maybe we should look further into Preston and Anthea's history. This business in Africa sounds a bit odd.'

Tilly remained silent, but jotted down the main points of their meeting, while Hettie gave a short version of Bonny's latest story concerning Granny Grubb and the implications of kittens having gone missing on the estate before. 'We have another lead to follow up in the shape of Bombazine Bright, an old witch who evidently lives in the woods and protects a Magic Tree,' she explained, without any conviction. 'We seem to be so wrapped up in magic, fairy tales and superstition that I think we're becoming blinded to the facts.'

The four cats sat and contemplated Hettie's words, and it was Tilly who eventually decided to add her thoughts. 'Well, there's all sorts of magic, isn't there?' she said.

'What do you mean?' asked Hettie, becoming more irritated.

Tilly thought for a moment, choosing her words carefully. 'The thing is, we can all do magic. Sometimes our mind plays tricks on us and we see things that aren't there, especially if we're tired or upset, and that's difficult magic. If you wish that something nasty will happen to someone you don't like and it does, that's black magic. Then there's nice magic, when you wish for something lovely and it arrives in the post or you win on a scratch card. I think we all have to believe in magic, otherwise nothing is possible.'

Hettie listened carefully to what Tilly had to say. She could tell that there was something troubling her friend, and if Tilly was upset it often led to a breakthrough in the case they were working on. Tilly was a lateral thinker, and often picked up on the tiniest of clues that Hettie had missed. 'So are you saying that magic is going to solve this case and we should pay a call on Bombazine Bright and her Magic Tree?'

'Yes, I think that's exactly what I'm saying.'

'OK, let's go and see Preston and Anthea again first thing tomorrow morning,' said Hettie. 'Then we'll get Bonny to introduce us to the witch in the woods. We should carry on the search in the house and immediate buildings here at Wither-Fork in the time left to us today. We need to look for any signs of kittens living rough, and I'll get Blackberry Tibbs to check her food stocks in the kitchen in case anything is missing.'

Hettie stood up, keen to conclude the search of Wither-Fork Hall, and Bruiser and Poppa agreed to face the snow again to check out the old stable block and buildings close to the house.

Hettie and Tilly made their way down a warren of tiled passages towards the Wither-Fork kitchen, where Blackberry Tibbs was busy wading through a mountain of washing up in the huge stone sink. The kitchen was vast, with a giant spit taking centre stage over an old fire pit, used in the days when the

Wither-Forks entertained on a large scale. The plaster walls were adorned with every possible cooking pot, the copper now dulled with age and lack of use, as Fluff had embraced a world of non-stick to make Blackberry's tasks a little easier.

Tilly was taken with the copper jelly moulds. 'There's just so many of them,' she said, sweeping her paw across the display. 'They must have liked jelly in the olden days.'

'That's because they had no teeth back then,' said Blackberry. 'They didn't have nice biscuits for cleaning teeth like we do now, so all their teeth went bad and fell out, and their food had to be mashed up and put into jelly moulds to make it look nice. Wither -Fork has one of the finest collections in the whole of England.'

Tilly was impressed, but Hettie brought the shared appreciation of jelly moulds to an abrupt conclusion by addressing Blackberry directly. 'I know you've been frantic with all the extra meals you've had to prepare, but have you noticed if any of your supplies have gone missing? Easy things, like cheese, bread and pies.'

Blackberry shook her head. 'To be honest, I don't think I *would* notice at the moment. The big fridge is packed with stuff, and the cold pantry is full as well. We took a big delivery from Malkin and Sprinkle just before the snow got really bad and I've been working my way through it without thinking, really. Why? Is someone stealing food?'

'It's a long shot, but if the missing kittens have run away from the Folly, they'd be hungry by now, so the kitchen here at the Hall might be a place they'd make a beeline for,' Hettie replied.

'Poor little things,' said Blackberry. 'If I was an orphan, I'd run away from the Munches. You only have to see those kittens being marched across the parkland to know how strict those cats are. She's worse than him, really – dressing them up so they all look the same, and those poor little girls in their stiff bonnets with their ears peeping through. What's really odd is that Anthea gets herself done up the same. Then there's the cleaning thing – she's obsessed with it. I took some buns I'd made for the orphans over there a couple of weeks ago. Preston invited me in and told me to put them on the kitchen table. Then he prayed all over them before Anthea took them up to the schoolroom. When she came back down, she noticed some crumbs on the table so she picked them off and threw them into the fire, then she got her scrubbing brush out and scrubbed away at that table until it was white with bleach. I couldn't get out of there fast enough, and he just stands and watches her. It's all a bit sinister, if you ask me.'

'Do you know where the Munches came from?' Hettie asked, keen to continue the conversation.

'There was some trouble about bringing orphans over from Africa, where I think they were missionaries. When they arrived in the town, there was some resistance at St Kipper's because Preston tried to set up a rival Bible group. I don't think the vicar or the congregation took too kindly to their approach to the scriptures, and they hijacked the Christmas carol service by parading down the aisle with real lit candles and setting fire to the nativity scene during "In The Bleak Midwinter". My friend Effie, who was there, said that Preston made a grab for the pulpit and told everyone that God had set fire to the nativity because he didn't like the way they were celebrating Jesus's birthday.'

'Perhaps he would have preferred a bouncy castle and a tea party,' said Hettie, unable to resist the sarcasm. 'So what do you remember about them moving into the Folly?'

'Well, as far as I know they sweet-talked Miss Wither-Fork by telling her that they needed a home for lots of homeless kittens. They wanted to put them in a shed on her allotments, but she offered them the Folly as no one was using it.'

'And do you know where the kittens actually came from?'

'I've no idea. They just arrived with the Munches.'

Hettie had found her conversation with Blackberry quite revealing. Although she hadn't learnt anything new, she was convinced that another visit to Preston and Anthea was imperative. 'Do you mind if we take a look around the pantry and the other rooms leading off the kitchen?' she asked.

Blackberry nodded. 'Go for it. There's lots of rooms we don't use any more – the still room, the butler's pantry, the dairy and the old boot room. They're mostly full of junk. The bakery's the nicest room, but it probably hasn't been used for years – certainly not in my time, anyway.'

Hettie and Tilly left Blackberry to her washing up and began a routine search of the below stairs rooms that had once been the very hub of running a house the size of Wither-Fork. The pantry was one of the rooms still in use, and Hettie could only admire the cooked hams hanging in muslin from hooks and the pork pies placed on marble slabs to keep cool – although there was very little need to worry about that with temperatures below zero outside. There was a whole shelf of bottled pickles, all labelled and clearly the work of Apple Chutney, one of Fluff Wither-Fork's tenants, who lived and breathed preserving things in vinegar.

Tilly's eye was drawn to the giant wedge of cheese resting under a glass dome, and she suddenly began to mourn the fact that she hadn't had a cheese dumpling with her stew. 'Everything is so big in here,' she said. 'You could feed an army on all this food. They could hold out here for months if the Winter Lands returned.'

'I don't think that's likely,' said Hettie, moving towards another door. 'My prediction is that all this snow will be gone in a week, and we'll forget it ever happened unless we find the bodies of three kittens out there when the thaw comes.'

'This must be the old bakery,' said Tilly. 'Just look at all those old flour sacks, and you could live in that giant oven – it's bigger than our little room. I bet the Butters would love a room like this to do their baking in. It's such a shame that none of it is used any more.'

Hettie was bored with the domestic history of Wither-Fork Hall and moved on quickly, opening the remaining doors along the corridor. It was clear from the cobwebs that none of the rooms had been disturbed in years, and there was certainly no sign of recent occupation in any of them. Blackberry was right: the nicest room was the bakery, and the two cats retraced their footsteps and perched themselves on a couple of flour sacks. 'I think we should give up for the day and go home for a Butters' pie and a video,' suggested Hettie. 'We can't even draw up a list of suspects because we don't know what to suspect them of. Is it a murder case, a kit-napping, or a bunch of runaway kittens doing their best not to be found? The more I hear about Preston and Anthea Munch, the more I believe that those kittens have done a bunk. I certainly would in their shoes. What do you think?'

Tilly was once again distracted by the giant bread oven and hadn't really been listening. She'd jumped down from her flour sack and was giving the old oven a closer inspection, staring into the glass window in the cast-iron door. For a moment, she thought she saw a pair of eyes staring back at her, and jumped as if the oven had burnt her.

'Whatever's the matter?' asked Hettie. 'You look like you've been stung by a bee.'

Tilly calmed herself and took another look at the glass panel, patting it with her paw. 'You'll just laugh at me,' she said, 'but I thought I saw a pair of eyes looking at me from inside the oven.'

Hettie heaved herself off her flour sack and joined Tilly. She reached up for the handle on the oven door and pulled it down. The door swung open with a juddering creak, and they both stared into the void. As Tilly had said, it was a capacious space with two sets of iron rungs, separated by some distance. A blast of cold air filled the room, clearly coming from the giant chimney pipe that sat inside at the top of the oven and climbed through the house to join the chimney stacks on the roof.

'Shall I crawl in and have a look?' said Tilly. 'I don't think you'll fit between those rungs.'

Hettie tried not to be too affronted, and was secretly pleased to see that Tilly also had difficulty in fitting into the oven. She tried to help by giving her a shove, but it was no use. Tilly backed out and was about to abandon the idea when she realised that her new snowsuit was the problem. She kicked off her wellingtons and struggled out of the padded suit, and was about to clamber back into the oven when Hettie burst out laughing.

'What's so funny?' asked Tilly, shivering with cold.

'You are,' said Hettie. 'I think you forgot to do something this morning.'

Tilly was getting upset as well as cold, but suddenly caught sight of her own reflection in the glass of the oven door. 'Bugger!' she said. 'I've still got my pyjamas on. No wonder I'm so cold. What if someone sees me dressed like this? It's so embarrassing.'

'Well, you'd better take a look in that oven before you catch your death of cold – then you can get your snowsuit back on before anyone notices. At least they're your *best* pyjamas.'

Hettie's words were of no great consolation, but Tilly was keen to get the job done. With another helpful push, she found herself in the centre of the giant oven. The rungs were uncomfortable, and she crawled her way deeper in to stare up at the chimney, which offered no sign of daylight, only a constant icy blast of air. In front of her, she could just make out a metal plate which seemed to be hanging on a hinge. She felt round it with her paw and it responded by swinging open.

'How's it going in there?' shouted Hettie.

'There's a small door at the back, and it looks like there's a tunnel, but it's very narrow and I don't think I'll fit. I might get stuck if I try,' came Tilly's muffled response.

Hettie was keen to get Tilly back onto safe ground. This might be the breakthrough they'd been hoping for, but there was no point in pushing their luck. 'Don't try going any further,' she counselled. 'We need to look at Fluff's tunnels to see if any of them lead into the bakery down here, and where they start from.'

Tilly was relieved not to have to pursue her tunnel explorations any further. Her limbs were seizing up with the extreme cold, and she couldn't wait to be reunited with her snowsuit. There wasn't enough room for her to turn round, so she slowly backed out of the oven, with Hettie assisting in the final drop to the floor.

Tilly grabbed her snowsuit and climbed back into it, instantly grateful for both the warmth and the concealment of her pyjamas. She sat on one of the flour sacks and pulled on her wellingtons while Hettie carried out a closer inspection of the main oven door. She ran her paw around the opening until she found what she was looking for. 'There's a release catch on the inside, which means that anything inside the oven can get out, and look at this.' She proffered her paw to Tilly; caught in one of her claws were several strands of grey fur. 'Could this belong to Windolene, I wonder? Preston Munch said she was a grey kitten, and the other two were gingers.'

'There's something else I was going to tell you,' said Tilly, 'but I thought you'd think I was being silly. It's about the dolls' house in the old nursery.'

'What about it?' asked Hettie, carefully placing the sample of grey fur in one of her pockets. 'Don't tell me you want one for your birthday?'

'That would be lovely, but I wouldn't want *that* one. You see, I think it might be haunted.'

Hettie laughed, 'I think all these fairy tales are getting to you. Why would you think that an old dolls' house was haunted, for goodness' sake?'

'Because things had been moved around between me looking at it for the first time and then again after Bonny's story.'

Hettie stopped laughing suddenly, realising what Tilly was trying to tell her. 'You mean that someone moved things round while we were in the next room?'

'Yes. I thought I was seeing things, but it was all a bit nasty. The dolls in the little nursery had been scattered around like they were dead. All their furniture had been tipped up, and worst of all there was a tiny pot on the stove that had strawberry jam in it.'

'What? Proper strawberry jam or just pretend stuff?'

'No, it was definitely real. I tasted it.'

'So that's why you were so quiet at lunch. I knew there was something wrong when you refused that cheese dumpling. Why on earth didn't you say something?'

'I didn't want to look silly in front of Bruiser and Poppa, and I was a bit frightened. I thought I might be going mad. Then that strange cat turned up to look at Fluff's wall painting and I tried to make myself forget what I'd seen,' said Tilly defensively.

'You're far from looking silly now. What you saw in that dolls' house is our first big clue. Stick that with what we think is happening in this old oven, and things are becoming a little clearer and much more hopeful. My guess is that the kittens are alive and well and running amok in Wither-Fork Hall. And we all know how tricky kittens can be. They obviously know about Albertine Chop and her crimes, and in their own silly way tried to warn you off by messing about with the dolls' house. They clearly don't want to be found in case they get returned to the Munches, so we'll need to box clever.'

Tilly was relieved that Hettie had managed to explain away the horror of the dolls' house and was now keen to pursue their new lines of enquiry. If the kittens didn't want to be found, she and Hettie would have to set a trap of some sort to make them reveal themselves. 'I suppose we'd better go and find Fluff and check out her map with the tunnels,' she said. 'She'll be pleased that we've made some progress at last.'

Tilly lifted herself off the flour sack, ready to follow Hettie out of the old bakery, when she noticed a light dancing round inside the oven. 'Look!' she whispered. 'There's something in there again. Quick!'

Hettie pulled the door open, only to be blinded by a flashlight in her eyes. 'Who's there?' she called. 'Come out where we can see you.'

The voice that came back at her was a familiar one. 'Watcha! It's Poppa here. Where are you?'

'We're in the old bakery, and this is the oven. You must be in the tunnel at the back of it – where does it lead?'

'We think it's an old coalhouse next to the stable block,' shouted Poppa. 'That would make sense. I s'pose they shovelled the coal in this way before they had gas and electricity to fuel up the oven.'

'So it's not a tunnel, as such?' shouted Hettie.

'No, it's a narrow chute. Why do you ask?'

'Because we think the kittens are getting into the house this way, through the oven, which isn't used any more. Before you come in, can you take a really good look round the coalhouse? They can't be far away, as one of them tried to get through here only a few minutes ago. We've found some fur, which we think might belong to Windolene. It's just a matter of catching them out.'

'Right-o,' called Poppa. 'We'll meet you back in the main hall. It's just started to snow again, so it'll be nice to get warm.'

Hettie and Tilly found Fluff in the kitchen with Blackberry. The two cats were deep in discussion over the meals planned for the next few days. The words 'hotpot', 'cottage pie' and 'custard tart' were all music to Hettie's ears, and the batch of scones that Blackberry had just pulled from her oven was a sure sign that afternoon tea was on its way.

When Fluff was satisfied with the menus, she turned to Hettie, who'd been waiting patiently to bring her up to date. 'We may have some good news,' Hettie began. 'We think the kittens are safe and sheltering in Wither-Fork Hall – or at least in the outbuildings

– but we also think they're hiding because they don't want to be found.'

'You mean they've run away from the orphanage?' said Fluff. 'That's worrying. I wonder why they would do that? And how do you know they're here in the house?'

Hettie explained about the dolls' house and the oven in the old bakery. Fluff listened carefully, coming to the same conclusion as Hettie. 'Well, this is excellent news. We must let Anthea and Preston know so they can stop worrying. Maybe they can shed some light on why they ran away? It was probably something really silly. We all know how kittens can be.'

Hettie nodded in agreement, but felt that she needed to share her concerns about Anthea and Preston. 'I thought we'd pay another visit to the Munches in the morning,' she said. 'By then, the kittens might have given themselves up, as I'm sure they know we're on to them. I do think we need to find out what made them run away, as it may have implications for the other orphans.'

'If you're suggesting that they might have been ill-treated that would be of great concern to me. I have to say, I took the Munches at face value when they made their approach. I thought they were just a couple of cats trying to put the world to rights by giving a home and an education to a pawful of homeless creatures. If you can bring me proof of anything untoward, I will instantly shut down the whole operation and turn the

Munches off my land. I won't countenance any form of cruelty from my tenants.'

'I don't suppose we'll be any the wiser until we've caught the kittens and given them a chance to explain,' said Hettie, as she watched Blackberry split the scones ready to fill them with cream and jam. 'I think we'll have to set a trap of some sort.'

'We could leave a message in the dolls' house, telling them we're not cross with them,' suggested Tilly. 'And maybe another message in the old oven.'

'That's a really good idea,' said Hettie. 'In fact, we should leave messages in all the places they might go, like here in the kitchen and in the cold pantry, maybe even in the fridge. I'm sure that wherever they're hiding they'll come out to look for food, probably after everyone has gone to bed.'

Blackberry nodded. 'I'll make sure I leave some scones out tonight with one of your notes.'

'Excellent, Blackberry, thank you,' said Fluff. 'Now we must leave you to cut the sandwiches for tea. I'll take mine in the small parlour before I go back to the Lodge. I've a mountain of paperwork to get through. Would you make sure that Hettie and Tilly have pens and paper and whatever else they need?'

She disappeared down the corridor. It was warm in Blackberry's kitchen, and Hettie and Tilly were in no hurry to return to the Great Hall until afternoon tea was ready to be served. Blackberry pulled a wad of paper out of one of her kitchen drawers, together with a selection of felt-tip pens, and Hettie and Tilly perched on the end of her preparation table to write the notes to be left for the kittens.

'What shall we put?' mused Tilly, sucking the top of her pen.

'How about "Give yourselves up and we won't be cross"?'

Tilly thought about it before replying. 'That sounds a bit strict, and they might think it's a trick. We could say: "Dear Windolene, Camay and Comfort, We just want you to be safe and happy, and we won't make you go back to the Folly".'

It was Hettie's turn to think before responding. 'That's a bit long-winded,' she said. 'How about "Dear Kittens, Whatever the problem is, we can fix it"?'

Tilly and Blackberry nodded, giving their approval. Hettie and Tilly wrote the notes while Blackberry cut a mountain of tinned salmon sandwiches. She laid out a small tray with two rounds of sandwiches, a scone and tea in a china cup, and delivered it to Fluff in her parlour before wheeling her trolley into the Great Hall, laden with afternoon tea for the hungry tenants.

Hettie and Tilly retraced their footsteps from earlier, placing the notes in the cold pantry and the old oven in the bakery; they left a note in the kitchen and the fridge, then made their way up to the attics. Tilly approached the dolls' house with extreme caution, still in shock from what she'd seen earlier. She opened the front and was almost relieved to see that there had been no change to the staged massacre, although it was still a scene of horror. Hettie joined her and was equally shocked by what she saw. 'That's what too many fairy stories do for you,' she commented. 'It makes you wonder what sort of monsters we're raising these days. Those kittens must be very disturbed to create something like this.'

Tilly left one of their notes in the miniature nursery and another on what they presumed to be Albertine Chop's bed, then the two cats returned to the Great Hall, where afternoon tea was well and truly underway. Seeing them arrive, Poppa approached with a bundle under his arm. 'Take a look at these,' he said. 'Bruiser found them under an old horse blanket in the stable block.'

Hettie and Tilly stared down at the bundle. It was a small red cloak and a crisp, white starched bonnet. On closer inspection, there was blood on the cloak, and a few tufts of grey fur.

Chapter Eleven

Hettie and Tilly were pleased to be back in their little room. The journey back from Wither-Fork Hall had been a difficult one, as the falling snow had once again transformed itself into a blizzard. Bruiser had done well to keep control of Miss Scarlet as she slid from one side of the road to the other, and the excitement of such extreme weather was wearing thin. The town was deserted, and behind closed doors many cats were cold and hungry as supplies of fuel and food ran out.

Living in the Butters' back room at the bakery brought many blessings, but the very fact that Hettie and Tilly had access to a constant supply of pies, pastries and cakes probably made them the luckiest cats in the town. And the Butter sisters always paid their debts: after such a difficult day at Wither-Fork Hall, the friends were delighted to find a chocolate trifle, a pair of cream horns and a boxed set of Agatha Crispy videos – starring Joan Hiccup as Miss Marble – on their doorstep. 'Ooh! That's lovely,' said Tilly. 'It was almost worth saving Lavender Stamp to get these lovely things.'

Hettie was pleased, too, but felt that there was work to be done before they could enjoy their evening. The shock of finding the blood-stained cloak had rather dampened their euphoria at the possibility of the kittens being alive and well, and she needed to go over the case so far with Tilly to see if there was anything obvious that they had missed. She built up the fire while Tilly brought her notebook up to date with the day's revelations. Hettie settled herself in her chair and filled her pipe with catnip, while Tilly relinquished her snowsuit for a comfy cushion and blanket by the fire, pleased to be wearing her pyjamas already.

'Right,' said Hettie, blowing a perfect smoke ring. 'Let's start from the beginning. We need to look at what we actually know, not what we think we know, so what have you got in your notes?'

'Well, I've called yesterday "day one",' said Tilly, turning to the relevant page. 'I've outlined the case first. Three female kittens missing in the snow, one grey striped, two gingers, Camay, Comfort and Windolene, all orphans living at the Folly with Anthea and Preston Munch. Then I've got a bit on the Munches and the Folly. Anthea a bit mad on cleaning products, names the kittens Brillo, Duster, Daz, Omo and Jaycloth etcetera, she seems very upset about the missing kittens. Preston also a bit mad, especially about God, not quite so bothered about missing kittens, thinks they're probably dead. The Folly, a bit dark and depressing, too clean and strict, more like a prison than an orphanage. Then I've got a bit on the kittens. Windolene is the oldest, a born leader and knows her scriptures; Camay follows her everywhere and Comfort is greedy, fat and blasphemous – according to Preston, that is.'

'That's a good point,' interrupted Hettie. 'Most of what we know is according to Preston Munch. Anthea was too upset to say much, but that might have been convenient. Maybe she knows more than he's telling us. After all, she was the one who discovered that the kittens were missing. Didn't he say he was in the woods gathering stuff for the fires?'

'Yes, that's right. He said he could hear the kittens playing in the snow from where he was in the woods, but that it was Anthea who discovered the girls were missing when she called them in for tea.' Tilly checked her notes. 'Preston said he raised the alarm at Wither-Fork Hall and they organised a search party. I've made some extra notes about the orphans that I found interesting. They're all dressed the same; their lessons are all about God. I couldn't see any other books except the Bible in the schoolroom or the dormitory, and there were no toys or anything for them to play with, no TV, and – as far as I could see – no radio either. It's like they've been cut off from the outside world.'

'You're right,' agreed Hettie, 'but I wonder why that is? Are Preston and Anthea trying to shield them from a world that made them into orphans, or are they deliberately creating a closed order where they can inflict their will on young, vulnerable cats? And I would love to know where those ten kittens came from in the first place. Are they really orphans, or have Preston and Anthea just rounded them up off the streets? I keep thinking about this Africa thing. They were obviously attempting to abduct a bunch of kittens from there and were foiled in the process. Why does their mission in life seem to be collecting kittens? I wonder if there's an endgame to all of this? We need some answers, and I think we need to adopt a harder line with them tomorrow. We should try and talk to them individually. What else have you written down?'

'I've made some notes on *The Ice Maid's Tail* and Albertine Chop, although you probably don't want me to read those out – but it *is* a good story, and it *is* about missing kittens,' said Tilly, trying to justify the space taken up in her notebook.

Hettie blew another smoke ring before responding. 'I think *The Ice Maid's Tail* is a bit of old-fashioned nonsense, but, as I've said before, I do find Albertine Chop interesting, especially after what Bonny had to say about her procuring girl kittens for Jenkin Cowdiddle to add to his collection of wives. If Granny Grubb was one of the missing Wither-Fork kittens, that does begin to sound like history repeating itself. But why should it all be happening now? Albertine Chop was hanged and Jenkin Cowdiddle must have been dead for years, along with Granny Grubb. All that's left behind is a fairy story which in itself is as far-fetched as they come. Ice Queens, giant snow cats, halls of glass, caves of jewels and sparkly things. The only thing that ties any of this together is the weather: all this snow seems to have thrown a blanket over any normal way of thinking. Everything has suddenly become so extreme along with the temperatures. Are we all seriously to believe that the Ice Queen in Cowdiddle's story has returned to enlist a bunch of girl kittens as Ice Maids to live in frozen tunnels under Wither-Fork Hall?'

Tilly could see that Hettie was getting cross, and suggested she refilled her pipe with catnip while she continued with her notes. 'I've put down some brief points about searching the attics, Bonny's story about Granny Grubb and the dolls' house, then I've gone straight to the old oven and the bundle of bloodstained clothes that Bruiser found. I've also added that we had a chocolate trifle waiting for us when we got home, but I don't suppose that's very important.'

Hettie laughed. 'It will be in a few minutes, after we've discussed the cloak and bonnet. The tuft of grey fur suggests it belongs to Windolene, and the bloodstain is bad news, but what about Camay and Comfort? Maybe Windolene was injured and the other kittens helped her. If they wanted to stay out of sight, abandoning the bonnets and red cloaks would be the first thing to do. Just because we've found only one set of clothes doesn't mean to say there aren't more bundles hidden somewhere. The one thing we do know is that someone is definitely using that old oven as a way of getting into Wither-Fork. We've just got to hope that we get a result with one of our notes.'

'Maybe Bombazine Bright will be able to help us,' said Tilly. 'I can't wait to meet her. I've never met a proper witch before.'

'Oh I think Lavender Stamp counts, although not in the traditional sense,' quipped Hettie. 'As for Bombazine, I don't hold out any great hopes there. Any friend of Bonny's is bound to be a little left field, and the fact that she talks in riddles, has a Magic Tree as a pet, and drinks moonshine doesn't really make her a reliable source of information.'

'But she does like catnip and cream cakes,' protested Tilly.

'Just the two redeeming features in a sea of old lady cat nonsense, then,' said Hettie, tapping her pipe out on the fender. 'And speaking of old lady cats, I think it's time for a Miss Marble and a large helping of chocolate trifle.'

Tilly clapped her paws together, pleased that their working day was over. 'Which one shall we have? We've got "The Murder at the Vicarage", "The Body in the Library", "A Murder is Announced" or "They do it with Mirrors".'

'What's that last one about?' asked Hettie, spooning the trifle into two bowls.

'It says it's set in an old Victorian mansion that doubles as a school for delinquent young cats. Miss Marble is visiting an old friend there and a mysterious visitor is shot dead, so she has to sort it out.'

'Old mansions, schools and delinquent young cats – sounds perfect, stick it on,' said Hettie.

The two cats settled down with their trifle, and Miss Marble unravelled the case as if she were pulling apart a tangle of knitting. 'I think Joan Hiccup does the best Miss Marble,' observed Tilly. 'She's a cat with a twinkle in her eye.'

'And you're a cat with trifle all over your ears,' said Hettie. 'I don't know why you even bother with a spoon.'

'I didn't,' said Tilly, getting down to some serious cleaning now that her trifle bowl was empty.

'What I want to know is how Miss Marble has the cheek to turn up on her friends' doorsteps with all her luggage without even being invited. She does it in nearly every story, and no one really asks what she's doing there. She joins in all the meals and country house parties, solves the murders, then clears off home to St Mary Mead, leaving all her friends high and dry – those that are still standing, that is.'

'That's the whole point,' said Tilly, defending her favourite author, whom she and Hettie had actually met during one of their recent cases. 'Miss Crispy has made her into a busybody so that she can poke her nose in anywhere. You just have to go with it. All the stories are different, even if the set-up is the same. And anyway, she has lots of friends to visit.'

'And countless nephews to help her out, it would seem, but I do agree – Joan Hiccup is the best Miss Marble. You'd better rewind a bit – I've lost the thread.'

Tilly did as she was asked and Miss Marble steered the case to a successful conclusion just as the clock on the staff sideboard was striking midnight.

Chapter Twelve

The new day brought no fresh falls of snow, and, as Miss Scarlet negotiated the town's high street, Bruiser sensed a definite thaw. The ice-packed pavements were slowly turning to slush and rivulets of water ran along the gutters, defining the line between road and path. The freeze had been terrible but the thaw threatened worse to come, as the melting snow would inevitably bring floods. Poppa had excused himself from another day at Wither-Fork Hall to take care of a multitude of burst pipes. Being the town's only plumber, he was much in demand.

As Bruiser headed for the bottom of Wither-Fork Hill, it was clear that the town was gradually coming back to life. Cats were out with shovels, clearing paths to their front doors; kittens were building snow cats and rolling giant snowballs; and, most importantly, several delivery vans were braving the weather to deliver much-needed supplies to the shops. Bruiser was in two minds about leaving the motorbike at the bottom of the hill; as the sun began to gain strength in the sky, the compacted ice was breaking up and there was already a constant stream of water coming down the slope towards them. In an instant, his decision was made: giving the bike full throttle, they climbed to the summit, with Hettie and Tilly leaning forward in the sidecar, willing Miss Scarlet on. The parkland was still very deep in snow, so Bruiser pulled the bike into the shelter of the backyard of the Lodge, and the three cats set off on foot across to the Hall. Hettie carried a small satchel containing a pot of her best catnip and the two cream horns that the Butter sisters had left the night before, hoping that they might serve as an inducement for Bombazine Bright. She was relying on Bonny Grubb for the moonshine and the introduction, although she was still sceptical about how beneficial to the case the witch would be – but she knew how much Tilly was looking forward to the encounter, and hated to disappoint her.

Their arrival in the Great Hall showed perfect timing. Blackberry had decided to serve a continental breakfast of freshly baked rolls, with slices of ham and cheese and some of Apple Chutney's sweet onion marmalade. 'No luck with the scones and your notes, I'm afraid,' she said as Hettie helped herself to a roll, cramming it with a slice of ham *and* cheese. 'I've checked the cold pantry and the fridge as well. There's no sign of anything being disturbed there, either.'

Tilly smiled at Hettie's keenness to make herself at home by joining in with breakfast. She couldn't help but think that there were some direct parallels between Miss Marble and her friend: Hettie wasted no time in settling herself in wherever the case they were working on took them.

There was much chatter about the prospect of a thaw and what that might mean for those who would soon be able to return to their plots on the Wither-Fork allotments, where many cats had set up permanent homes. They were grateful to Fluff for offering them food and shelter from the bitter weather on such a grand scale, and most of them had enjoyed the practical diversion of uncovering the Great Hall's wall painting, but home was home and they were now all keen to return to their everyday lives. There was also a very real concern about the damage the thaw would bring to their assorted dwellings. Apple Chutney voiced concerns regarding her pickling shed and the fact that she had sacks of vegetables waiting to be soused in vinegar. Gladys and Dahlia Mulch were concerned for the newly covered fireside chairs in their small but homely cabin; Dahlia had spent most of the early winter stitching the new material onto the chairs and had been particularly pleased with the result, although her sister had railed against her choice of a hunting scene in the fabric. Rooster, Desiree and their little son Blight were confident that their houseboat would withstand any amount of potential flooding; when Rooster Chit had ended his days at sea to grow prizewinning potatoes up on Fluff's allotments, it had seemed the most natural thing in the world to house his family in a boat that he'd hauled from the sea and settled in dry dock; the Chits' home was admired by every cat visiting the allotments, and was a particular favourite of Tilly's for its imaginative built-in bunks and cupboards, and for the fact that Desiree made the best potato cakes she had ever tasted. Hettie and Tilly had enjoyed several batches during their investigations on the Michaelmas Murders case a couple of years before.

Bonny Grubb was perhaps the only one of Fluff's residents who would have preferred to spend the rest of her days in the comfort of Wither-Fork Hall rather than returning to her caravan. 'This spell in the warm 'as done wonders for me lumbago and me siattiks,' she said. 'If it wasn't for me moonshine still, I could live 'ere quite 'appily, scrapin' Miss Wither-Fork's walls.'

Hettie wondered how Fluff might feel about that, but was pleased that Bonny had mentioned the moonshine. 'We're hoping you might introduce us to Bombazine Bright later, Bonny,' she said. 'We've brought catnip and cream cakes, so if you could spare some moonshine, we'll have all the things you say she likes.'

''Cept other cats,' responded Bonny. 'If she don't take to you, no amount of treats will loosen 'er ancient tongue. She's special, see. Answers to no one. What time were you thinkin' of visitin'? I'll need to get to me van to pick up some of me brew.'

'There's no hurry,' said Hettie. 'We need to pay a call on the Munches this morning, so some time after lunch would be good.'

The gypsy cat nodded and shuffled off to help Blackberry clear away the breakfast things. 'I think we'd better go and check the old oven and the dolls' house to see if we've had any luck there with our notes before taking on the Munches,' Hettie said, reaching for the last bread roll and filling it with ham. 'I'll do the oven and you can check the dolls' house and the old nursery if you like?'

Normally Tilly would have been delighted to return to the attics, but the shock of her discovery the day before made her wary. 'I think we should look at everything together today,' she said. 'I'm not sure I want to visit the attics on my own.'

Hettie could see that Tilly was having one of her shy, thoughtful days, and agreed that they would stick together for the various tasks ahead. Before leaving the hall, Hettie spoke to Bruiser. 'It's just occurred to me that we haven't checked the allotments in our searches. You could go over with Bonny and have a look round some of the buildings before the residents return to them. It's possible that the kittens may have sheltered up there.'

They left Bruiser finishing his breakfast and decided to check the oven in the old bakery first. Blackberry stopped them in their tracks with a message. 'Miss Wither-Fork has just phoned from the Lodge to ask if you'd take tea with her later. She's not coming over to the Hall today, but if you could stop off on your way home, she'd be pleased.'

Hettie was pleased, too, as it signalled another pleasant hour of eating, but it did mean that they would have to make some sort of progress on the case if they were to have something to report. More importantly, no discussion had yet been had over their fee, but Hettie knew that Fluff would be fair – and most likely generous – eventually.

The old bakery was as they'd left it. Hettie pulled open the oven door and checked the note; it was still there, and there was no sign of it having been moved or altered in any way. She was beginning to think that they'd been wrong about the kittens coming and going, but if that wasn't the case, who had been messing around with the dolls' house? And more especially, why?

They walked through the attic rooms until they came to the nursery. On first sight, the dolls' house seemed to be missing from the toy box it had stood on. Tilly was visibly upset – for her the toy house had become the most sinister aspect of the case – but Hettie was pleased to see that at least something had changed in the room, supporting their original theory. With no sign of the house in the nursery, they moved into Albertine Chop's room – and there it was, in the middle of the floor.

'I'm not opening it,' said Tilly. 'I bet there's something nasty in there and I don't want to look.'

'But it could be a real breakthrough – there might be an answer to our note. I'll have a look first.' Hettie pulled open the front of the house and stared in dismay, while Tilly stood behind her with her paws over her eyes. 'Oh dear,' said Hettie. 'This is a real mess. Why would anyone want to be so destructive?'

Tilly couldn't resist a peep, and was as shocked as Hettie by what she saw. The whole house had been rearranged, with furniture stacked in corners as if the occupants were packing up to leave. The tiny books were piled up in the middle of the floors like bonfires waiting to be lit, and worst of all the ground floor had been hacked away to reveal a cavity in the floorboards beneath, giving the house a basement which it hadn't had before. The draught coming up from the missing floorboard was icy, and Hettie put her paw into the cavity retrieving several small cat dolls which she passed to Tilly. 'It's wet down there,' she said, putting her paw back in to see what else she could find. 'I can feel something else, but it keeps sliding away from me. Just a minute – I think I've got it.' With much fumbling about, Hettie eventually managed to retrieve the object that had eluded her. Bringing it up from below the floor, she couldn't quite believe what was sliding around in her paw. 'It's a bloody ice cube!' she exclaimed. 'And there's more of them down there.'

Tilly stared down at the melting ice cube, then at the collection of tiny cats in her own paw. 'Look,' she said. 'Their tails have been cut off just like in the story. What does all this mean?'

'If I knew that, we'd be tucked up at home eating the Butters' pies and watching more Miss Marbles, having banked our fee at Lavender Stamp's post office,' said Hettie, inspecting the house a little closer. 'Interestingly, the note's gone, but if it's connected to the case at all, why hasn't whoever did it left a proper message rather than this mess?'

'What do you mean?' asked Tilly. 'What else could it be connected to?'

Hettie let the half-melted ice cube fall back into the hole. 'I just don't know,' she replied with a sigh. 'Maybe young Blight Chit fancied a game. He's been cooped up here at Wither-Fork for days in all this weather, and maybe he discovered the dolls' house and is playing some sort of game that only makes sense to him. I'm just clutching at straws here.'

Tilly placed the tiny kittens back in the top storey of the house and Hettie closed it up. The two cats searched the rest of the room for the note they'd left, but found only the one that had been placed on Albertine's bed. The dolls' house note was definitely missing; it might have been shoved out of reach under the floorboards, of course, but Hettie felt they'd wasted enough time when clearly there were now more practical matters to address. 'Let's leave this and have a think about what we've found. We should keep it to ourselves, too. It might all be one big joke to someone, and I don't want to be seen rising to the bait. We'll get ourselves across to the Folly and have a detailed conversation with the Munches like we planned. After all, that's where this mess began.'

Tilly was pleased to leave the Wither-Fork attics – and more especially the dolls' house – behind to pay another visit to the Folly. On their way out, Blackberry announced that lunch would be served at one o'clock, and that it would be sausage and mash with small peas and extra gravy, which put a spring in Hettie's step as they crossed the park. The snow was fast turning to slush beneath their feet, and Fluff's cherub statues were once again beginning to spout fountains of water as the sun melted the ice. The world was waking from its frozen slumbers, and, as the snow retreated, the parkland became alive with creatures catching up with their lives after being entombed for so long in the return of winter. The fields were full of scurrying rabbits and hares, finally released from their burrows to go about their business.

When Hettie and Tilly neared the Folly, they were instantly aware of some form of celebration taking place in Wither-Fork Woods: the cacophony of birdsong was deafening as the crows and rooks emerged from their roosts to feel the sun on their feathers at last. 'This must be how Hugo Nightspark and the Ice Maid felt when they came up from the ice tunnels,' observed Tilly. 'You forget how lovely it is to feel the sun on your face again.'

'Let's just hope that this fairy tale or nightmare that we're living through has a happy ending like that one,' said Hettie.

Chapter Thirteen

An eerie silence greeted Hettie's knock on the Folly's door. There had clearly been some activity around the building recently, with a multitude of slushy footprints leading into the woods and across the park. It occurred to Hettie that – like the rest of the world – Anthea and Preston were out with their orphans, taking advantage of the thaw to indulge in some sort of educational nature walk or even a foray into town for much-needed supplies. She knocked again, then turned the iron ring door handle. It twisted with an obliging creak and the door opened.

'They can't have gone far if they've left the door unlocked,' said Hettie, kicking the slush off her wellingtons against a well-placed door scraper. Tilly did the same, and the two cats entered the Folly. The kitchen was deserted; the only sign of life came from a giant stew pot on the stove which rattled and puffed, sending plumes of meaty vapour into a row of identical kitten smocks drying above the range.

Hettie called up the first flight of stairs, which led to the schoolroom, but there was no answer.

'Well, this is all very annoying,' grumbled Hettie. 'I wonder where they are?'

'Maybe they're out looking for the kittens,' offered Tilly, 'or maybe they're all collecting kindling. They can't be far. Some of those tracks went into the woods.'

'It's a shame not to have another look round while we're here,' said Hettie, climbing the stairs.

Tilly was a little concerned. 'What if they come back?'

'Then we'll just say we were looking for them. We *are* supposed to be detectives, after all.'

On reaching the schoolroom, it was a great surprise to both cats to discover that the Folly was by no means uninhabited. Seven boy kittens sat at their desks in absolute silence, as if they were made out of clay. Hettie greeted them with a bright 'good morning', but none of them moved and all stared straight ahead in some sort of trance-like state.

Hettie clapped her paws, adopting a schoolmistress approach of authority. 'Now then, boys,' she said, 'who's going to tell me where Preston and Anthea are?'

There was still no response, and Hettie found their silence more than a little unnerving. 'Let's take a look in the dormitory,' she said, moving to the second flight of stone steps, quickly followed by Tilly. 'Maybe Anthea's up there.'

The dormitory was as before, with ten neat little beds laid out in a circle, but the beds belonging to Windolene, Camay and Comfort had clothes across them – red cloaks, bonnets, blue smocks and socks, all neatly folded and waiting for the kittens to return. Hettie was quite pleased to see that as far as the Munches were concerned there was still hope for a happy outcome, but her train of thought was derailed minutes later by the sound of footsteps on the dormitory stairs and the familiar tones of Preston Munch. 'Now then, girls – up you go. Let's get you changed into the nice new clothes that God has provided.'

Hettie and Tilly backed into one of the window recesses and froze as the first of three little kittens emerged at the top of the stairs. The kitten was very small, her face tearstained and her eyes bulging with trepidation. 'I just want my ma!' she cried pitifully, as two more kittens followed her into the dormitory, both looking as upset as she was.

Preston was too busy with his new charges to notice Hettie and Tilly straight away. All three kittens began to cry as they stared at the beds, and one darted behind Preston, making an attempt to escape down the stairs. Preston caught her by the scruff of her little neck, dangling her in the air as he delivered what he clearly thought was a speech of calming reassurance. 'Now you don't want to upset God, do you? He has blessed you by bringing you here to do his work, and for that you will be allowed to sit with him in heaven one day. He's marked out a very special place for you, and you must be silent and obedient to keep it. You don't want to make him angry, do you?' The little kitten squirmed in his paw, shaking her head, and Preston put her down on the floor, satisfied that the rebellion had been quelled.

Hettie and Tilly looked on in horror at the heartbreaking scene, waiting for the right moment to make their presence felt, but one of the kittens gave them away. 'Miss Tilly,' she said, pointing across the room.

Preston immediately turned round, and Hettie and Tilly moved away from the window, not wanting to give the impression that they had concealed themselves in some covert way. 'Ah, Mr Munch – we'd almost given up on you,' said Hettie, adopting a forthright approach. 'Please forgive the intrusion, but we have some more questions regarding the missing kittens and we thought you might be up here.'

Preston was visibly rattled by his unwanted guests, even more so when the kitten who had recognised Tilly ran to her and started sobbing into her snowsuit. Tilly comforted her while Hettie widened her conversation with Preston. 'I see you have some new orphans,' she said. 'Where did you find them?'

Preston was taken aback by such a direct question, for which he clearly had no direct answer. He procrastinated a little with his favourite topic. 'Suffer the little kittens to come unto me, for…'

Hettie held her paw up, bringing the sermon to an abrupt and premature end. 'Yes, yes – I'm sure for those who believe that's all lovely, but I'll ask you again: where did you find these little kittens?'

'In the town this morning,' said Preston, realising that he'd have to respond. 'They'd been turned out and left on the streets to starve. God was merciful and showed them to me, and I knew that Anthea and I could help them.'

Hettie tried very hard to contain her anger as the other two kittens joined the first one for a group sob under the protection of Tilly and her snowsuit. 'Are you telling me that you just snatched these kittens off the street without making any enquiries as to where they came from? God or no God, what gives you the right to decide if they are homeless? Perhaps they were just out playing in the snow – had that occurred to you? Maybe you should have adopted the old priest's attitude in the story of the Good Samaritan and passed by on the other side.'

Preston Munch backed towards the stairs, giving the perfect impression of a rabbit caught in headlights, then changed his mind and decided to stand his ground. He moved forward towards Hettie, forcing his face into hers. 'I'll ask you just once to leave, if you know what's good for you,' he hissed.

Undaunted by his approach, Hettie squared up to him. 'Or you'll what?' she challenged. 'Bring the wrath of God down upon me? Look at me – I'm shaking in my wellingtons. You should know that if I leave now I will return with Miss Wither-Fork. The orphanage, for want of a better word, will be closed and you and Anthea will be turned out.'

The stand-off had silenced the crying kittens. Tilly moved them over to the stairs, keen to get them out of harm's way, but Preston darted back to block their exit. 'Those kittens are staying here under my protection. You can leave whenever you like.'

Tilly obliged him with a beaming smile before moving in for the kill. 'I'm sorry to say that these kittens have a perfectly good home in the town. They often come into my friend's shop with their mother, who I'm sure will be very pleased to get them back.'

Preston crumpled to the floor and put his head in his paws. 'I just wanted to cheer Anthea up,' he sobbed. 'She's been so sad since the kittens went missing, and I wanted to surprise her by getting some more. These little ones looked so helpless in the snow, and we can give them so much more here at the Folly – an education, lovely food, and a spiritual pathway directly to our dear Lord. I honestly didn't think they had a home. I just wanted to do my Christian duty.'

Hettie nodded to Tilly, who took the kittens downstairs and settled them in the kitchen, knowing that the conversation wasn't over. Hettie sat on one of the beds and waited for Preston to pull himself together before opening up the subject of the orphans again. 'I can understand that you might have made a mistake with the kittens you brought here today,' she said, trying to be generous, 'but what about the others? Where did they all come from?'

'Most of them were begging in the streets in town just before Christmas,' said Preston. 'It broke Anthea's heart to see them, so we rounded them all up and gave them food and warm clothes. That's when I asked Miss Wither-Fork if we could have a shed on her allotments, and she gave us this place instead so we could do things properly. Anthea's always wanted to set up a proper school, and this Folly is like a dream come true.'

'And what about Windolene, Camay and Comfort?' asked Hettie. 'Were they out begging, too?'

'Well, Windolene was sleeping rough in Malkin and Sprinkle's shop doorway, and we found Camay and Comfort sheltering under an old wheelbarrow in St Kipper's graveyard. Their mother had just been buried there, and they had nowhere to go.'

'So Camay and Comfort are sisters?' said Hettie. 'Why didn't you say that before?'

'I didn't think it mattered,' said Preston. 'We're all part of God's family.'

Hettie chose to ignore Preston's attempt to return to his favourite subject and pushed on with her questions. 'What more can you tell me about Windolene? You said she's good at her scriptures, but what else is she good at?'

'Not much, to be honest,' Preston replied. 'She knows her scriptures off by heart, but she's no use at anything else. Anthea was trying to teach her to read, but she was so slow with her letters that she couldn't even write her name.'

'How come she was so good at her scriptures if she couldn't read or write?' asked Hettie, feeling a little confused.

'Because she learnt them off by heart. Anthea would read to her and she would remember every word, just like learning a poem.'

'And what about Camay and Comfort – can they read and write?' asked Hettie.

'A little bit,' said Preston. 'The thing is, Anthea's a bit old-fashioned. She believes that boys should have the opportunities to learn their letters and girls should learn to keep things clean and tidy and cook. As long as they know their scriptures and can write their name, there's no need for anything else.'

Hettie was finding the Anthea Munch school of drudges a little hard to take, and it was becoming very clear that the missing kittens had craved a life beyond the oppressive regime that the Munches had set up for them. It was interesting that Windolene couldn't read: that might explain why she and Tilly had had no success with the notes they had dotted around Wither-Fork Hall. 'Tell me about Africa,' she said, changing the subject. 'What happened there?'

'What do you mean?' Preston asked defensively.

'I understand that there was some trouble over bringing orphans back here?'

'Ah, that was a misunderstanding,' Preston insisted, looking for the right words. 'We were out there spreading the word, and Anthea set up a pop-up school in one of the villages. Lots of kittens travelled miles to come to the school, although it was really only an old shack. The kittens' parents tried to sell them to us as they were very poor. We said we couldn't buy them, but offered to bring them back to England for a better life. Anthea chose mostly girls, and we were all set to board the ship when a whole tribe of African cats stopped us from taking the kittens. They said we were stealing them, and that if we wanted them we would have to pay for them. We fled for our lives, as things got quite nasty.'

Hettie wasn't convinced by Preston's explanation, but thought she'd stick with the subject of school. 'When we arrived at the Folly just now,' she said, 'the boys in the schoolroom seemed rather unresponsive. I asked them a question and they just sat at their desks, staring straight ahead, which I thought was rather odd.'

Preston shook his head. 'That's not odd, that's discipline. Our orphans are told not to speak to strangers and, if Anthea and I have to go out for any reason, they are to sit still and be quiet until we return. You can't have a school without discipline. I always tell them that if we're out we leave God in charge, and He sees and hears everything.'

have to organise the return of the three kittens to their mother – and Blackberry Tibbs's sausage and mash would wait for no cat. Tilly was finishing off a truncated version of *The Ice Maid's Tail* for the kittens when Hettie joined her in the Folly kitchen, and all clapped their paws at such a lovely story. Without another word to Preston, Hettie and Tilly gathered up the kittens and marched them across the park to Wither-Fork Hall.

When it came to food, Hettie's timing was invariably perfect: as the two cats and their three small charges arrived at the French windows into the Great Hall, Blackberry was wheeling in her trolley ready to serve the lunch. Bruiser had just arrived back from a fruitless trip to the allotments, having searched the sheds and assorted buildings, but Bonny had drawn off a large bottle of her best moonshine in anticipation of her visit to Bombazine Bright, and Bruiser obliged her by carrying it back to the Hall.

Most of Fluff's residents had decided to return to the allotments after lunch, fearful of the thaw and eager to protect their homes from the inevitable flooding. They had all enjoyed their time at Wither-Fork Hall, protected from the blizzards and freezing temperatures, but they were equally pleased to be going back to what they all regarded as home. There was quite a party atmosphere over the sausage and mash, and Hettie and Tilly's three little kittens joined in the feasting, heavily swathed in napkins as the mashed potato and gravy kept narrowly missing their mouths. The kittens seemed to have recovered from the trauma of being kit-napped by Preston Munch, and were now looking forward to being reunited with their mother.

'I think we should get them home as soon as possible,' said Hettie. 'It's a nuisance, really, as I was hoping to get Bombazine Bright out of the way this afternoon, then speak to Anthea Munch.'

'I could take 'em in Miss Scarlet and pick you up later,' suggested Bruiser after he'd licked his plate clean.

'That would be such a help, but I'm not sure we know where they live.'

Tilly turned to the kitten sitting next to her. 'Where do you live with your mummy?' she asked.

The kitten giggled, then the other two joined in and they began to sing, banging their spoons on the table to add extra percussion. 'Cheapcuts, Cheapcuts, Cheapcuts.'

Blackberry brought their song to an end by placing a bowl of banana custard in front of each of them, and while the kittens tucked in to their puddings, Tilly came up with a plan. 'They must live in Cheapcuts Lane, near Jessie's shop. She'll know where, so if Bruiser takes them to her, I'm sure she'll be happy to take them home.'

Hettie and Bruiser were pleased with Tilly's plan and, after giving the kittens a cursory wipe with a damp tea towel provided by Blackberry, they waved Bruiser and his three new friends off as they headed towards the Lodge and Miss Scarlet. 'I wonder how things would have been if we hadn't rescued them from the Folly?' mused Hettie, as she watched them scamper around Bruiser, throwing snowballs and squealing with delight. 'I just can't get over the silence in that schoolroom. Those poor little things have had the spirit knocked out of them, and Preston obviously doesn't expect Windolene and her friends to turn up. He seemed mighty keen to grab some replacements, and that's beginning to worry me.'

Tilly thought for a moment. 'Do you think Preston has murdered the kittens, and that's why he isn't expecting them to come back?'

'It's a possibility we have to consider. He behaved rather oddly about where Anthea was, as well. Maybe he's done away with her, too, although that doesn't explain why he went out and got another set of replacement kittens. It seems this whole orphanage thing is Anthea's idea, and he just goes along with it – according to him, anyway.'

'If he *has* killed the kittens, that doesn't explain what's going on here at the Hall, either, or that awful thing with the dolls' house.'

'Ah, but I did find something out which might explain why our notes didn't work if the kittens are sheltering here. Windolene can't read or write, and the other two – who are sisters – can't do much more than sign their names. Anthea's teaching methods for female kittens appear to be firmly fixed in the dark ages. She likes them to cook and clean, evidently.'

'Sounds like she's turning them into Ice Maids,' joked Tilly.

Hettie laughed. 'Well, all I can say is heaven help her come the revolution. She might get a shock if those orphans decide to turn on her *en masse*.'

Bonny Grubb ended Hettie and Tilly's speculative conversation by approaching with a large bottle of moonshine. 'This is one of me best brews,' she said, pushing the bottle into Hettie's paws. 'I s'pose we'd better be makin' tracks if you wants ta catch 'er in the right mood. She 'as a selection of moods, dependin' where the moon is, see. Full moon would be no good – too busy witchin' then – and the new moon's right out 'cos she's busy with 'er spells.'

Hettie, who had never had much faith in the prospect of a visit to Bombazine Bright, had even less now that Bonny was complicating the issue. 'So where are we currently in the lunar cycle?'

'Slap bang in the middle,' replied the gypsy. 'She should be at 'er best right now, if you can work through 'er riddles.'

'Well, let's get it over with, then,' said Hettie, picking up the satchel containing the cream horns and catnip and passing the moonshine to Tilly to carry.

The three cats set off towards Wither-Fork Woods, keeping the Folly on their right and this time giving it a wide berth. At the edge of the trees, Bonny took the lead, but their progress was slow as the snow was deep here, still frozen in places where the sun couldn't reach. The bottle of moonshine became increasingly heavy in Tilly's paws as they dragged themselves through snowdrifts and tangled branches, and the black starkness of leafless trees that had stood for centuries gave no comfort or shelter to the small party, picking their way deeper and deeper into the heart of the wood. There were small frozen pools to negotiate, with icy mists rolling across them, and giant icicles hung from the lower branches of trees like strange sculpted fruits.

Hettie's heart began to beat faster as a threatening silence descended upon them. The birds had stopped singing, and only the occasional thud of melting snow – falling from a branch and halting their progress – had any effect on the frozen landscape. Suddenly, Bonny stopped dead. Craning her neck, she sniffed the air. 'Not far now,' she said. 'Wood smoke.'

Hettie could smell nothing except the faint aroma of catnip coming from her satchel, and Tilly was too exhausted after carrying the moonshine to care, but both cats kept up with the gypsy as she quickened her pace, following her nose until they came to a clearing.

The little stone cottage stood watchful and not at all welcoming. A faint trail of smoke from its chimney was nothing more than the slightest hint of occupation, and the snow that lay around the cottage was deep and showed no sign of anything having recently left or approached. Bonny hesitated. 'You sure you want ta go on with this?' she whispered.

Hettie wasn't at all sure and Tilly had quite changed her mind about meeting the witch, but they had gone to a lot of effort to get to the cottage and now was not the best time to turn and run back to civilisation. 'Let's just get it over with,' said Hettie. 'The worst that can happen is she won't see us.'

Bonny cackled. 'If she takes agin you, you'll see what 'er worst can be.' With her barbed comment still ringing in the frosty air, Bonny moved forward across the virgin snow to the cottage door, where she knocked so loudly that the noise unseated a giant avalanche of snow from the thatched roof, missing Hettie and Tilly by inches as it slid to the ground in front of them. The door appeared to open by itself; only after they had all stepped inside the cottage did they realise that Bombazine had hooked the door open with a gnarled walking stick while remaining seated in her chair by the fire. She waved the stick at them, as if counting her visitors, and pointed it directly at Tilly, beckoning her forward with a crooked claw.

Tilly was mesmerised by the cat in front of her. She was clearly very old; her eyes were misted and the fur covering her face was almost white, and she had unruly tufts of fur growing from her chin in long strands and hardly any whiskers at all. She was swathed in knitted blankets against the cold, and a shawl covered her ears and the top of her head, fastened at her throat with a silver brooch.

Tilly approached with caution and Bombazine lurched at her, clawing the bottle out of her paws and offering a toothless grin that could have been interpreted in several ways. Tilly was shocked by Bombazine's keenness to wrestle the moonshine from her, but the witch was already training her misty eyes on Hettie's satchel. Bonny nudged Hettie, and she responded by opening the satchel. Once again Bombazine pounced, hooking the pot of catnip and the cream horns away from Hettie, and this time offering a deep-throated cackle before she spat into her fire, creating a cascade of coloured sparks. She clawed the top off the catnip and sniffed it, then opened the bag and took a good, long look at the cream horns, allowing strings of saliva to escape from the corners of her mouth. Her visitors stood silently watching, wondering if their gifts had gained them favour for an audience with the witch.

Bonny decided to make some introductions. She moved closer to Bombazine and shouted: 'Good day, Bombazine. I brought some visitors lookin' for lost kittens. We was wonderin' if you could 'elp or if you'd seen anythin' of 'em? This is Tilly and Hettie.'

Bombazine moved forward in her chair to take a closer look at Hettie and Tilly. She sniffed at the air around them before addressing them directly in a cracked and broken voice. 'Lost kittens are only lost to them that thinks they're missin'. We're all lost till we finds ourselves. Some say it's better never to be found.'

Hettie was tempted to turn on her heel and walk back into the woods; a philosophical witch was not what the case needed, and her patience had run out much earlier in the day with Preston Munch. It was Tilly who suddenly summoned up the courage to take the witch on by giving her some background to their enquiries. 'Miss Bright,' she began, 'there are three kittens missing from the orphanage at Wither-Fork Folly – Windolene, Camay and Comfort. They've been gone for several days in this terrible weather, and we wondered if you'd seen them or could shed any light on their disappearance?'

Bombazine cackled again before responding. 'Pretty little things, danced for their stories.'

Tilly waited for Bombazine to continue, but instead the witch cat reached for a slice of burnt toast, abandoned in the grate, and proceeded to scrape it into an old battered teapot. She added water from a black kettle that swung over the fire, and turned the pot three times before pouring the liquid into a dish which she offered to Tilly. 'Drink,' she said.

Tilly did as she was told. The concoction tasted bitter, and it burnt her tongue. Hettie and Bonny looked on, not daring to interrupt the understanding that was developing between Tilly and the ancient cat. When all the drink was gone, Bombazine clawed back the bowl from Tilly's paws and sniffed at the black residue in the bottom. 'Bad things come to thems that waits below. This is not the time for crystal crowns and icy queens. Two is left, and one has gone to bring the house down. Mark well the little house that's never warm with words or deeds. Their faces lie, one to serve and one to wield the power, forever frozen in time. And time is running out. The stage is set for tragedy and revenge. The play is well rehearsed, but the mantle may be hard to wear.'

While Bombazine was incanting, Tilly reached into her snowsuit pocket and pulled out her notebook and pencil, quickly scribbling down as much as she could remember of the riddle and hoping that Bonny and Hettie would fill in the gaps later. When Bombazine finally fell silent, she decided to ask a question. 'Miss Bright, can you tell us if the missing kittens are alive or dead?'

Bombazine spat into the fire again and reached for a clay pipe, packing it with Hettie's best catnip. She lit a taper from the fire and sucked hard on the pipe, filling the cottage with smoke. Several minutes elapsed as the witch enjoyed her pipe, ignoring the visitors who stood waiting for an answer to Tilly's question. Eventually, after the catnip had burnt down, Bombazine cast the pipe aside and picked up her walking stick, waving it at her visitors in a rather aggressive manner. It would appear that the audience was over, and the three cats decided to leave without an answer to Tilly's question.

Hettie was pleased to be out in the cold air, but, as they made their way across the clearing, heading back into the woods, it was obvious that Bombazine Bright hadn't quite finished with them. There was suddenly an intensity of light which grew brighter as they approached. 'Look!' cried Tilly. 'It's the Magic Tree!'

The cats stood stock-still and gasped at the vision before them. The tree was small and resembled an oak, its branches spread like tendrils and twisted with age. It was silver, a joyful contrast to the tall, black-barked trees that surrounded it. Some of the branches reached low to the ground and were decorated with ribbons, bits of string, fir cones, several dead birds and a mouse. Although the tree was still, it gave the impression that it could uproot itself at any minute and perform a pagan dance for its onlookers. 'So this is the tree where they hanged Albertine Chop,' said Tilly. 'It seems to have just landed from somewhere. I'm sure it wasn't here earlier when we were looking for Bombazine's cottage.'

'Well tha's 'cos it's magic,' said Bonny in a rather matter of fact way.

Hettie rubbed her eyes, wanting to make sure that the passive smoke from Bombazine's catnip hadn't affected her, but the tree was still there when she looked again, and on closer inspection it wasn't just decorated with ribbons, string and dead things from the woods. To her horror, Hettie found herself staring at two small ginger cats' tails, hanging from one of the branches.

Chapter Fourteen

The discovery of the ginger tails meant that Hettie and Tilly would have to have a complete rethink of the case. It was clear that at least two of the missing kittens had been harmed – possibly even murdered – and the bloodstained clothes found in Wither-Fork's stables might now suggest that Windolene had suffered the same fate.

Throwing caution and magic to the wind, Hettie pulled the tails from the tree and put them in her satchel. 'I think we definitely need to have a conversation with Anthea Munch before the day is out,' she said, turning her back on the Magic Tree and striding off through the woods, leaving Tilly and Bonny to stumble after her in the snow.

Bonny was keen to return to her caravan up on the allotments before it got dark, and bid farewell to Hettie and Tilly when they reached the edge of the woods. She cut across the park, leaving the two friends to approach the Folly. The earlier warmth had drained from the sun. Underfoot, the going was a slushy, slippery mess, and it was growing noticeably colder as they drew closer to their next port of call. 'What's the plan with Anthea?' asked Tilly, wanting to be prepared.

'The important thing is to get her on her own,' said Hettie. 'I'm going to come clean about our various discoveries so far, as I want to see how she'll react, but I don't need Preston adding his little religious insights into the conversation. If necessary, you'll have to distract him while I deal with her, but I'll take your notebook, even if I just use it to intimidate her. At least she'll know we mean business.'

The Folly looked as it always did, bleak and isolated. Hettie knocked on the door and it was opened immediately by Preston. 'I'm afraid Anthea is still out,' he said. 'I suggest you come back tomorrow.'

Hettie felt that she had wasted enough time on the Munches already, and stringing things out for another day was not on her agenda. 'That's not a problem,' she said, forcing her way over the threshold, quickly followed by Tilly. 'I need to speak to Anthea today, and I'm very happy to wait for her.'

Preston seemed disturbed by Hettie and Tilly's invasion of his kitchen, even more so when the two cats placed themselves firmly on a pair of kitchen chairs as if they were in a waiting room. 'I'd be happy to pass on any message to Anthea to save you time,' Preston offered, hopping nervously from one foot to another and wringing his paws. 'You see I'll have to start the kittens' teas soon, and I'm in the middle of a lesson with them at the moment.'

'You go ahead, and don't mind us. We wouldn't want to interfere with the kittens' education.'

Hettie made no attempt to hide the sarcasm in her voice. By now, Preston was almost beside himself, and the frustration of not being able to get rid of his unwanted visitors turned him into a jabbering wreck. He paced up and down the kitchen, then suddenly stopped as if a welcome idea had presented itself. His whole demeanour changed. 'Actually, I've just had a thought,' he said. 'Perhaps you'd like to talk to the boys about being detectives. I'm sure they'd find that a really interesting subject.'

Hettie was a little taken aback at Preston's willingness to have his orphans polluted with the seamier sides of life, but agreed on the principle that it would kill some time and perhaps give her a chance to discover the true circumstances that had brought the kittens to the Folly in the first place. She and Tilly followed Preston up the stairs to the schoolroom, and he addressed the kittens, who immediately stood to greet their visitors. 'Blessed be the fur,' they incanted, and sat down again at their desks.

'Boys,' said Preston, 'for your last lesson today, I've engaged two detectives from the town who are going to talk to you about the evil they encounter in the course of God's work.'

Hettie and Tilly exchanged looks as Preston beat a retreat back downstairs to the kitchen. It wasn't the first time that Hettie had been called upon to give a talk: she had awkwardly mumbled her way through several friendship club gatherings and library events during crime week, as well as a rather unfortunate encounter at the town's annual garden fete which still haunted her on sleepless nights; to take on Anthea and Preston's orphans was a big ask, and as she and Tilly made their way to the front of the class, she had absolutely no idea what either of them was going to say.

It was Tilly who came to the rescue. 'We are The No. 2 Feline Detective Agency,' she began. 'My name is Tilly Jenkins and this is Hettie Bagshot. We spend our days solving mysteries and catching nasty cats who do terrible things.'

Hettie had to admire Tilly's mission statement and made no attempt to interrupt her flow, but a kitten on the front row raised his paw to ask a question. Tilly responded by nodding her head, and the cat rose from his seat. 'My name is Jaycloth, Miss, and I was wonderin' if you had any news on Windolene and the other girls?'

This was an unexpected question, but one that Hettie was happy to take. 'We are continuing our enquiries, Jaycloth, and we hope to solve the mystery very soon.' Looking at the kitten in front of her, Hettie suddenly had an idea. 'Maybe we should all get to know each other a little better,' she began. 'Let's start with you, Jaycloth. Is that your real name?'

It was Tilly's turn to look on in admiration as Hettie managed to turn an awkward situation into a full-blown enquiry. Jaycloth looked round at the rest of the class, as if seeking solidarity before answering the question. 'We're not supposed to say anything about before,' he said.

'Before what?' pressed Hettie gently.

Jaycloth turned again to his classmates, and the kitten sitting next to him gave him an encouraging nudge with his paw. 'Before God took us in and Jesus was our friend,' he mumbled, lowering his head to focus on the desk.

Hettie shot Tilly a meaningful look and touched her ear, nodding towards the stairs. Tilly excused herself on the pretence of fetching a glass of water, returning almost immediately without the water but with the glad tidings that Preston Munch was nowhere to be found and the kitchen was unoccupied. She whispered the news into Hettie's ear, giving her the confidence to continue with her questions. 'And what happened to your mother, Jaycloth?'

'I don't think I have one. Mr Preston said that the mother cat who was looking after me gave me away to him because she didn't like me any more.'

The kitten's little voice cracked, and tears began to roll down his face. Tilly moved over to comfort him and Hettie spread her net wider. 'What about you?' she asked, pointing her paw at the kitten sitting next to Jaycloth. 'What's your story?'

The kitten stood, but, like Jaycloth, lowered his head, fearful of speaking out. Eventually he found some courage. 'I was very naughty,' he admitted. 'I stole cakes from my Ma's baking tin, and when she found out I ran away. Mr Preston found me in an old shed. He said my Ma was so angry that she didn't want me to go home, and that I was to be put in an orphanage to teach me a lesson.'

'The same happened to me,' came a squeaky voice from the back of the class. 'Mrs Anthea told me that my Ma asked her to take me away because I stole some sweets from my little sister.'

'And did you steal the sweets?' asked Hettie.

'No, Miss, and I don't have a little sister, but it all happened so quickly and Mrs Anthea is quite kind. One day I'll be big enough to run away from here, so I try not to cry. Mr Preston shouts when we cry.'

There was a unanimous nodding of little heads in agreement with the kitten on the back row. Hettie and Tilly were appalled at what they'd just heard, and Hettie was about to ask for more stories when she heard the sound of footsteps on the stairs. The kittens froze as Preston Munch appeared. 'Anthea has returned,' he said, in a rather breathless fashion. 'She's happy to talk to you while she makes the teas in the kitchen if you'd like to go down.'

It was more of a command than an invitation. Hettie and Tilly moved swiftly towards the stairs and Preston took over at the front of the class, seemingly unaware of the conversations that had passed between the orphans and the detectives in his absence.

There was something different about Anthea Munch. She seemed less fragile than the last time Hettie and Tilly had spoken to her, and had obviously wasted no time in tidying the kitchen on her arrival home: the floor was wet, and she was wielding a mop as they arrived at the bottom of the stairs. She stowed it away in a bucket and invited Hettie and Tilly to sit down. 'Preston says you need to talk to me, although I don't know why. You'll have to excuse me while I get on with the kittens' teas. I don't want them up too late – it's not good for them.'

Hettie could have come up with a whole list of things that were harming the kittens more than a late night, but she resisted the temptation and took a professional line instead. Deciding to adopt shock tactics, she pulled the two ginger kitten tails out of her satchel and placed them gently down on the kitchen table. Anthea was slicing bread, and accidently cut into her paw at the sight of them. Staunching the blood with a dishcloth, she stared at the body parts, seemingly lost for words. Eventually she found some. 'What does this mean? Where did you find them?'

'Dangling from a tree in Wither-Fork Woods,' said Hettie. 'We'd just paid a visit to Bombazine Bright, who has been helping us with our enquiries.'

'Oh, that ridiculous old hag! You should never believe a word she says,' scoffed Anthea. 'She's the one you should be talking to about those tails. I bet she knows more about our missing kittens than any other cat, her and her Magic Tree.'

'I didn't say it was a Magic Tree,' said Hettie, nodding to Tilly, who made much of getting her notebook and pencil out of her pocket and turning to a clean page. 'Bombazine was very helpful, actually, and we've made several discoveries in the last couple of days that we'd like to discuss with you.'

'You are supposed to be detectives, so I imagine that's not unusual, but why bring these grotesque things to *my* door? Are you telling me that Camay and Comfort are dead?'

'We're not telling you anything. We needed you to identify the tails, which you've just done, but we also want to talk to you about Windolene.'

'What about her?' Anthea looked more than a little on the offensive. 'Have you found her?'

Hettie thought for a moment before replying. 'Not exactly, but we are cautiously optimistic that she may be hiding in Wither-Fork Hall.'

'Well, good riddance to her is what I say,' responded Anthea. 'She's been nothing but trouble from the start. She lives in a fantasy world, leading the other kittens on and telling terrible lies about cats who care for her. If anything *has* happened to Camay and Comfort, you can be sure it's her fault. That's probably why she's run away – she's done something wicked.'

Hettie was taken aback by Anthea's vitriol towards Windolene, and said so. 'The other day, when we first came to the Folly, you were distraught about the loss of all three kittens. Now you seem to be marking out Windolene as the villain of the piece. Has anything changed to make you feel that way?'

Anthea looked a little caught out, but recovered quickly. 'I was in shock that day, what with the weather and everything else. It was all too much. This school means the world to me, and when kittens go missing in terrible weather, you can hardly blame me for being upset.'

'I'm not blaming you for anything,' countered Hettie, 'but I am a little confused by how quickly you and Preston gave up the search for the kittens – and more especially, by how quickly you tried to replace them with new kittens who weren't orphans at all.'

This time Anthea rose to Hettie's bait. She slammed the bread knife down on the kitchen table and looked her interrogator directly in the eye. 'I've given my life to the care and well-being of these young cats,' she said. 'Kittens come and go, but there are always those who make something of themselves and prove to be worthy of my attention. I am always looking for those who wish to serve with diligence and humility, but those who flout the rules of this house shall eventually burn in the fire of their own making.'

'Powerful words indeed,' said Hettie, 'but a little too constricting for an orphan who just wants to be loved.

And while we're on the subject of orphans, it seems to me that you and Preston have a very different definition of what one is to the rest of us. You will, perhaps, be pleased to know that Preston's latest acquisitions are being returned to their mother as we speak, and I wouldn't be the least bit surprised if some of your boy cats don't wend their way home in the next couple of days under the protection of Miss Wither-Fork.'

Anthea picked up the bloodied dishcloth and immersed herself in a concentrated bout of frantic cleaning, scrubbing first at the kitchen table, then moving on to the sink before taking down all the food jars from a shelf and wiping every single one. It was clear to Hettie and Tilly that their interview was over for the time being, and Hettie was satisfied that – after their meeting with Fluff Wither-Fork later – the orphanage would be dismantled and the Munches forced to look for pastures new.

She put the kitten tails back in her satchel and Tilly closed her notebook. Such was the cleaning frenzy that Anthea hardly noticed as they left the Folly, shutting the door firmly behind them.

'What a thoroughly nasty pair of cats those Munches have turned out to be,' said Tilly, zipping her snowsuit up to her chin against the biting cold. It was later than they had planned, and they were rapidly losing the light as they crossed the park to Wither-Fork Hall.

'They are nasty,' agreed Hettie, 'but we're still no closer to finding out what happened to the missing kittens. Just because the Munches have washed their paws of them, it doesn't mean the case is solved. We still have to figure out what that dolls' house set-up is all about, and then there's the nonsense from Bombazine Bright and her bloody Magic Tree. Are we to believe that Camay and Comfort are dead, or are they running around without tails after some weird satanic or pagan ritual? And where does Windolene fit in to all of this? We've no proof that she's hanging out at Wither-Fork, and she could easily be dead. We've got to try harder. It's strange – I keep forgetting that these kittens are small and vulnerable, but when you hear the testimonies of some of those boys in the schoolroom, the whole thing is heartbreaking.'

Tilly smiled to herself. Hettie rarely showed her soft side, and certainly never did so publicly for fear of seeming weak, but Tilly could see that her friend was deeply troubled by the plight of the kittens at the Folly and admired her for it, although she couldn't resist a bit of teasing. 'I thought you couldn't stand kittens?' she said.

'Well, I'm not keen on cheese and onion crisps but I'm happy to watch you eat them,' Hettie replied, reverting to her usual belligerence.

Chapter Fifteen

Blackberry Tibbs was the only cat in the Great Hall when Hettie and Tilly got back from the Folly. She was busy tidying up after the residents had said their farewells before going home to the allotments. There was still a decent fire crackling and spitting in the giant fireplace, and Hettie and Tilly warmed themselves before contemplating a trek across to the Lodge for tea with Fluff. 'I suppose you're quite pleased to be rid of all that extra cooking?' Hettie remarked, as Blackberry stacked the chairs and folded up the trestle table.

'It's been a lot of work, but I'll miss them all. I've had fun, really, and watching the wall painting being revealed has given me an idea. I thought I'd make models of all the characters in *The Ice Maid's Tail* and see if Miss Wither-Fork would put an exhibition on in the summer. It would make a fantastic project, and it would be great to feature some of Wither-Fork's ancient history for the visitors. We could even get Albertine Chop's book reprinted to sell, and do Ice Maid teas.'

Hettie could see why Blackberry was so valuable to Fluff, and more especially to the prosperity of Wither-Fork Hall. Not only was she an excellent cook and housekeeper, but she had a real flair for marketing; there was no doubt that *The Ice Maid's Tail* was a brilliant theme to sell to the many visitors who loved their history, particularly if it had a macabre twist. 'I don't suppose there's been any sign of our mysterious visitor today?' Hettie asked. 'We've managed to establish that the missing kittens can barely read, which might explain why our notes are being ignored. Sadly, at least two of them have lost their tails.'

Blackberry threw her paws up to her face in horror. 'You mean just like the story? How do you know that?'

Hettie reached for her satchel, but before she could pull the tails out Blackberry backed away. 'No, please – I don't want to see. How could anyone be so cruel? Poor little things. Do you think they're dead?'

'That question has cropped up many times today,' said Hettie. 'I only wish we had an answer.'

'If there's anything I can do, just say,' said Blackberry. 'I've been in the kitchen for most of the day and I haven't seen anything out of place, but I'll keep an eye on things.'

'That would be really helpful, especially as you're here at night. If you could leave some food out and check the old bakery and the nursery now and again, we might get lucky.'

'And the dolls' house,' added Tilly, pleased to pass the job to someone else. 'It's been moved into what we think was Albertine Chop's bedroom.'

Blackberry hadn't really considered how it might feel to stalk the empty rooms in Wither-Fork Hall at dead of night, let alone tamper with what appeared to be a haunted dolls' house, but the offer had been made and now she felt obliged to go through with it. Hettie and Tilly promised to return the following day, just in case anything occurred overnight, and reluctantly left the fire in the Great Hall to join Fluff for a welcome but late afternoon tea.

Surprisingly, it was Bruiser who answered the door at the Lodge; he'd been waiting in Miss Scarlet's sidecar for Hettie and Tilly to conclude their business for the day, and Fluff had invited him in out of the cold. 'She's in her kitchen,' he said, 'makin' cheese on toast. She says to go through to the parlour.'

As he closed the door behind them, it occurred to Hettie that Bruiser would have made a rather fine butler in another life; being the doorkeeper at Wither-Fork Lodge suited him. 'How did you get on with returning the kittens?' she asked, sinking into Fluff's sofa next to Tilly.

'I was just tellin' Miss Wither-Fork – there's been a lot of it goin' on round them Cheapcuts Flats.'

'What do you mean?' asked Hettie, leaning forward to warm her paws at Fluff's blazing fire.

Bruiser sat himself down on an ornate footstool before recounting his afternoon adventure. 'Well, I took meself to Jessie's shop an' she knew straight away who them littl'uns belonged to, so she leaves me keepin' shop and fetches their mother, who lives in Cheapcuts Flats, see? Kittens was all over 'er like their Christmases 'ad all come at once, and their mother hugged me till I could 'ardly breathe. She said she'd let 'em out to play in the snow, as they'd been cooped up fer days in the blizzards, and next time she'd looked they was gone – just like the others.'

'What others?' asked Tilly.

'Ah well, that's the point. She told me that several kittens 'ad gone missin' from the flats just before an' after Christmas, and she'd 'erd that there was one or two missin' from Sheba Gardens, as well. Said Hacky Redtop from the *Daily Snout* 'ad run one of 'is articles on 'em, askin' if anyone 'ad seen 'em.'

'I don't know how we missed that,' said Hettie indignantly.

'You stopped our daily paper because you said the *Sunday Snout* was much more interesting and you preferred the TV news,' Tilly pointed out, with a hint of waspishness in her voice.

Reluctant to get involved in a domestic tiff between Hettie and Tilly, Bruiser pulled a folded newspaper page out of his pocket and opened it. ''Ere it is, with photos of them that's gone missin'.'

Hettie clawed the page from Bruiser and stared at the row of little faces. Although they all looked very similar in black and white, she thought that she recognised Jaycloth and possibly two others from the schoolroom at the Folly. 'Did you show this to Fluff?' she asked.

Bruiser shook his head. 'I only told 'er about returnin' the ones to Cheapcuts, and that there were others missin'. I thought I'd leave the rest of the business to you.'

Tilly pulled the page closer to read the editorial, written by Hacky Redtop himself. 'That doesn't add up,' she said, having digested the article. 'According to this, at least sixteen kittens are missing and that doesn't include the ones Bruiser returned today. Nine female and seven male kittens, it says here.'

'I suppose we have to allow for those who have quite simply run away from home,' said Hettie. 'The Munches might not be responsible for all of them, but sixteen is rather a lot and there's only space for ten at the Folly – which begs the question…'

'Where are the rest of them?' chimed in Tilly, finishing Hettie's sentence for her. 'If we allow for Camay, Comfort and Windolene, that still leaves six girl kittens unaccounted for. If the Munches have snatched them, where are they now?'

The question went unanswered, as Fluff Wither-Fork barged the parlour door open with a laden tea trolley. 'I'm afraid you'll have to put up with a scratch effort put together by me,' she said. 'Blackberry has so much on at the Hall that I didn't have the heart to ask her to prepare tea as well. She's been a Trojan through all this weather, and now she's faced with the big clear-up.'

Hettie, Tilly and Bruiser surveyed the tea trolley while Fluff offered an inventory of the delights on offer. 'We've cheese on toast, as I thought you'd appreciate something hot. I've warmed the sausage rolls through, too, along with the meat pasties – they're Blackberry's, as are the Madeira cake and the chocolate buns. She baked those last night, although goodness knows where she finds the time. Please tuck in.'

The friends didn't need a second invitation. Bruiser passed the plates round and all four cats chewed and licked their way through the mountain of hot, sizzly cheese on toast, before attacking the pastry items with equal enthusiasm. Pausing to drink a cup of milky tea, their final offensive was aimed at the cakes; in no time at all, the trolley was redundant except for a pile of empty plates and cups and the odd stray crumb.

Satisfied that her guests had enjoyed her scratch tea, Fluff sat back in her armchair, keen for Hettie to update the case of the missing kittens. 'Bruiser tells me that he has been returning kittens to their homes and that more are missing in the town,' she began. 'I understand that you rescued some from the Folly. I really am at a loss for words to think that this sort of thing has been going on right under my nose.'

Hettie nodded. 'I'm afraid it seems to be much worse than just a few kittens. We've interviewed Preston and Anthea Munch today, and it's very clear that they've been snatching kittens from the town at the slightest opportunity to enrol them in their school. The worst part is that they've convinced the kittens that they're unwanted by their own families, and are now orphans under so-called "protection".'

She gave a full account of the investigations at the Folly, including her brief conversations with Jaycloth and his classmates, before handing over the newspaper article. Fluff stared at the line-up of tiny faces and allowed several tears to fall onto Hacky Redtop's story. 'I remember seeing this, but it never occurred to me to make the connection,' she said, reaching for the hanky which was tucked in the sleeve of her cardigan. 'I just feel so responsible. I trusted the Munches – they seemed so genuine, if a little too worthy, perhaps. I would never have suspected them of such wickedness.'

Fluff blew her nose, giving Hettie time to reach for her satchel. She was keen to get all the bad news over with so that they could collectively come up with a plan. There were things that Fluff would need to instigate regarding the Munches, and the search would have to continue for Camay, Comfort and Windolene, alive or dead. 'We also visited Bombazine Bright this afternoon,' she added.

'Bombazine Bright!' exclaimed Fluff. 'I'd quite forgotten about her. I used to visit her in the woods when I was very young. She insisted on my dancing for her, then I'd get a wonderful story about magic and that sort of thing. How on earth did you find out about her? She's one of Wither-Fork's best-kept secrets, and she must be very old by now.'

'Bonny took us there. We haven't managed to digest what exactly it was that she told us yet, but on our way out of the woods we found these hanging from an old oak tree.'

Fluff looked at the tails in disbelief, then reached out and touched them with her paw to make sure they were real. She recoiled in horror and Hettie put them back in her satchel, not wanting to cause more upset than was necessary. 'This whole business is an absolute nightmare,' said Fluff. 'Do you think those tails belong to the missing kittens?'

Hettie nodded. 'We're almost certain they do. Anthea Munch appeared to recognise them as belonging to Camay and Comfort, who are both ginger kittens.'

'So does that mean they *are* dead?'

There was that question again, thought Hettie before responding. 'We honestly don't know, and we have no firm evidence that Windolene is still alive either. It's as if someone is trying to mirror Albertine Chop's book – this tail-docking business, added to the severe weather, the wall painting in the Great Hall and the Magic Tree.'

'But that's just a story,' said Fluff. 'You surely don't believe that the Ice Queen has returned to seek her revenge on the Nightsparks and the Wither-Forks, do you?'

'I honestly don't know what to believe any more,' admitted Hettie, 'but we're not giving up until we find those three missing kittens.'

'I really am most grateful for all you're doing,' said Fluff, 'and it's clear to me that I will have to take action. It's too cold and late to do anything tonight, but I'll deal with this first thing in the morning as far as the Munches are concerned. The kittens who are still at the Folly will have to be returned to their homes, and it's time that Anthea and Preston moved on. I just hope they don't try the same scam in another town.'

'We could give the story to Hacky Redtop,' Tilly suggested. 'If his photographer, Prunella Snap, captures their images for the newspaper, the story will go national and no one will ever let the Munches near a kitten again.'

'What an excellent plan,' said Fluff. 'I'll call Mr Redtop in the morning and ask him to join me for the showdown at the Folly if he's free.'

'I'm sure he will be,' said Hettie. 'He never shies away from a good headline. What shall we do about the kittens?'

'I'll put Blackberry in charge of them at the Hall until we can get in touch with their families to come and collect them. Of course, there may be some genuine orphans amongst them, but I'll cross that bridge when I come to it. Wither-Fork Hall might benefit from some young blood rattling around the place.'

There was a wistful look in Fluff's eyes. The landowner had no family of her own, and perhaps caring for her tenants wasn't quite enough for her. Hettie knew that whatever the fate of the kittens left at the Folly, Fluff would have their best interests at heart and they would no longer be at the mercy of Anthea and Preston Munch's cruel, closeted regime.

Before they left the Lodge, Fluff took Hettie to one side and assured her that their fee would be paid, no matter what. She had been generous in the past, and she gave Hettie twenty pounds on account for any expenses incurred so far, promising to settle in full once the case had been solved. The three cats said their thank yous for an excellent tea and sped off into the icy darkness, intending to return the next day to witness the departure of Preston and Anthea Munch. But as things turned out, nothing was going to be that simple.

Chapter Sixteen

They arrived home to a freezing cold room after a nightmare journey in Miss Scarlet. The roads were a mixture of black ice and floods. At the bottom of Wither-Fork Hill, they'd encountered a foot of water which – even though Bruiser drove carefully through it – flooded the sidecar, making the rest of the journey wet and uncomfortable for Hettie and Tilly. At the head of the high street, the motorbike skidded on a patch of ice, sending it into a spin which Bruiser eventually managed to control, bringing the bike to an unscheduled stop just inches from the door to Meridian Hambone's hardware store. Tilly banged her head on the sidecar's windscreen, but Hettie managed to brace herself in time to avoid injury. They were pleased to arrive at the Butters' bakery in one piece, and Hettie decided to treat them all to a fish and chip supper, which Bruiser fetched from Elsie Haddock's when he'd finished baling out Miss Scarlet.

'If you crack on with the fire, I'll hang our wet things over the radiator next to the bread ovens,' Hettie said, kicking her wellingtons off. Tilly clambered out of her snowsuit and wrung it out in the sink before passing it to Hettie. She pulled on a random winter cardigan from the bottom drawer of the filing cabinet and set about lighting the fire. Within minutes, the room was transformed into a warm and cosy sanctuary from the extremes of the day.

After draping the Butters' radiator with wet snowsuits and socks, Hettie pulled on her dressing gown and sank into her armchair, grateful that the day was almost over. Tilly switched on the TV and was delighted to find that it was working again. They were just in time to catch the end of the news – a bunch of feline reporters placed strategically round the region bemoaning the floods and warning everyone to fill sandbags and stock up on supplies. The worst hit areas showed rivers bursting their banks and whole families perched on their rooftops, waiting to be rescued.

'Looks like we've got off lightly in the town,' said Hettie. 'I hope Poppa's OK on his narrowboat. He might end up floating down the high street if things don't calm down.'

The weather cat swung into view on the screen, offering more misery for several days to come before his chart collapsed on top of him, bringing the presentation to an abrupt conclusion and catching the newsreader out while he was enjoying a Cornish pasty. He recovered well, managing to say his goodbyes through a mouthful of chuck steak and pastry, much to Hettie and Tilly's amusement.

'Bruiser should be here with the supper soon,' said Tilly. 'I'll get the mugs ready for some tea. He'll be frozen when he gets back. I bet his shed isn't very welcoming at the moment.'

'He'd be better off sleeping by that radiator in the hall,' said Hettie. 'We could ask Betty and Beryl to lend him their inflatable lilo.'

'I thought they'd get rid of that after Beryl was swept out to sea on it last summer. Thank goodness for the cat on the Paddlo.'

'Not a great way to emerge from the waves, though, being towed by a Paddlo.'

They collapsed in a bout of giggles until Bruiser interrupted their merriment with a polite knock at the door. The fish and chips were lovely and hot, and the three friends enjoyed them in front of the TV, while Crusty Allslop offered a lesson on how to make over your downstairs cloakroom using potatoes and poster paint.

'I wonder what planet that cat lives on,' remarked Hettie, through a mouthful of crispy batter bits. 'For a start, who has a downstairs cloakroom? And if you did have one, why would you want to do that to it? And just look at the mess she's made! It'll cost a fortune to put that right. She's already knocked through the kitchen and put a conservatory on the parking space. If I owned a proper house, I wouldn't let her within a mile of it.'

They congenially debated the pros and cons of Crusty Allslop's programme, then watched another Agatha Crispy from the Butters' boxed set. Hettie knew that they should be working on the case, as they still had to decipher Bombazine Bright's riddle, but, after the horrors of the day, she felt that they needed to indulge in some normality.

Bruiser fell asleep long before Miss Marble had wrapped up the case, and Hettie and Tilly saw no reason to disturb him. Tilly banked up the fire while Hettie cleared away their fish and chip papers and switched off the light. All was peaceful, until the telephone began to ring in the staff sideboard.

Chapter Seventeen

Blackberry Tibbs had watched the same programme on the small TV in her bedsitter next to the kitchen at Wither-Fork Hall. She enjoyed Crusty Allslop's makeovers; anything creative pleased her, and Crusty's use of paint and colour was very similar to her own. She loved making things with her paws, and working for Fluff gave her the time to explore her artistic leanings while having a roof over her head, a decent income and no real worries. Tonight was different.

Since moving from her old railway carriage up on the allotments, life had been so much easier. If she wanted it, she had the run of Wither-Fork Hall, and – with Fluff choosing to live a simpler life at the Lodge – she was often left to her own devices for days on end. She was busier in the summer, when visitors arrived in their hordes to explore the house and gardens, but in the winter, when the mansion was at rest, her main job was just to make sure that all the valuables were dusted, the floors swept and the carpets hoovered. There was the occasional bout of cleaning at the

Lodge to be fitted in when Fluff required it, as well as the preparation of most of her food, but Blackberry enjoyed cooking and Fluff Wither-Fork was always appreciative and never made her feel in the slightest bit like a servant.

In the late afternoon, when Hettie and Tilly had left, she found herself viewing the house in a very different way. For the first time since moving in, she was aware of being completely alone and isolated. Her bedsitter was filled with the trappings of her life, all familiar and safe, but now she found herself staring at the closed door, fearing the thirty empty rooms that lay beyond; some were set up to give the average cat in the street an ancestral home experience; others she had never visited, shut up years ago to store the mementos of lives long ago extinguished.

Most of her winter evenings were spent by her fireside, watching TV or making one of her models. Fluff had installed a telephone in case she needed Blackberry at short notice, but it rarely rang at night, which until now had been a blessing. Sooner or later, Blackberry knew she would have to face those empty rooms; she'd promised Hettie and Tilly, and if there were frightened kittens on the loose, she was keen to do her bit to help.

She wished she'd asked Bonny to stay another night. The gypsy cat had been reluctant to return to her caravan, and right now Blackberry would have welcomed her endless stories; more especially, they could have searched the house together, but that Romany ship had sailed back up to the allotments. Resigned to her fate, Blackberry reached for her torch and checked that the batteries were still strong. The installation of electricity was somewhat sporadic at Wither-Fork, and Fluff saw no reason to spend money on rooms that never saw the light of day, let alone after dark. Pulling a shawl round her against the cold, Blackberry opened her door and felt for the light switch in the kitchen. The blaze of light was a comfort and she had no qualms about checking the cold pantry, but the rest of the original servants' work rooms were in darkness.

She was about to make her way down the corridor, checking the rooms that led to the old bakery, when she noticed that there was a scone missing from the plate on the kitchen table. They had been left in a prominent position since the day before and had begun to gather dust, but one had definitely been taken. Blackberry's heart began to thud in her chest, and she couldn't decide whether it was out of excitement or fear. Her first thought was to call Hettie and Tilly, but it was late and anyway, what was there to say? She had no idea when the scone had gone missing, and one of the residents could easily have helped themselves before leaving for the allotments.

Blackberry took a deep breath, switched on her torch and made her way down the dark corridor, kicking the doors open one by one and sweeping the rooms with the flashlight until she came to the old bakery. At first sight there was nothing out of place. She opened the oven door and the rush of icy air made her gasp. The cold was extreme, but she shone her torch into every crevice before shutting the door with a clank that echoed through the corridor, unnerving her even more. She longed to return to the warmth and comfort of her room, but that wasn't an option; she knew she would have to see this through, and reasoned that the worst she could encounter was three frightened little kittens. With that in mind, she retraced her footsteps back down the corridor, training the torch onto the old, uneven flagstones to light her way. Then she stopped dead. There, on the worn down grey stones, was a set of small, wet footprints, gradually drying out as they reached the kitchen.

Feeling only slightly more confident about her mission, Blackberry strode through the kitchen and headed for the Great Hall, turning lights on as she went. There was never enough light to fill the Hall at night: the three giant chandeliers that hung from the high ceiling did very little for the corners of the room, and threw dark shadows across the walls. The figures of Hugo Nightspark and the Ice Queen became almost animated in the strange glow as they towered above Blackberry, reminding her of a Wither-Fork history she'd rather not address; in the oldest part of the building, what by day was a simple nursery story somehow turned itself into a nightmare after dark.

Most of the visitors' rooms were off the Great Hall, and Blackberry made quick work of them. The library, games room, morning room and old study were all perfectly peaceful. Satisfied that nothing was out of place, she left the lights blazing and headed for the grand staircase, which swept its way up to the long gallery, where the notable Wither-Forks now resided in youthful poses as gilt-framed oil paintings. Blackberry was familiar with them all, as she dusted them once a week and even held conversations with them. There were uniformed cats returned from the wars, proudly displaying their medals; studious ones, bespectacled in their leather armchairs and surrounded by books; and the chatelaines, beautiful in their gowns and adorned in the family jewels that Fluff had had to sell to keep the house afloat.

The bedrooms occupied by the family in the glory days were all off the long gallery, and were set up now to impress the visitors with four-poster beds, dressing rooms, and ornate, gilded furniture. Blackberry took her time, making sure that nothing was hiding under the beds or in any of the wardrobes, then lifting the dust sheets on some of the more precious vases and statues that were clothed against the ravages of winter.

Leaving the lights on and all the bedroom doors open, she progressed to the part of the house that she most feared. At the end of the long gallery was the door to the attics, a set of servants' rooms that she had never visited. Fluff had closed the attics long before

Blackberry arrived at Wither-Fork; she deemed them unsafe, impossible to heat and surplus to requirements. As Hettie and Tilly had discovered, they were now mostly storage areas for unwanted and forgotten bits of the mansion's past.

From the moment that Blackberry opened the door, she was thrown into darkness. The stairs in front of her were steep, and – as she entered the servants' domain – the luxury fell away to reveal a bare wooden staircase with damp, bulging walls of wet plaster. Her torch lit the way, and she pulled open the door at the top to find a suite of long narrow rooms, closed in on either side by the shape of the roof. She listened in silence to see if she could detect the slightest movement or sound. If the kittens had sought sanctuary in the attics, they might have heard her coming up the stairs and scuttled out of sight. There was nothing and she moved forward, checking the rooms as she went until she came to what was clearly the old nursery. She remembered what Tilly had told her about the dolls' house being moved into the former nanny's room, and she shone her torch in the direction of a closed door. She hesitated, sensing for the first time that she wasn't alone, and swept the beam of her torch around the nursery again before approaching the door. She put her ear to it, listening for the slightest sound before turning the knob. No sooner had she opened the door than she was knocked backwards by something that rushed past her. She cracked her head on the floorboards, and lay for several minutes seeing stars and waiting for her head to stop spinning. Her torch was out of reach, but she managed to recover herself sufficiently to crawl forward and pick it up. She felt sick, her head was thumping and she sat up and cried, not caring who or what may hear her.

After a while, Blackberry struggled to her feet and forced herself to walk through the attic rooms, down the stairs and back to civilisation. The lights from the long gallery were more welcoming than anything she'd ever known. She dragged herself down the grand staircase, through the visitors' rooms and back to the Great Hall. As she headed towards the kitchen, she was suddenly aware of a strange light reflected in the French windows, which came from the other side of the parkland. She moved towards the windows for a closer look, and there in the night sky was a red and orange fireball. She stared at it, trying to understand what she was looking at, and ran back to her room as realisation struck. Dialling the Lodge, she waited for Fluff to pick up the phone; when she did, there was no time for niceties. 'It's the Folly!' she shouted into the receiver. 'It's on fire!'

Chapter Eighteen

The muffled sound of the telephone woke all three cats, but it was Tilly who responded by kicking off her blankets and crawling into the staff sideboard to answer it. 'Hello, The No. 2 Feline Det…'

Fluff Wither-Fork's commanding voice cut across her. 'I'm so sorry to wake you, but the Folly is on fire and I would appreciate it if you could come as soon as you can,' she barked. 'I've called the volunteer fire brigade, but heaven knows when they'll get here. I'm on my way to the Folly now.'

With that, the phone went dead and Tilly replaced the receiver. 'That was Fluff,' she said, crawling out of the sideboard. 'She wants us to go to Wither-Fork now. The Folly's on fire.'

'Bloody marvellous!' cursed Hettie as she stumbled to the door to collect their snowsuits from the radiator. 'Why these things can't happen in daylight, I'll never know. Let's just hope the orphans haven't gone up in smoke.'

Tilly resisted the temptation to laugh at Hettie's outburst and pulled on her clothes. Bruiser, who'd taken a moment to work out where he was, found his coat and went out to fire up Miss Scarlet, arranging to meet Hettie and Tilly in the high street at the front of the bakery. Hettie grabbed her satchel and glanced at the clock on the staff sideboard; it was just after midnight.

Bruiser drove carefully, not wishing to repeat the slide that had almost brought them to grief earlier. It was bitterly cold and the roads were treacherous. He was concerned about even attempting Wither-Fork Hill, but circumstances overtook them in the shape of the town's fire engine, clanging down the high street with its motley crew of volunteers on board. Bruiser's friend, Lazarus Hambone, was driving the ancient engine, and his crew consisted of Clippy Lean, the town's award-winning bus conductress, who had the honour of ringing the bell; Morbid Balm from Shroud and Trestle, the town's undertakers; and Turner Page, chief librarian, with his partner, Mr Pushkin. Lazarus slowed the fire engine alongside Miss Scarlet and suggested that Hettie, Tilly and Bruiser hop aboard.

Bruiser was relieved not to have to negotiate the icy roads and parked the bike outside Elsie Haddock's fish and chip shop. The three cats joined the reservists in the cab, and Lazarus put his foot down as they headed towards Wither-Fork Hall. There were a few scary moments along the way, as the old fire engine coughed and spluttered down the icy roads, but Lazarus knew what she was capable of and gave her every encouragement. The daunting prospect of Wither-Fork Hill was soon a reality, and Lazarus increased the revs on his approach; with screaming gears, the fire engine climbed the Hill and rattled through the Lodge gates. It was clear where the fire was, and Lazarus made a beeline for it. Taking no account of paths and roads, he crossed the parkland, doing his best to avoid Fluff's ornamental statues on the way.

The Folly was well alight on all four floors when the firefighters arrived. Hettie was relieved to see Fluff and Blackberry, surrounded by a group of kittens wearing blankets against the cold. There was no sign of Preston or Anthea Munch.

Lazarus leapt out of his driver's seat and began connecting a hose to the water tank on the fire engine. Bruiser helped him roll it out, and Morbid and Clippy started pumping the water through. Turner Page and Mr Pushkin unstrapped the fire blankets and began beating the flames back at the door. Very soon, Lazarus and Bruiser had a continuous jet of water trained on the upper storeys, and slowly but surely the inferno began to submit to the volunteers. Hettie and Tilly watched with admiration as the most unlikely set of firefighters began to win their initial battle against the flames.

Fluff and Blackberry were standing away from the intense heat, silent as they watched the flames die down, to be replaced by an acrid black smoke that rose up into the sky. The kittens chattered excitedly, treating the disaster as a real adventure and seemingly none the worse for their experience. Hettie and Tilly joined the group as the firefighters continued their work. 'Where are Anthea and Preston?' asked Hettie.

'I've no idea,' said Fluff. 'When Blackberry and I got here, the kittens had escaped the fire but there was no sign of the Munches. I fear they may well have perished. They have a room at the top of the Folly, and Blackberry says that's where she first saw the flames.'

Hettie looked up. The glass from the windows had shattered in the heat. The stone structure was still intact, but it was clear that the fire had raged from within, blackening the outside walls as the flames licked through the empty window slits. As she surveyed the damage, a small paw tugged at her snowsuit. She looked down to see one of the kittens, keen to get her attention. 'It's Jaycloth, Miss. He's still in there.'

Hettie swung round and quickly counted the kittens. To her horror, there were only six and Jaycloth was nowhere to be seen. She ran towards the Folly but Bruiser stood in her way. 'You can't go in there; it's too dangerous!' he shouted.

'But there's still a kitten in there!' protested Hettie. 'It's Jaycloth!'

Bruiser reacted immediately, shouting for Lazarus. The two cats tried to gain entry by the front door, but it was blocked by fallen roof beams. Lazarus sprang onto the back of the fire engine, pulling the ladders down to the ground, and Bruiser helped as Lazarus extended them. 'Try for the third storey,' called Hettie. 'That's where the kittens slept.'

Fully extended, the ladders just about reached one of the dormitory windows. Before Lazarus could argue, Bruiser shot up the rungs, leaving everyone below with their hearts in their mouths. The stone walls were hot and he burnt one of his paws as he forced his way in through the window hole. The fire had devoured everything in the dormitory except for the metal bedsteads; some of the floorboards still glowed, threatening to ignite again at any minute. Keeping to the edge of the room, where less damage had been done, Bruiser moved slowly round towards the stone stairs. Pulling his scarf up in front of his nose and mouth to protect himself from the thick black smoke, he made his way down the steps to the schoolroom. The desks were burnt to a cinder, but there was a stone bench in front of where the blackboard had been. Through the smoke, Bruiser saw a blanket bundled underneath the bench and it appeared to move. 'Jaycloth!' he shouted. 'Is that you?'

The bundle wriggled and gave a piteous cry. Bruiser crossed the room and grabbed at it, revealing a small, singed head. Jaycloth threw his arms around Bruiser's neck and offered a mixture of coughing and crying. Bruiser pulled the blanket back around him and surveyed the room, looking desperately for a way out.

In places, the fire was beginning to catch hold again. There was falling debris everywhere and Bruiser cradled the kitten in his arms, using the blanket to protect him from the smoke that was now closing in on them both. He could no longer see the stairs, and the wooden beams above his head were bursting into flames and cracking in the intense heat. The little bundle in his arms squirmed and wriggled, and Bruiser knew that he would have to risk them both to survive. He looked across at the window, just managing to make it out through the smoke, then moved slowly towards it, hoping that the floor wouldn't give way beneath his feet. A stray piece of flaming plaster from the ceiling fell onto his head, setting his fur alight. He beat it off with his paw, refusing to give in to the searing pain: if he was going to die, he'd go down fighting – but first he must save the kitten in his arms; at least then it would be worth it. The window was almost in reach when another beam crashed to the floor in front of them, sending sparks up into Bruiser's face. He closed his eyes and leapt for the opening, clearing the beam by inches.

The cold air was invigorating as the inferno built behind them. Pulling the blanket from around the kitten, Bruiser forced it through the window in the hope that Lazarus would see it. Seconds later, a jet of water flooded the schoolroom, soaking them both; the water was swiftly followed by Lazarus himself. Below, Turner Page and Mr Pushkin were training the hose on Bruiser's only means of escape, while Morbid Balm and Clippy Lean pumped furiously to make sure that the water supply was continuous.

Bruiser bundled the kitten into Lazarus's arms and climbed out of the window, following him down the ladder. Looking back up, he could see that the rescue had only just succeeded: the window they'd escaped from was now entirely engulfed in red and orange flames. The jet of water was redundant as the fire claimed the building, and even the stonework began to surrender to the heat.

There was a joyful reunion at the bottom of the ladder. Jaycloth was carried away by his classmates to a safer distance, where they were keen for him to give his account of being trapped in the burning building. On the ground, Hettie and Tilly had watched as the fire spread through the building, fearing that Bruiser was about to make the ultimate sacrifice. Tilly stood and sobbed for the cat who had saved them from so many dangers in the past, believing that this time his luck had run out. Hettie waited for the worst news, knowing that Bruiser had saved her from the horrible death that he was now facing. The joy that both cats felt as their friend climbed down the ladder to safety could probably never be expressed to its full extent. From the moment he'd joined their detective business, he'd been their personal hero – but now his bravery would be written down and celebrated for years to come. Hettie watched as the firefighters slapped him on the back and clapped. He looked suddenly old, she thought – old, and vulnerable. Admittedly he wasn't looking his best: his grey fur was blackened with smoke, there was a sore patch on the top of his head where he'd been burnt, and he was soaked to the skin and limping – but Hettie saw more than that in her old friend; he looked haunted by his own mortality. She pushed through the well-wishers and took his paw, leading him away from the Folly, and there as the moon lit up the snowy parkland, turning it icy blue, she hugged him and wept.

Chapter Nineteen

The fire at the Folly continued to burn, in spite of the volunteer brigade's best efforts, and Fluff Wither-Fork was happy to concede that the building was lost. She was also convinced that the Munches had died in the fire, and – although it was tragic – justice had been done. Shepherding the kittens, she walked slowly back to Wither-Fork Hall with Blackberry, having announced to the firefighters that there would be hot soup and sandwiches in the Great Hall when they'd packed their kit up. Her offer was gratefully received.

Hettie and Tilly flanked Bruiser as they walked across the parkland. He was shivering from a mixture of cold and shock, and Hettie wanted to get him into the warm as quickly as possible. Bruiser hated fuss of any kind, but this time he was pleased to lean on his two best friends. Being a hero was punishing work at the best of times, but now, in the freezing cold as he moved away from the inferno that had nearly claimed him, he wondered just how many of his allotted nine lives he had left.

Blackberry stoked the fire in the Hall and it soon responded as the survivors gathered round it, pleased to be in front of a blaze that was under control rather than the one they'd just abandoned. Fluff was busy wielding a butter knife in the kitchen, cutting a mountain of ham sandwiches, having tipped Blackberry's entire stock of tinned chicken soup into a large saucepan on the stove.

Hettie and Tilly had been left in charge of the kittens. They set about putting up the camp beds that had so recently been taken down, hoping that the young cats might settle for the night. Tilly bathed Jaycloth's and Bruiser's burns, plastering them in ointment from Blackberry's medicine cabinet. Bruiser was grateful to shed his soaking wet coat, and was given the best place by the fire to eat his supper and thaw out.

The kittens squealed and licked their way through their late-night suppers, showing little sign of the night's horrors; only Jaycloth sat apart from the group, and Hettie could tell by the look on his face that his had been the greatest trauma. She went to sit beside him. 'Are you all right?' she asked. 'Do your burns hurt?'

The kitten shook his head. 'No, Miss, not now the cream's on them.' His voice was husky and clearly affected by the smoke he'd breathed in, but he was keen to talk and Hettie let him. 'We were in bad trouble from Mr Preston after you left,' he squeaked. 'He was angry about what we'd said to you. He told us we would all burn in the fires of hell for it, because we were wicked. Mrs Anthea was nasty, too. She said she was going to cut our tongues out and feed them to the foxes in the woods, then she sent us to bed without our tea.'

Hettie felt the guilt consume her as she listened. She'd gone too far with her questions, and she berated herself for assuming that Preston hadn't heard any of her exchanges in the schoolroom. She took Jaycloth's paw to reassure him. 'I promise that whatever happens next, you won't have to be unhappy again,' she said. 'We're going to try and return you all to your families as soon as we can.'

'But my Ma doesn't like me any more. Mr Preston said so.'

Jaycloth began to cry, and Hettie – feeling a little awkward – pulled the kitten towards her until the sobbing subsided into a bout of violent hiccups. Her nursery skills were limited and Tilly was much better suited to the soft approach, but she was keen to understand how the fire had started and stuck with the hiccups until they also stopped. 'Can you remember how and where the fire started?' she asked gently.

'I think it was my fault,' said Jaycloth.

'Why?'

'Because when Mrs Anthea came up to read us a Jesus story, we thought she was going to cut our tongues out so we pounced on her and I clawed her face and made it bleed. She was so angry. Mr Preston came up and tied us all into our beds with rope. He said God always punishes sinners, and that's what was going to happen to us. He switched our lights off and left us tied up in the dark. I didn't cry, but Duster and Ajax did, and Mr Preston came back and threw icy cold water on them till they nearly drowned. He pushed ice cubes into their mouths to shut them up. After that, we all pretended to go to sleep, but then there was thick smoke and we all cried but no one came. I got loose from the rope and untied the others, but flames were coming from the stairs to Mrs Anthea and Mr Preston's room. We grabbed our blankets and ran down the steps to the schoolroom, but the fire chased us. The others managed to get down to the kitchen, but I was last and I got trapped. I hid under the stone bench to get away from the flames. It was so hot I thought I was going to melt.'

Shocked again at the cruelty meted out by the Munches, Hettie had so many questions for Jaycloth, but he was just a small, frightened kitten, too young to understand the evil regime that he'd been locked into through no fault of his own. It was clear that Bruiser wasn't the only hero of the night: if it hadn't been for Jaycloth's quick actions, all the kittens would have perished in the fire. They stood no chance, tied to their beds, and would have suffered the worst death imaginable. She asked just one more question before encouraging Jaycloth to join the other kittens in time for a bedtime story from Tilly. 'What happened to Mrs Anthea and Mr Preston?'

'I think Jesus must have saved them. Mrs Anthea told us that Jesus saves and God punishes.' Hettie picked the kitten up and carried him to join his friends, doing her best not to let him see the tears in her eyes.

Tilly had a captive audience for her impromptu bedtime story. She'd decided on a section from her favourite book, *The Wind in the Willows*, in which Mr Toad acquires himself a motorcar. The kittens joined in with the 'poop poops', and laughed and giggled themselves to sleep, leaving the grown-up cats to ponder on the night's events. When she was sure that all the kittens were settled, Tilly joined Hettie, Fluff and Blackberry by the fire. Blackberry had convinced Bruiser to rest on one of the camp beds, and he'd fallen asleep the moment he put his head down. The volunteer fire brigade had enjoyed their late supper and said their farewells, and Lazarus fired up his engine, ready to drop his crew off at their homes in the town.

Now that all was relatively peaceful, Blackberry chose her moment to recount her experience from earlier. 'I think you were right,' she began, turning to Hettie. 'I did as you asked and checked out the rooms last night. There was a scone missing from the plate in the kitchen, so I thought I might get lucky with our unseen visitor.'

'And did you?'

'Well, not exactly,' Blackberry replied, rubbing the back of her head as she remembered the moment she'd cracked it on the floorboards in the attic. 'It was all a bit creepy, really. I checked the old bakery and there were wet footprints coming away from it. I was a bit spooked by that, so I put as many lights on as I could and looked through all the staterooms where the visitors go. To be honest, I was putting off the attics. I've never been up there until now, and I wish I hadn't really.' She rubbed her head again, realising that it was actually very sore and there was a sizeable lump forming.

Hettie, Tilly and Fluff were all waiting for her to continue, but Tilly interrupted her flow. 'It's the dolls' house, isn't it?' she said, becoming noticeably distressed.

Blackberry shook her head, even though it hurt. 'No, nothing like that. I didn't even see the dolls' house. Something rushed at me from the nanny's room in the nursery. It knocked me backwards, and I banged my head. It all happened so quickly, and I just lay on the floor for a minute or two, too shocked to move. When I got back down to the Great Hall, I saw the fire from the window and called Miss Wither-Fork straight away. I didn't give whatever rushed at me a second thought after that. All I could think of was those poor little kittens in the Folly. I ran all the way there, and I was so relieved to see them standing in the snow with their blankets round them. Miss Wither-Fork came across from the Lodge, and then we heard the fire engine and knew help was on its way. I was stupid, really. I should have counted the kittens; then we'd have known that one was missing. Thank goodness for Bruiser.'

Everyone nodded sagely. Hettie updated them on Jaycloth's account of the fire and the Munches' cruel threats. 'The big question is – did they start the fire on purpose?' she said. 'If they did, they probably escaped. If they didn't, they'll be toast by now.'

'Are you really suggesting that the Munches tied those kittens to their beds, hoping they would burn to death?' asked Fluff in horror.

Hettie shrugged her shoulders. 'I think it's definitely a possibility. When we spoke to Anthea and Preston yesterday, they knew the game was up and that it was only a matter of time before they'd be thrown out of the Folly and the kittens returned to their proper homes. Dead kittens don't tell tales, and who knows what else they've been up to? We still don't know what's happened to Camay, Comfort and Windolene. If Blackberry's visitor was one of them, what's happened to the other two? Then there are the tails. A barbaric thing to do to any cat, but did it happen before or after death, and why would you do such a thing? If Preston and Anthea have flown the nest, we may never know. All we have to hang on to is the knowledge that a kitten seems to be on the loose here at Wither-Fork Hall, and if we can convince it to trust us, we might be able to solve the case once and for all. It's clearly frightened, and I think it's been trying to tell us something. Perhaps now the Folly has gone, whoever it is will feel safe enough to reveal themselves.'

Hettie reached for her satchel and pulled the two kitten tails from it, then placed them on the fire where the flames consumed them instantly. They were macabre trophies which she no longer needed to keep as evidence; alive or dead, she had to find the kittens. The four cats were silent, staring into the fire as if it would somehow offer a solution – but the solution was listening intently in the corridor that led to the kitchen.

Chapter Twenty

Fluff had opened one of her best bedrooms for Hettie and Tilly to rest in for what was left of the night. It was a treat to sleep in a four-poster bed, but Tilly was uneasy about the bed curtains so they kept them open. Hettie slept well, but Tilly was wide awake, listening to every creak the old house offered. She worked through the case in her mind, laying out all the characters: Anthea and Preston Munch; Bombazine Bright and her riddles; the Magic Tree; Albertine Chop and her *Ice Maid's Tail*, borrowed from Jenkin Cowdiddle. Then there were the characters in that story: Hugo Nightspark; the Ice Queen and her maids; the Halls of Glass; the cave of jewels and sparkly things; the frozen tombs and the Winter Lands. Her head was full to bursting with the combined images of fairy tales and the very real evil that manifested itself in the shape of Anthea and Preston Munch. She hoped with all her heart that they had perished in the fire, but somehow she doubted it. Someone must have started the fire: the kittens were all tied to their beds, which only left the Munches free to set the Folly alight. Tilly was exhausted, but her mind had kicked into overdrive. She knew that they had missed something in the investigation, but, try as she might, she just couldn't put her claw on it.

Sleep finally came just as Blackberry Tibbs was firing up her biggest frying pan, filling it with as many rashers of bacon as would fit. She'd cracked and beaten two dozen eggs into another pan, adding milk and butter in preparation for the scrambled eggs, and now she was slicing bread to toast. The kittens would be awake at any moment, and wanting to be fed.

Hettie and Tilly's room was immediately above the Wither-Fork kitchen, and Hettie's nose detected the bacon at the moment it hit the pan. She sat up and rubbed her eyes with her paws, trying to get her bearings. Gradually, the night's horrors returned to her; her fur smelt of smoke, and she brought to mind Bruiser's heroic rescue and Jaycloth's infant testimony of the Munches' cruelty, then she remembered Blackberry's encounter with Wither-Fork's unseen visitor. She lay wide awake now, staring up at the ornate plaster ceiling. The mouldings displayed dancing cats, trees and fruit, and she found herself wondering about the artist who had taken on the wall painting in the Great Hall. Did Albertine Chop's book come before or after the fresco? Why would the Wither-Forks want to celebrate a fairy story in their Great Hall? Or did it all have a more sinister significance? Hettie decided that there were just too many questions for whatever time of the morning it was, and she intended to tackle none of them before she'd properly investigated the smell of bacon which was now filling their room.

She climbed out of the four-poster and pulled on the snowsuit that lay abandoned on the floor next to Tilly's. The room was icy cold after the warmth of the blankets, and she crossed to the window and pulled the thick curtains open to reveal another winter's day. The thaw had made very little impression on the snow that still covered the parkland, and now there was a new sculpture to add to Fluff's cherubs: the blackened remains of the Folly stood out like some brooding, dark, satanic presence against the backdrop of Wither-Fork Woods.

'Do you think it's late?' came a voice from the bed.

Hettie turned from the window as Tilly sat up. 'I've no idea,' she replied, 'but I do know there's bacon if my nose serves me well.'

Tilly licked her paws and attempted to dampen down the tufts of fur that were sticking up from her head. She caught her reflection in a large mirror on the wall opposite the bed, and hardly recognised herself. 'I don't feel very presentable,' she said. 'My fur smells of smoke and I haven't had enough sleep. I'm not sure I can face bacon.'

Hettie laughed at her friend and held her snowsuit up, hoping to coax her out of the four-poster. 'There might be scrumbled eggs as well – you love those.

And after last night, I doubt that any of us looks good today – but we've a case to crack, and my hackles tell me that the ice is beginning to melt, metaphorically speaking.'

'That's a very big word for this time of day,' observed Tilly, as she stumbled to the floor and dived into her snowsuit. 'I might have to write that down in my notebook and use it later.'

She was delighted to see that scrumbled eggs were indeed on Blackberry's breakfast menu. The kittens were all seated at the trestle table when they arrived, eating noisily, and Blackberry looked rushed off her feet as she charged around with a jug of orange juice, making sure that everyone had their vitamin C. It was a real contrast to the silent, frightened, zombie-like creatures that Hettie and Tilly had encountered in the schoolroom at the Folly. Even Jaycloth seemed to have shrugged off his cares and was giggling along with the other kittens.

'What a difference a day makes,' observed Hettie, pulling a couple of chairs up to the fireplace, where a giant log crackled in the grate. 'If we don't get any further with this case, at least we've set these kittens free from the Munches' tyranny. If those other kittens hadn't gone missing, Anthea and Preston could have been at it for years without anyone noticing.'

Tilly nodded in agreement as Blackberry approached. 'Scrambled eggs, bacon and toast OK?' she said. 'There's orange juice, but I'm making a big pot of tea if you prefer it. If you could keep an eye on the kittens for me, I'll go and fetch it all. I'd forgotten how lively kittens can be, and they don't seem any the worse for their time at the orphanage. I've given them paper and crayons to keep them occupied for now. Bruiser's had his breakfast, and said to tell you that he's gone to fetch Miss Scarlet. He'll see you back here later.'

'How is he?'

'He looked much better this morning and I gave him three extra rashers. Miss Wither-Fork is on her way over from the Lodge. She's got Hacky Redtop and Prunella Snap from the *Daily Snout* with her. They're going to take pictures of the kittens for today's front page, in hopes that their parents will come forward to claim them.'

'That's a great idea,' said Hettie, as a paper aeroplane landed in her lap, followed by the over-excited kitten who came to claim it. 'The sooner the better, by the looks of things! It's good to know that Bruiser's up and about. I don't think he was happy about abandoning Miss Scarlet last night.'

Fluff arrived minutes later, at the same time as their breakfast. She nodded from across the hall, not wanting to disturb them while they ate. Prunella Snap wasted no time in setting up her mobile photo booth, which consisted of a camping stool and a roll of plain white wallpaper that was used as a backdrop. Hacky Redtop waved a greeting at Hettie and Tilly. He seemed to be busy talking into his Dictaphone, and was clearly treating the case of the abducted kittens as a big story.

They tucked into their food, and watched the kittens posing one by one on Prunella's camping stool for their photographs. When all seven images had been taken, Hacky called for a group photo, which he intended to use the following day when he'd had the chance to speak to Hettie and Tilly about how their case was progressing. Fluff had pushed for the seven kittens in her care to be highlighted ahead of the more lurid copy that was to follow; she knew that the goings-on at the Folly would make the front pages, but she made it clear to Hacky that her priority was to see the kittens safely returned to their homes, before the tabloid assassinations and recriminations began.

When the photo session was over, Fluff returned to the Lodge, asking Hettie and Tilly to call in on her later with a progress report. Hacky and Prunella lingered to enjoy one of Blackberry's frothy coffees before leaving to set the presses rolling on their big story. Hettie promised to call Hacky the following day, when she hoped the case would be concluded. She had convinced herself that the more she said it out loud, the more likely it was to happen.

The kittens settled to a game of hide and seek. Blackberry had made it clear that they were to go nowhere near the attics, and that they should come out of hiding when she banged the dinner gong to call them for lunch. They all scampered off like an excited school party, leaving Hettie and Tilly to make some sort of plan. 'I know I've been avoiding the Bombazine Bright issue,' admitted Hettie, 'but I think we should take a look at this riddle of hers. Heaven forbid that we should rely on the ramblings of an old witch to solve a case, but just now I'll take any help we can get.'

Tilly pulled her notebook out of her snowsuit pocket, and turned to the page where she'd hurriedly scribbled down Bombazine's riddle. 'I'm sure there are bits missing, but this is what I've got,' she said, trying very hard to read her own writing, which was worse than a doctor's prescription at the best of times. 'She said: "bad things come to them that waits below". That could be tunnels, do you think?'

'Could be,' said Hettie, not convinced that the exercise was going to bear fruit.

'Then she said: "it's not time for crystal crowns and icy queens", or something like that.' Hettie stared up at the figure of the Ice Queen, towering over them as it dominated the fresco, and Tilly continued. '"Two is left, and one has gone to bring the house down, mark well the little house that's never warm with words or deeds". That might be the dolls' house, but I'm not sure what that first bit could mean.'

Hettie repeated the words. '"Two is left and one has gone to bring the house down". I suppose that could refer to the missing kittens. What else have you got?'

'Well, it's a bit of a mess after that. I couldn't remember what she said next, but I think I got the end bit,' said Tilly apologetically. 'She said that "time is running out, and the stage is set for tragedy and revenge, the play is well rehearsed but the mantle may be hard to wear". That's it, I think.'

'That last bit sounds a bit theatrical to me,' responded Hettie. 'Mantle is an interesting choice of word, though. It could mean a burden of some sort, or a cloak.'

'Like those red ones that Anthea made the kittens wear, do you think?'

'Possibly,' said Hettie, not sounding convinced as she looked at the red-cloaked Ice Maidens in the painting above her. 'Can you remember *The Ice Maid's Tail* well enough to give me the basic facts of the story?'

'I think so,' said Tilly, amazed that Hettie was interested. 'There's a copy up in the old nursery. I could read it to you if you like, but I'm not fetching it.'

Hettie laughed at Tilly's refusal to venture anywhere near the attics. 'No need to read it all,' she said. 'Just lay it out like any other crime we're investigating.'

'You mean as if it were real?'

'Exactly.' Hettie sat back in her chair and made herself comfortable.

'Well,' said Tilly, 'to begin with, I should say that all this happened during the time of the Winter Lands, when the sun appeared for only one day a year. We've got a community of ice cats living in ice caves under

Wither-Fork Woods, ruled by an Ice Queen who lives in the Halls of Glass below where we're sitting now. She has Ice Maids as her servants, who all have to have their tails docked. The tails were hung in a special cave of jewels and sparkly things, guarded by a giant snow cat called Hugo Nightspark. One of the Ice Maids decides to poison the Queen, and on the day she dies the sun returns and melts all the ice, so almost everyone drowns and gets washed into the cave of jewels and sparkly things, where they freeze up again. Hugo and the killer Ice Maid feel guilty and emerge from the ice tunnels. The sun returns for good, and Hugo builds a big house above the ground. They live together happily ever after and have lots of kittens, but the Ice Queen broods below and haunts the woods on snowy days, stealing kittens to turn them into Ice Maids.'

Hettie sat for a moment, staring into the fire, before commenting on Tilly's truncated story. 'The thing is,' she said, 'as Fluff pointed out originally – Albertine's book is really about stolen kittens, and that's actually what we're dealing with. The rest is the stuff of fairy tales – except for the weather, of course. Like I've said so many times before in this case I think we may quite simply be dealing with kittens who ran away from Anthea and Preston's hateful cruelty. All this Ice Queen stuff has just confused us.'

'But what about the tails and the things going on in the dolls' house?'

'I can see that Preston or Anthea might have chopped the kittens' tails off as some sort of punishment,' Hettie reasoned. 'That would be a good reason for them to run away, and just because we haven't found a grey striped tail doesn't mean that Windolene escaped the chop, either – we did find a cloak stained with blood. As for the dolls' house, I can understand that a kitten might like to recreate the story of Albertine Chop's fall from grace as some sort of game, but the last set-up with ice cubes and the broken floorboard was quite extreme. To be honest, I just don't know what to think. I just wish this unseen visitor here at the Hall would show itself and stop messing about. The Folly's gone, and hopefully Anthea and Preston with it, so if one or all of the missing kittens are on the loose here, there's no reason for them to hide any more.'

'We haven't explored any of the tunnels on Fluff's map yet,' Tilly pointed out. 'Bombazine talked about waiting below, and the dolls' house was suddenly given a cellar with ice cubes. That could be the ice tunnels in the story.'

Hettie shook her head. 'We can't keep going down that route. It's just a story, and it never happened. It's one of those old tales told to keep kittens out of woods and tunnels, invented by grown-ups. Fluff said that the old tunnels were probably long gone, anyway, and all these big old houses had tunnels and secret passageways. I don't think the answer to this case lies in a tunnel.'

Tilly wasn't convinced, but she could see that Hettie was getting cross about the inclusion of *The Ice Maid's Tail* in their investigations.

The two cats were suddenly distracted from their deliberations by the arrival of Bonny Grubb, who joined them by the fire. 'Miss Wither-Fork wants me to tell some of me stories to the littl'uns – says they need to be kept occupied till their ma's come for 'em. Bad news about the Folly, though. Bombazine warned us, didn't she?'

Tilly grabbed her notebook and turned to the page where she'd written Bombazine Bright's riddle down. She read it out to Bonny. 'That's all I could remember,' she said. 'Can you add anything to it?'

Bonny asked Tilly to read it out again as she listened intently. 'Ah, you've missed the bit about the faces that lie, and one to serve and one to wield power, forever frozen in time,' said Bonny. 'That was the best bit – that's why I remember it.'

'So what makes you think that Bombazine warned us about the fire?' asked Hettie.

''Cos she mentions bringin' the little house down, never warm in words or deeds. That's got to be the Folly and them Munches. Miss Wither-Fork says they tied them kittens to their beds – that's settin' the stage for tragedy, if ever I heard it. Just plain wicked if you ask me.'

Hettie wasn't really in the mood for Bonny's tenuous connections, but the smell of cooking suddenly lifted her spirits. It signalled that lunch was on its way, and to confirm her hunch, Blackberry rattled into the hall with her trolley and proceeded to lay up the trestle table. 'I've catered for the kittens today,' she said. 'We're having fish fingers, spaghetti hoops and a jam sponge with custard for afters if you'd like to join in?'

Hettie, Tilly and Bonny chorused an enthusiastic 'Yes please!'

Blackberry laid an extra three places and returned to the kitchen to haul a huge catch of fish fingers out of her oven. She then headed for the grand staircase, where she banged a dinner gong that was almost as big as she was. The noise reverberated through the house and, within seconds, kittens started to emerge from every direction, keen to take their places at the table.

The fish fingers went down very well indeed, and the spaghetti hoops certainly hit the spot, covering most of the kittens and Tilly in tomato sauce. Blackberry offered damp napkins all round to wipe away the residue before bringing in a tray bake jam sponge and two large jugs of custard. She cut the sponge into squares, allowing the jam to ooze out from the incisions she'd made, then filled the bowls and passed them round. Bonny followed on with the jugs of custard, and the kittens waited patiently for the signal to begin. When it came it was a joyful sight, and Hettie couldn't help but think that the food must taste so much nicer without Preston Munch's religious fervour preached all over it.

There was much licking and banging of spoons as the kittens delighted in Blackberry's cooking, so much so that it was some time before anyone noticed the poor little creature who stood silently in the middle of the Great Hall. It was Jaycloth who reacted first. Slamming his spoon down on the table, he leapt off his chair. 'Windolene!' he cried, bounding across to the small, dishevelled grey kitten. She looked half dead: her fur was matted, her blue smock torn and dirty, and her eyes dull and unseeing. Jaycloth hugged her but she hardly noticed, and when he released her, she collapsed on the floor like an old abandoned piece of rag.

Hettie and Tilly rushed over to her as Bonny, Jaycloth and the rest of the kittens stared in silence. 'She's barely breathing!' shouted Hettie. 'Get Blackberry to phone the nurse and tell her it's urgent!'

Tilly ran to the kitchen while Hettie pulled a blanket off one of the camp beds and gently wrapped the kitten in it before carrying her to the fire. She was no weight at all, and Hettie was horrified at the state of her. Her little pink tongue was peeping out between her front teeth, and her eyes – now closed – were crusted over. When Tilly returned from the kitchen with the news that Nurse Featherstone Clump was on her way, Hettie was convinced that it was probably too late. 'Just look at the poor little thing,' she said, opening the blanket to let the warmth from the fire reach the kitten – and then she noticed. 'How could anyone be so cruel? Just look at her tail.'

Tilly felt sick to her stomach as she looked at the half-severed grey striped tail.

Chapter Twenty-One

Nurse Featherstone Clump was good to her word and arrived within the hour, accompanied by Fluff Wither-Fork, who'd been informed of Windolene's appearance in the Great Hall. After gently examining the kitten, the nurse said she was suffering from severe cold and malnutrition, as well as a serious infection caused by an accident to her tail. She bathed her eyes, bound the mutilated tail and prescribed lots of beef tea, but cautioned that the kitten would probably not last the day as she had no real strength left to fight the infection. During her examination, Windolene was barely conscious and strangely silent; when the nurse bound her tail, she didn't even cry. It was as if she'd given up her fragile hold on life and was content to slip away in the comfort and kindness now being offered to her.

To give Windolene the peace she deserved, Bonny kept the rest of the kittens occupied at the other end of the hall with one of her long-winded stories. Satisfied that she could do no more, the nurse promised to return in the morning if the kitten was still alive. She left with Fluff Wither-Fork, who was keen to sit by her phone; now that the *Daily Snout* was out, she hoped to get some responses from the families of the kittens rescued from the Folly.

Blackberry sat with Windolene, tipping the occasional teaspoon of warm beef tea into the side of her mouth to give her strength. The kitten struggled with the liquid, but managed to swallow some of it. Hettie and Tilly sat in silence as they watched for the slightest improvement, but there was very little change. Suddenly Hettie got to her feet. 'Come on,' she whispered to Tilly. 'I want to take a look at that Folly before we lose the daylight. Get your wellingtons on.'

Tilly had no time to ask questions as Hettie pulled on her own boots and strode towards the French windows. She gave every appearance of a cat on a mission, and Tilly followed her out onto the parkland. They struggled through the snow, which was wet underfoot and still quite deep. The winter sun was high in the sky and created a blinding, magical light, which glistened and sparkled across the snowy landscape. As they neared the ruins of the Folly, Hettie paused to take in the enormity of the terrors from the night before. The acrid smoke still permeated the air, and the blackened structure stood defiantly, threatening an otherwise beautiful scene.

'Why are you suddenly interested in the Folly?' asked Tilly. 'There's hardly anything left of it.'

'Several reasons,' said Hettie, moving forward again. 'Blackberry talking about wet footprints and you going on about tunnels – and then there was all that nonsense from Bombazine about power and service.'

Tilly was still confused, but it was clear to her that Hettie was on to something and she was happy to go with her. The door to the Folly was long gone; none of the wood in the building had survived, and much of the stonework had suffered, too. Hettie carefully picked her way across bits of twisted metal and deep patches of black ash until she found what she was looking for: the place where the kitchen table had once stood. She looked around for something to clear the ash from the floor and found a blackened saucepan, then bailed the worst of the ash to one side and got down low onto the floor, feeling the old bricks with her paws. Tilly watched as Hettie's strange behaviour continued. Suddenly, she lifted her head in triumph. 'There we are! A good old-fashioned trapdoor!'

Tilly looked closer and could see the outline in the brickwork. 'What made you think there was a trapdoor?'

'It's that jigsaw thing – all those pieces we have to fit together when we're on a case. Do you remember yesterday, when we finally got to interview Anthea Munch? She'd been washing the floor, and that's because it was wet. I think she'd just come up through the trapdoor and it's obviously wet underneath the Folly. Then there's Bombazine, going on about bad things coming to them that waits below. She must have meant below the Folly. And the dolls' house, of course.'

'What about the dolls' house?'

'Think about it – if that poor little kitten knew about this trapdoor, then what she did to the dolls' house was just trying to tell us that there was a cellar under the Folly with ice in it. It also explains why there was no sign or trace of the Munches at the fire last night. My guess is that they escaped this way before it took hold. They could be anywhere by now, planning to set up another of their bloody orphanages.'

'Or they could be living in the ice tunnels,' said Tilly quietly to herself.

A familiar sound suddenly caught their attention, and Tilly stepped out into the snow to see Bruiser heading towards them on Miss Scarlet. The fire engine had made tracks across the park from the Lodge the night before, and Bruiser had decided to follow in them to see if Hettie and Tilly needed a lift back to the Hall.

'Perfect timing as always,' said Hettie, emerging from the Folly. 'How did you know we were here?'

'Blackberry said, and she told me ta tell you that the kitten's drinkin' beef tea.'

'That's wonderful news,' said Hettie. 'Have you got your toolbox with you?'

'I got some basic stuff in Miss Scarlet's boot,' said Bruiser. 'What do yer need?'

'Ideally I need a jemmy, but a big screwdriver would do. It's to lift a trapdoor.'

Bruiser opened the boot in the sidecar and was soon able to offer an assortment of screwdrivers. Curious to see what the job was, he followed Hettie and Tilly into the Folly. It felt strange to be back in the building that had almost killed him, but it was a very different place now – open to the sky, a blackened shell which held very few memories of its former self. The heat of the fireball that had engulfed it was gone, replaced by an icy coldness common to any derelict building. He stared down at the outline of the trapdoor. 'Must 'ave been a rope or an iron ring to pull it up originally. We'll 'ave ta find somethin' better than them screwdrivers to shift it.' Bruiser left the Folly and returned minutes later with a spade. 'This should do the job. I found it round the back. I reckon Preston Munch 'ad been clearin' snow with it.'

Hettie and Tilly stood back as Bruiser jammed the spade into one of the edges of the trapdoor. It resisted at first, but he pulled and tugged at the spade handle until eventually the trapdoor surrendered. Jamming the spade further into the hole, he eased the door open far enough to get a purchase on it. It was heavy, as it had been bricked over to fit in with the rest of the kitchen floor, and Hettie and Tilly helped to pull it away from the hole. The three cats stood looking down into the Folly's cellar.

It was dark, but they could make out stone steps leading downwards. Hettie was ready to explore, but Bruiser caught her with his paw. 'You don't know what's down there. I'll fetch me torch and go first.'

Hettie knew that Bruiser was right and waited for him to lead the way. With the comforting beam of his torch to light their way, the cats descended into the cellar. It was freezing cold, and the walls and floor were thick with ice. The room was quite small, and Hettie was disappointed to see that – except for ice – there was nothing in it at all. They were about to return to the burnt-out kitchen, when Bruiser spotted something. 'Looks like a door in that ice wall,' he said.

Hettie and Tilly followed the beam of light, and there, nestling in the ice, was indeed a door. 'Do you think it's an ice tunnel?' asked Tilly, beginning to feel a little vindicated.

'There's only one way to find out,' said Hettie, giving Bruiser the nod to open it.

The door opened easily, suggesting that it was in constant use. It revealed a long passageway, which could easily be described as an ice tunnel. Like the cellar, the walls and floor were thick with ice and the ceiling was arched, giving just enough height for the average-sized cat to walk through. Hettie shivered. The cold was intense now, and she was beginning to feel claustrophobic. She desperately wanted to turn back, but she knew it wasn't an option. Tilly seemed to be coping, and she took strength from that as Bruiser pushed on ahead of them. The tunnel was long, with what seemed to be a never-ending journey of twists and turns. In places, the walls ran with water, creating ice pools, and Tilly found out to her cost that some were deep, coming up over her wellingtons as she splashed through them. Eventually the tunnel began to widen out, and Hettie's keen hearing became aware of strains of music – coming and going at first, then becoming more continuous. Bruiser heard it too and looked back at Hettie, waiting for instruction. She hesitated, trying to decide whether to go on and follow the music or to retreat and enlist extra help: Bruiser was a fighter and could handle most situations; Tilly had been known to strike out with her claws on occasions; and she, Hettie, had a credible temper that could easily turn to violence if necessary. Her mind was made up. If Anthea and Preston Munch were at the end of the tunnel, she and her friends were ready for them.

The three friends moved forward together. There was now a glimmer of light at the end of the tunnel, and Bruiser switched off his torch. The music grew louder, and Hettie detected a chorus of infant voices as well. For some unknown reason, she thought they would find themselves back in the Great Hall, where the rescued kittens were having a sing-song, but she was wrong.

The tunnel opened out onto a balcony overlooking a giant cave, decorated with huge sparkling stalactites hanging from the roof. Like the tunnel, the walls were thick with ice, and leading down from the balcony where they stood was a staircase sweeping to the floor below. To one side was a frozen blue waterfall that reached from the top of the cave to the bottom, and the whole effect was breathtakingly beautiful.

Hettie moved forward to peer over the balcony, and gasped at the scene below. In the centre of the cave's floor was a glass throne, mounted on a dais. Upon the throne sat Anthea Munch, wearing a golden gown bedecked with jewels. The gown had a giant white fur collar, which stood up against her neck, and above that the crown sat on her head. Below her stood eight little kittens, dressed in red cloaks and white bonnets, all singing their hearts out to an old-fashioned wind-up gramophone operated by Preston Munch, who seemed to be wearing some sort of royal livery in gold and midnight blue; as Hettie would say later, he looked even more ridiculous than Anthea. The whole ensemble was like the grand finale in a rather lavish pantomime, and Hettie had to use every ounce of self-control not to laugh and give the game away. She signalled to Bruiser and Tilly to follow her back into the ice tunnel, where they could discuss what to do next.

Once they'd reached a safe distance, Hettie gave her first impressions. 'They are both completely off their trolleys,' she said, not wanting to mince her words. 'Clearly Anthea Munch thinks she's the bloody Ice Queen reincarnated, and I suppose he fancies himself as Hugo Nightspark. The whole set-up is just like Fluff's wall painting.'

'There were eight kittens,' said Tilly. 'That means that two of them might be Camay and Comfort.'

'Are you saying that we've been looking for kittens who haven't gone missing?'

'Well, we only had Anthea and Preston's word for it, and if they've been keeping the other six girl kittens in that ice cave, goodness knows how long they've been there. It must be weeks since they all went missing from the town. Camay and Comfort can only just have joined them.'

Hettie shook her head. 'We've been taken for fools in all of this. Bombazine was right again about the lies and this business of one to serve and one to wield power. Preston was clearly under Anthea's control all along – she obviously wears the crown. The big question is why? What are they trying to achieve? The school at the Folly was a good idea, so why would they want to burn it down and scuttle off to play some weird dystopian parlour game?'

'Because it's not a game to them,' said Tilly. 'They've created a parallel world with their rules, using the Folly as a front. We got too close to rumbling them, so they burnt the Folly down and took refuge in the world they've created, using those poor little kittens as Ice Maids to wait on them paw and foot.'

'They're welcome to it, but we've got to rescue those kittens. We need to be careful, though – we know that the Munches are more than happy to sacrifice kittens to save their own necks, so we need a plan.'

It was time for Bruiser to add a few words of wisdom. 'The singin's stopped, so we'd better head back to the cellar in case they get wind of us. I think we need more help. These tunnels are like rabbit warrens. We gotta get all exits covered and smoke 'em out.'

Hettie could see the sense in what Bruiser said. Her instinct was to attempt a rescue there and then, but, if they failed, she knew that the kittens would be the first to suffer. They made their way back to the cellar and climbed up to the kitchen, replacing the trapdoor and leaving it how they'd found it. It was good to get out in the air again, and the temperatures – though cold – were positively tropical compared with those in the ice tunnel. Hettie and Tilly clambered into Miss Scarlet's sidecar, and Bruiser drove them across to Wither-Fork Hall, where Blackberry was putting on a nursery tea, assisted by Bonny.

The number of kittens at the Hall had dwindled. Fluff had received two calls so far in response to Hacky Redtop's front page, and Daz and Omo had been joyously reunited with their families, leaving five kittens to tuck into sausage sandwiches and chocolate cake. Windolene was awake and taking tiny sips of beef tea, but she still looked very weak and ill.

Bonny piled up three plates, but Hettie uncharacteristically waved hers away. 'Thank you, Bonny,' she said, 'but I need to speak to Fluff urgently.'

'Why don't you phone her from the kitchen?' suggested Blackberry, sensing Hettie's keenness to get to the Lodge. 'It'll be much quicker.'

Leaving Bonny with Windolene, Blackberry took Hettie into the kitchen and dialled the Lodge for her. Fluff was engaged to start with, but Blackberry got through on the second attempt and left Hettie to discuss the bizarre subterranean world of the Munches and the need for more paws on deck. After a long silence, just to take in what Hettie was telling her, Fluff agreed to send some of the residents over to the Hall from the allotments, reminding Hettie to take a good look at the tunnels marked on the Wither-Fork map. Before ringing off, she asked for a progress report on Windolene; Hettie was able to say that there was a very small improvement.

In Hettie's absence, Tilly took a much closer look at the fresco. She was astonished by how alike the painting was to the ice cave, even down to the blue waterfall, which she now recognised to one side of the image. It was as if the artist knew the cave well, and had painted what he or she recalled from memory rather than illustrating an old story.

When Hettie returned to the Great Hall, she found Bruiser and Tilly tucking into their sausage sandwiches. She polished hers off in record time, allowing herself an extra large slice of chocolate cake while she waited for Fluff's rescue party to arrive from the allotments. 'I think we'd better take a look at this map before the others arrive,' she said, posting the last piece of cake into her mouth. 'We need to know where that ice cave is in relation to all these tunnels.'

Bruiser was much more savvy when it came to maps, and cast an eye across the maze of tunnels. 'My guess is that the cave is below Wither-Fork Hall,' he said, tracing the map with his claw, 'and there are several tunnels leadin' from it as far as I can make out. One of 'em comes up in this icehouse marked here. There's another underneath the church, and some really long ones that stretch away into them woods.'

'So we'll need cats stationed at all those entrances,' said Hettie. 'I just hope we'll have enough troops to cover them.'

'There must be other caves,' suggested Tilly. 'We've only seen the big one, but the kittens must sleep somewhere. I can't see Queen Anthea putting up with them in her throne room.'

'If she lets them sleep at all,' Hettie pointed out.

'I think we should go in by this icehouse,' said Bruiser. 'That tunnel from the Folly's a long one. We could station someone over that trapdoor to stop 'em escapin', but the icehouse is much closer to the Hall – and if we're rescuin' kittens, it's less distance to get 'em out.'

'That sounds like a plan,' agreed Hettie. 'If we focus on the rescue and get as many cats as we can to cover the entrances to the other tunnels, we should stand a good chance of sorting this nightmare out. I agree with Tilly – there must be other areas where those kittens are kept, and with a bit of luck we'll be storming the tunnels around their bedtime. Hopefully we'll find them all together, without any help from the Munches.'

'What will we do with the Munches when we've caught them?' asked Tilly.

'Off the top of my head, I honestly can't think of a punishment bad enough to fit their vile crimes,' said Hettie, looking over to where Windolene was still fighting for her life. 'The most important job at the moment is to get those kittens out of their clutches.'

Fluff arrived minutes later with reinforcements, and two female cats whom Hettie didn't recognise. Brillo and Duster obviously knew them, though; they both abandoned their chocolate cake and bounded across the hall to be reunited with their mothers. There was much screeching and crying, more from the mothers than the kittens, and Fluff escorted them back to her Lodge to await a taxi home.

'Just Jaycloth, Vim and Ajax to go,' said Tilly. 'How lovely to see some happy endings. I hope the other mothers turn up soon. It would be nice to see Jaycloth go home. He's been so brave, and he deserves a happy ending.'

Hettie agreed, but had other things on her mind. There were still eight kittens to be rescued, and it was getting dark. They needed to find the entrance to the icehouse, and station all the helpers at the other tunnel entrances. Bruiser called everyone to order, telling them that their mission was to stop anyone escaping; he then allocated the stake-outs. Rooster Chit agreed to guard the trapdoor at the Folly; Apple Chutney and Desiree Chit were sent to the crypt in Wither-Fork Church; and Bonny Grubb grudgingly agreed to station herself in the woods, as long as she could borrow an extra warm shawl from Blackberry.

The party set off in various directions, taking walking sticks and garden tools to defend themselves should – as Bruiser put it – a 'situation' arise. Blackberry had plundered the kitchen drawers for enough torches to go round, and Hettie had chosen a lantern to carry, which she lit before leaving the Hall. Jaycloth, Ajax and Vim watched anxiously from the French windows as the cats disappeared in the fast fading light, not truly understanding what lurked beneath them in the cave below Wither-Fork Hall.

Oblivious to the danger they would soon have to face, Anthea and Preston Munch sat down to a grand dinner in their cave, served by eight little Ice Maids who bowed their heads, did as they were told and hoped that Jesus would eventually come to save them.

Chapter Twenty-Two

With the help of Fluff's map, Hettie, Tilly and Bruiser quickly located the icehouse. It looked like a giant snow mushroom, and stood in a dip close to Wither-Fork Lake. Since the introduction of fridges and freezers, it had become redundant in the life of the mansion. No longer did the kitchen maids have to chip away at giant blocks of ice to preserve the food they served, and there was no need for the ice to be hauled from the lake in winter and stored in the strange-looking building.

The icehouse had a short, brick-built tunnel entrance, leading to the giant dome. Bruiser went ahead, followed by Hettie and Tilly. The tunnel opened out into a deep well with a rounded ceiling, and Hettie was the first to stare down into it. 'Well, I don't fancy climbing down there, for a start,' she said. 'I can't even see the bottom.'

'There's a ladder we can use,' observed Bruiser, 'but we'll 'ave to be careful as it's all iced up. You'll 'ave ta leave that lantern at the top, 'cause you can't climb an 'ang on to it. I'll go first.' Without waiting for any further comment from Hettie, Bruiser pushed his torch inside his jacket and began to descend slowly into the bottom of the icehouse. Hettie abandoned her lantern and followed on, but Tilly hesitated at the top.

On reaching firmer ground Hettie looked back up the ladder. 'What are you waiting for?' she asked.

'I'm not happy about heights,' said Tilly. 'I'm not sure I can manage.'

'This isn't the time to lose your nerve. You managed the ladder to rescue Lavender Stamp, didn't you? So pull yourself together and climb down – you're holding us up.'

Hettie knew that her strict approach was the only way to get Tilly to abandon her fears, and it worked. Tilly put her torch in her pocket and began the descent. There was one heart-stopping moment when she slipped and lost her footing, but she soon recovered herself and completed the task successfully, earning a pat on the back from Bruiser and a look of great relief from Hettie.

At first they could see no evidence of a tunnel entrance, and Bruiser examined the walls carefully. There was a small ice pick lying on the floor, clearly used by the servants in days gone by to chip away at the ice. Bruiser picked it up and began hacking away at the frozen walls, which came away in giant chunks, splintering and flying in every direction. Hettie and Tilly looked on, ducking to avoid some of the larger shards as Bruiser continued to wield the pick. He was about to concede defeat when a large section of ice fell away from the wall in a single lump – and there was the tunnel entrance, guarded by a rusted grille that gave way easily in Bruiser's paws.

The tunnel was similar to the one under the Folly, but with less headroom. Bruiser stooped as he took the lead, shining his torch onto the frozen floor as he went and avoiding the ice pools. He stopped every few yards to listen for something that might indicate a sign of life. The tunnel was surprisingly noisy, with the constant dripping of water magnified by a hollow echo that reverberated around them. Soon there were choices to make: the tunnel split in two directions and Bruiser shone his torch onto Fluff's map, but this time it was no help.

Bruiser elected to take the tunnel on the right. The three cats continued in silence, not knowing what or who they might find at the end of it. Eventually it opened out into a small chamber, which – surprisingly – had no ice on the walls. It was a cavern of rock, and much warmer than the tunnel. There were signs of habitation: a bundle of rags had been tossed into a craggy recess, and there was a cauldron of what looked like black tar in the centre, next to a wooden block. Tilly moved to investigate, sweeping the beam of her torch across it and shrinking back when realisation dawned. 'Look!' she whispered. 'There's blood on it. Lots of blood.'

Hettie and Bruiser examined the block. Tilly was right, and Hettie suddenly knew exactly what she was looking at. 'It's a butcher's block,' she hissed. 'This is where they chop the tails off. Look – there are bits of fur mixed with the bloodstains, and tufts all over the floor, too, so the poor little things must have put up a fight. And this pot of tar – I bet they've been using that to cauterise the wounds. It's like a bloody chamber of horrors!'

Bruiser decided to investigate the bundle of rags. They were also covered in blood, and had presumably been used for mopping up after the docking took place. Next he found a small axe; the implement – also bloodied – was clearly the weapon that had parted the kittens from their tails. 'Poor Windolene,' said Hettie. 'They must have brought her here and botched the job. Obviously she managed to escape somehow. No wonder she went into hiding.'

Bruiser decided to arm himself with the axe. He put his claw to his mouth, warning the others to keep quiet, having detected the faint sound of something in the distance. Hettie and Tilly could hear it as well, and they crept slowly towards it, out of one chamber and into another. This room was stacked from floor to ceiling with enough food supplies to last for several winters: tins, packets, boxes, jars and bottles, and – in the colder parts, where ice had formed – dead rabbits, hares and even a small muntjac deer hung from hooks hammered into the wall. Hettie was astonished by how thoroughly the Munches had set up their underground world. 'They must have been planning this for months,' she whispered, as they moved forward into yet another tunnel.

The faint sound suddenly became much louder, and it was clearly the monotone voice of Preston Munch. Hettie, Tilly and Bruiser walked on, taking care not to make a sound. The chamber ahead of them was bathed in candlelight, and the three cats stood in the shadows and watched as Preston Munch systematically chained eight little kittens by their necks to metal rings in the walls, reciting the Lord's Prayer as he went. One by one, the kittens sank to the floor in their chains, taking comfort from a thin layer of straw and their red cloaks. Their bonnets had been removed to reveal bright, staring eyes and tiny heads, giving them back a hint of individuality which was normally obscured by the starched hats. Hettie noted that there were two ginger kittens amongst them, and hoped that they had finally found Camay and Comfort.

'May Jesus keep you safe till the morning,' intoned Preston, blowing out the candles. 'Blessed be the fur.'

'Blessed be the fur,' came the weak reply from the kittens. Preston's footsteps receded, and only the occasional pitiful snuffle from the bedchamber broke the silence.

Bruiser turned on his heel and led his party back the way they'd come, where it was safer to discuss their next move. Back in the chamber of horrors, he offered his thoughts. 'Them chains are goin' to be impossible to break without makin' lots of noise,' he whispered. 'I think I can do it with this axe, but it'll take time and them Munches'll be on us before we've got any of them kittens free. Best plan is ta knock out the Munches first, I reckon.'

Hettie could see the sense in what Bruiser was saying; she was concerned that the kittens might give them away just from the sheer joy of being rescued. 'So what do we do?' she asked.

Bruiser thought for a moment, weighing up the possibilities. 'I think Tilly should stay with the kittens and keep 'em quiet. They need ta know we're on their side and that we're goin' ta get 'em out. You and me will find out where the Munches are and sort 'em out. We might even get the key to them chains if we're lucky.'

Tilly was pleased to get the best job, and Hettie – though a little nervous – welcomed the opportunity to have a go at the Munches with Bruiser by her side – or more especially in front of her. And so it was decided, and the three friends made their way back to the bedchamber. Tilly moved swiftly from one kitten to another, putting them at ease and asking them to stay silent. As she shone her torch at them, she could see how scared they were and how much their movement was restricted by the metal collars around their necks. She was happy to stay with them, but felt cheated of the chance to strike her own blows at Preston and Anthea for meting out such cruelty.

Hettie and Bruiser left the bedchamber, and – after negotiating a short tunnel – found themselves in another cave which was clearly used for the preparation of food. There was a giant fire basket stacked with logs in the centre of the room, and as Hettie looked up at the craggy ceiling, she could see a deep fissure in the rock above that allowed the smoke to escape. The logs smouldered, giving out very little heat, but there was evidence that cooking had recently taken place. It would seem that the Munches had enjoyed their dinner before chaining up their servants and putting them to bed for the night.

They listened for an indication of how close they were to the Munches, but everything was strangely silent. Another short tunnel led to the giant ice cave where Anthea had been sitting on her throne. The cave was lit with candles, and Hettie and Bruiser crept towards it, feeling a radical change in the temperature as they progressed along the tunnel.

'Welcome to the Halls of Glass,' came a voice from behind them. 'Thought you'd drop in on us unannounced, did you?' Hettie felt a sharp point in her back as Preston Munch used a long-bladed kitchen knife to encourage her to move forward. Bruiser looked back, but there was nothing he could do in the narrow tunnel except step into the ice cave, where Anthea's gaze fell upon him. She sat on her throne and nodded as Preston forced their unwanted visitors to stand in front of her, making Bruiser drop the axe. 'Bow down to your Queen,' he ordered, 'and ask for mercy before I cut your throats.'

Hettie and Bruiser lay motionless on the icy floor in front of the dais, and Anthea Munch looked down on them. 'So, you dare to enter my kingdom and sneak around my ice palace?' she said. 'The penalty is death, of course, but I shall allow you three questions before you die. Who will speak?'

Hettie lifted her head. 'I will.'

'Very well,' said Anthea. 'Ask your questions and go to your grave with my answers. They will do you no good there.'

Hettie sat up and Bruiser tried to do the same, but Preston sprang on top of him, pulling his head back and putting the knife under his chin. 'No need for you to move a muscle,' he hissed. 'As soon as the questions are over, I'll pull this knife across your throat nice and deep and slow, so your friend here can see what she's getting next.'

Hettie's mind was racing, and she wondered what had happened to Tilly. Had Preston discovered her? Was she lying somewhere with her throat cut? And there was nothing she could do to help Bruiser. The situation was hopeless, and all she had between her and oblivion was three questions. She dug deep for some courage, and asked her first. 'What made you want to set up an underground world in the ice caves?'

Anthea put her head on one side as if considering the question, then quickly straightened it again when her crown threatened to topple off. Hettie wanted to laugh, mostly out of hysteria for the predicament she found herself in, but she managed to control herself as the self-appointed Ice Queen began to speak. 'I am descended from the Ice Queen of the Winter Lands,' she said. 'This is my destiny, and in this place my word is law. I command my subjects, and they serve me to the end of my days. One shall inherit my crown when I go to rest in my ice tomb. What is your second question?'

Hettie wanted clarification on all the points that Anthea had raised, but she realised that it wasn't a two-way conversation. She was dealing with a cat who was completely insane, devoid of any normal thought and totally schizophrenic, and who clearly believed that she *was* the Ice Queen; in her delusionary world, she was capable of anything. Choosing her words carefully, Hettie asked her second question. 'Why do you choose female kittens to wait on you and dock their tails?'

'It is the highest honour I can bestow on my subjects to offer them eternal life as my Ice Maids. The tail-docking ceremony is sacred, and gives the maids the joy of knowing that they belong to me. It is their badge of honour,' Anthea added. 'In time, they will multiply into an army of Ice Maids and will fight for their Queen and rule the earth in my image. Your final question?'

Hettie looked at Preston and realised just how instrumental his role was in Anthea's master plan: as the only male cat, he would be the father of her Ice Maid army. His knife was still across Bruiser's throat and she knew that this was the final curtain, but what should she ask? Then it came to her. She prostrated herself on the icy floor and began to pray out loud. 'Dear God, please forgive Preston for breaking your commandments. May he find peace in heaven after this terrible deed is done.'

Preston's resolve to cut Bruiser's throat wobbled long enough for a tin of baked beans to crack him on the back of his head, followed swiftly by a tin of sardines which hit Anthea between the eyes. The knife slid across the ice, and Anthea toppled from her throne with a crash. Hettie hardly dared move but twisted her head to see Tilly, armed with a selection of tins which she was lobbing indiscriminately at the Munches. Anthea received an additional tin of spaghetti hoops between her shoulders, followed by a can of cream of mushroom soup, and Preston succumbed to some marrowfat peas before being knocked to the ground by a tin of meatballs in tomato sauce.

The Munches lay in a tangled heap at the foot of the dais with their paws above their heads, pleading for Tilly to stop her canned food onslaught. Bruiser grabbed the set of keys that dangled from the belt of Preston's livery, then retrieved the knife and the axe from the floor. Hettie joined Tilly, hoping that there were still some tins left to throw at the Munches, but she had to make do with a small can of mixed vegetables and a jar of pickled onions; they both found their mark with a satisfying thud and an even more satisfying cry from Anthea, who now looked more like an Eton mess than an Ice Queen.

Hettie moved forward again to deliver a little message of her own. 'We're going to relieve you of your Ice Maids now and leave you to your evening. We have all the exits covered, so there's no point in trying to escape, and the best news is that the thaw has begun and the tunnels are running with water. It's only a matter of time before the caves flood. When they freeze again, you'll be part of the ice walls, just like your so-called ancestors.'

Hettie, Tilly and Bruiser left the Munches licking their wounds and headed back to the kittens in their bedchamber. Bruiser made light work of unlocking the collars, and the kittens – pulling their red cloaks tightly around them – were marched through the larder cave and the chamber where their tails had been docked, with Hettie in front and Tilly at the rear. Bruiser hung back to make sure that the Munches weren't attempting a counter-attack.

The tunnel which led to the icehouse was filling up with water; as Hettie had said, the thaw was well and truly underway. Hettie made the kittens hold paws to form a chain as they sloshed through the tunnel. The ice on the ladder at the bottom of the icehouse had melted, making it easier to climb, and the lantern which Hettie had had to abandon was now a comforting light to aim for. One by one, they emerged into the open, where they were greeted by a half moon and a sky full of twinkling stars. Bruiser secured the grille to the tunnel, then leapt up the ladder to join Hettie and Tilly as they shepherded the eight little kittens across the melting snow to Wither-Fork Hall for a blazing fire, a hot supper and the comfort of clean warm beds.

Chapter Twenty-Three

It was quite some years since Bonny Grubb had spent a winter's night under the stars. These days, the gypsy cat preferred her home comforts and had no thought of moving on. She'd put roots down at Wither-Fork, and made friends she could trust. Her van was comfortable, she enjoyed her allotment, and she loved working with Blackberry up at the Hall when circumstances arose. Tonight, she was cold. The woods dripped from every branch and bush as the snow turned to pools of water, bringing a dank and desperate isolation to the landscape. Gone were the beautiful, folded drifts of snow and the magical eerie silence they created, only to be replaced by the death of what seemed to be a long ago summer – black and dark in its intensity, and offering as yet no hope of spring.

The tunnel entrance that she'd been sent to guard was little more than a hole in the ground, overgrown with brambles and barely visible. She was pleased to have the light of the moon for company, but it was no comfort as she shivered beneath Blackberry's borrowed shawl. She decided to light a fire, and found some dry wood and moss in the hollow of an old oak tree. After several attempts to get it going, she succeeded with the last match in her box. Soon the fire was established and she settled by it, staring into the flames and mesmerised by the colours which the burning wood threw up into the night sky. Very soon she was asleep.

Chapter Twenty-Four

Anthea and Preston Munch lay bruised and beaten at the foot of the dais. Their ice cave, like their dream, was melting before their eyes: the giant frozen stalactites that hung from the ceiling were crashing around them, and the blue ice waterfall was beginning to wake from its suspension, sending rivulets of water onto the cave floor. Anthea's elaborate gown was already soaked, and the fallen Ice Queen could only whimper as the waters approached like some advancing army, come to claim her crown. She had lost her power, and now she would die in a watery tomb of her own making.

'This is all your fault,' she hissed, throwing her crown across the floor, 'letting those cats into the Folly to poke their noses in, and worst of all allowing Windolene to escape during the ceremony, then pretending she'd gone missing with Camay and Comfort. I trusted you, and this is my reward.'

Preston wasn't listening. He was concentrating on a much higher power. Hettie's last-minute intervention before he'd managed to slit Bruiser's throat had made him think, and now, in this hour of crisis, he was praying for forgiveness. The list of his sins was a long one. He hoped his prayers would be heard, and that God would understand how difficult it had been to say no to Anthea's demands. She had dominated him from the moment they'd met, hatching her schemes for supremacy in all things and coercing him into a way of life that he knew was wrong. He thought he loved her, but – as the waters filled the cave – he realised it had all been for nothing. All he wanted now was a sign that God had at least forgiven him. It came from the heavens, swift and painless. A giant icicle fell from the roof of the cave and embedded itself in Preston's heart. He died instantly, while Anthea was still blaming him for her downfall.

The shock of his instant death didn't immediately register, but when it did her howls brought down a rain of icicles and her cries echoed around the cave. For the first time in her life, she was completely alone. Her kingdom was melting around her, the Halls of Glass was shattering before her eyes, and soon she would be washed away to some deep underground rock pool, where her body would freeze and melt with the seasons until there was nothing left of her at all.

Anthea had always regarded herself as a survivor. In her right mind she was aware of the demons that beset her, but more recently they had become the driving force in her existence. They'd discovered the ice caves by chance after moving to the Folly. The old copy of

Albertine Chop's book – which she'd found when they were converting the schoolroom – had become her bible, and she had grown to believe that anything was possible. Now that Preston was dead, there was no one to support the extreme and radical life for which her other self yearned. She shrank further into the gown she'd so regally worn as the Ice Queen, but the game was over; she could allow the waters to take her, or she could try to escape the punishment which she knew in her heart she deserved.

As the cave began to fill with water, her mind was made up. She'd find her way back to the cellar under the Folly and surrender to whoever was guarding it. She'd explain that Preston had forced her into the whole scheme, that he'd lied about the missing kittens to cover his tracks, that he had set light to the Folly and murdered the boy kittens when his plans began to unravel; now he was dead, she was free of him and ready to put things right in any way she could. The more she thought of her latest plan, the more convinced she was that it would work. Without Preston to mess things up, at least she stood a chance.

She pulled off the gown that was now heavy with water and threw it over Preston's body, pleased to be relieved of his staring eyes. It left her naked and vulnerable, which was perfect for the role she was about to play: poor Anthea Munch, survivor of a controlling relationship, saved by fate and set free of the cat who had consumed her life and made her do unspeakable acts of cruelty. She would play the victim and bring the house down.

Anthea climbed the giant staircase up to the balcony – just in time, as the waterfall finally broke free of the ice and gushed down into the base of the cave. She didn't look back, but entered the ice tunnel that would take her to the Folly. It was colder here, and she shivered. The walls were intact for some distance, but as she progressed towards the Folly, she could see that the tunnel ahead was full of water and impassable. Anthea began to panic. She couldn't turn back, and the route ahead was impossible to wade through. As she studied the walls of the tunnel, she noticed recesses where the ice had fallen away and, to her relief, she found one that she could crawl into. It was a tunnel of sorts, and it appeared to climb upwards. The aperture was narrow, and there was no light to give her any indication of what lay ahead. She scrabbled with her front paws, and crumbling bits of rock gave way to soil as the tunnel climbed to the surface. Soon she sensed a change in the fetid air; there was a freshness, and – unless her eyes deceived her – a flickering light ahead. She paused to rehearse her new role in her head: victim; repentant survivor. Of course they would believe her. She clawed her way along the final few feet and popped her head up into a thicket of brambles. The light she'd seen was a small campfire, and she recognised the gypsy from the Wither-Fork allotments, wrapped in a shawl and sleeping soundly.

This was the luck she had never expected. Anthea pulled herself free of the brambles and tiptoed past the sleeping cat. Perhaps no explanation would now be required, she thought; she was free, and it would be assumed that she had drowned in the ice cave along with Preston. She was born again, given a second chance – and she meant to take it.

The wood was a relief after the horrors of the caves and tunnels, and she decided to follow a well-trodden path rather than strike out into the tangle of bushes and fallen trees. She was convinced that the sleeping gypsy was her only companion in such a vast area of woodland, and she hoped to put as much distance between them as possible.

'You look lost my dear,' came a craggy voice from behind her. Anthea froze, then slowly turned to see Bombazine Bright. The ancient cat leaned heavily on a knotted walking stick. 'You look in need of a warm fire and a cup of my special tea.'

Anthea had been caught out, but her original plan could still be easily executed. Instantly she became the victim she'd rehearsed, agreeing to follow the witch back to her cottage. There she told her story, and Bombazine listened through clouds of catnip, puffing thoughtfully on her clay pipe. The tea she'd brewed was bitter, but Anthea drank it nevertheless, wanting to look grateful. It was the very last thing that she ever did.

Chapter Twenty-Five

Hettie, Tilly and Bruiser received a hero's welcome when they returned to Wither-Fork Hall with their eight rescued kittens. Blackberry sprang into action immediately with hot tomato soup and nursery sandwiches which she'd cut the crusts off. The kittens joined Jaycloth, Vim and Ajax, and there was a grand reunion of sorts. Hettie was thrilled to see that Windolene was sitting up, sucking noisily on a cheese triangle and looking much better.

There was much discussion around the fire after the kittens had been put to bed. Blackberry had managed to establish that Camay and Comfort were amongst the new arrivals, which was a great relief to Hettie, who was now able to call an official end to the search. Fluff had come over from the Lodge to congratulate The No. 2 Feline Detective Agency on a magnificent rescue mission. Tilly beamed as much praise was given to her tinned food assault on the Munches, which had saved Bruiser and Hettie, and Fluff was satisfied that Anthea and Preston had got what they deserved. To be left to die in the flooded caves somehow seemed perfect justice for the cruelty and terrors they'd put the kittens through, and now there was no chance of their repeating their crimes elsewhere.

Fluff rose from the fire. 'I'll bid you all a goodnight,' she said, turning to Hettie. 'You're most welcome to stay if you can't face the trek home. It seems to have been a very long day for all of us. I daresay tomorrow will be busy, too. It appears that I now have ten kittens to reunite with their families – a joyful task, but not without its complications. And I had some bad news about Jaycloth earlier. It seems that his mother was so distraught when he went missing that she simply stopped eating and died. Her neighbour called me after seeing his photo in the paper. His real name is Archie – my late father's name, actually, and altogether nicer than Jaycloth, but he's now a genuine orphan unless I can trace some extended family.'

'Does he know?' asked Hettie.

'No,' said Fluff. 'I thought he'd been through enough at the moment, but I'll have to say something because his friends, Vim and Ajax – or should I say Miles and Monty – are being collected by their mothers in the morning, which means he'll be the only boy kitten left.'

Fluff looked like she was about to say something else, but changed her mind. She crossed to the row of camp beds, where all the kittens were fast asleep, and took a closer look at Windolene. She was snuffling contentedly into her blanket, and looked so much better after Blackberry's care. Fluff hoped with all her heart that she, at least, would have a happy ending. She turned towards the door, and left without another word to sit and think long into the night in her armchair at the Lodge.

It was nearly midnight, and Hettie decided that she would much rather wake up in her own armchair than spend another night at Wither-Fork Hall, even though the breakfasts were excellent. 'I think we'd better be making tracks,' she said, tearing herself away from the fire. 'Before we leave, we'd better just check all those tunnel entrances to make sure that the Munches haven't made a final bid for freedom. The tunnels and caves will be well under water by now. It should be safe to stand our stake-outs down, as I'm sure they'll be wanting to get to their beds.'

Bruiser fired up Miss Scarlet, and Hettie and Tilly clambered into the sidecar, weary but pleased that the Ice Maid's Tail case – as it would be called from now on – was finally solved. There were a few loose ends, of course, but most of those belonged to Fluff Wither-Fork herself, and Hettie knew that all the rescued kittens were in a very safe pair of paws.

Bruiser drove to the church first, and Hettie skipped out to tell Desiree Chit and Apple Chutney that they could return home. She checked the old tunnel entrance in the crypt, and was satisfied to see that the water level was high and that the grille guarding the entrance was securely locked. Bruiser headed for the Folly next, and Rooster Chit came out to greet them, announcing that the cellar under the kitchen was full of water and that he'd had no sign of trouble throughout the evening. Relieved of his post, he set out across the parkland to his boathouse on the allotments, where Desiree – who'd just got home – had put the milk on for his bedtime drink.

'Just the woods to go,' said Hettie. 'I think Bonny drew the short straw. I wouldn't want to be stuck in there on my own at night. We'd better give her a lift back to her caravan on the allotments.' The three cats left Miss Scarlet parked by the burnt-out Folly, and – guided by Fluff's map – set a good pace through the woods until they could smell smoke. Bonny's fire had dwindled, but she was still fast asleep.

'Bonny!' shouted Hettie. 'Wake up!'

Bonny Grubb jumped at the sound of her name. She was disorientated for a moment, trying to work out why she was in the middle of a wood with Hettie, Tilly and Bruiser. 'Sorry,' she muttered. 'I must 'ave nodded off there for a minute. I got cold, see. I lit me a fire and just shut me eyes for forty winks, that's all.'

Hettie was taking a close look at the tunnel entrance, barely listening to Bonny's excuses. 'Shine that torch on this,' she said to Tilly. ' I thought so! This bramble's got some ginger fur caught in it.'

Bonny blinked, realising that she might have fallen down on the job. 'Maybe it was a ginger rabbit,' she offered. 'Or a stoat? Or weasel?'

Hettie shook her head. 'No, Bonny – this is cat hair. Did you check the tunnel when you got here?'

'I did 'ave a look over it, but I didn't go down there on account of them brambles. I didn't see no ginger fur, though. I'd have noticed that.'

'Then we have to assume that a ginger cat has come out of this tunnel while you were asleep,' said Hettie crossly.

'Maybe it's one of them gingery kittens that's gone missing?' suggested Bonny, trying to put a positive spin on the situation.

'No, that's not possible. All the kittens are tucked up in bed at Wither-Fork Hall.' Hettie was trying to keep her temper under control. 'There's only one ginger-haired cat likely to come out of that tunnel.'

'Anthea Munch!' chorused Bruiser and Tilly.

'Exactly!' said Hettie. 'So we'd better start looking. For all we know, Preston might be with her as well, which means we've failed miserably.'

Bonny now understood the enormity of her indolence and stood up, ready to help with the search. Bruiser kicked the fire out and the four cats spread out in a line, moving forward with their torches trained on the woodland floor for anything that might offer a clue.

Hettie's mind was racing. The Munches had proved to be a formidable enemy, and if they had escaped a watery grave in the ice cave, she was certain that they would stop at nothing to put their vile schemes back on track. Searching Wither-Fork Woods was a thankless task: it was dark, slippery from the receding snow, and now it was starting to rain.

Bonny spotted it first, as everyone else had their heads down. 'Look!' she cried. 'Through there – it's the Magic Tree!'

All eyes turned to a blazing light up ahead, and there, as if it had just landed from another planet, was the Magic Tree, shining its light on an open patch of ground. They approached with caution and, as they grew closer, the tree revealed more than just ribbons and dead birds hanging from its branches. Hettie had mixed feelings about what she was seeing, relieved and horrified in equal measure. The ginger cat hung by its neck from one of the lower branches, her fur drenched from the rain. She looked strangely peaceful.

'Not a pretty sight,' came a familiar voice from behind them.

Hettie turned to find Bombazine Bright standing on the edge of the glade. 'Do you know what happened here?' she asked.

Bombazine grinned, and hopped from one foot to another in some sort of shuffling dance, her eyes now as bright as the buttons on a military cat's tunic. In that odd moment, it occurred to Hettie that Bombazine had been a very beautiful cat once, inside and out. The hag they'd met the day before had somehow transformed herself into something very different. 'You'll take some tea out of the rain?' she said, waving her stick at a path through the wood before turning on her heel and moving away into the darkness.

As if in some sort of trance, the four cats followed her and were soon settled by the fire in her small cottage. The kettle seemed to boil as soon as Bombazine touched it, and this time she spooned proper tea into an old teapot that had lost its lid before Hettie and Tilly were born. The milk came from a tin. It was thick and sweet, and the witch cat stirred it into five cracked mugs and passed them round her visitors. The tea tasted good, and was very welcome. Slowly they began to dry out after the rain, but no one spoke; all were waiting to see what Bombazine would say or do next.

She sat back in her chair, savouring her tea and enjoying the warmth of the mug on her arthritic paws. Her claws were extended and long, like the talons of an eagle. Under different circumstances, Hettie would have loved to quiz her about her own history, but just now she needed to know how Anthea Munch had ended up hanging from the Magic Tree.

Bombazine obliged after noisily draining her mug and spitting into the fire. 'Them's that tinkers with fires gets burnt,' she began. Tilly reached for her notepad, expecting another riddle, but Bombazine's words held no mystery this time. 'She came out of that thicket like a rat,' she continued. 'All pleased with 'erself, past the sleepin' gypsy, thinkin' she'd got away with it. I took 'er in and she gave me 'er sorry tale, tellin' me 'ow he'd forced 'er into wickedness, stealin' them young'uns, torturin' them, burnin' them in their beds. The lies just fell out of 'er! She cried and wrung 'er paws as she sipped me special tea, then just like the old Ice Queen in Albertine's story, she died.'

'You mean you poisoned her,' said Hettie.

Bombazine smiled again before replying. 'Some teas don't suit all. I was just bein' hospitable. P'raps it wasn't me special tea – who can say?'

'So how did she end up hanging from your Magic Tree?'

'I puts all sorts of things that I finds in the woods on that old tree. I found 'er in the woods, so I puts 'er up there with the rest of the bits and pieces. I found them cats' tails in the woods, too. There's more, but I 'aven't got round to them yet 'cos of the snow.'

Surprisingly, Hettie found everything that Bombazine Bright said perfectly reasonable. Perhaps it was because she was exhausted and in need of sleep, but she felt that there was real justice in what the witch cat had done. There was still a question to be answered, though. 'Did Anthea say what happened to Preston Munch?' she asked.

'She said 'e was struck dead by an icicle and lies in the 'alls of Glass,' Bombazine cackled. 'Nice end to 'is story.'

'And a perfect end to ours,' agreed Hettie, relieved to know that the Munches' reign of terror was now over. She was pleased that none of them seemed to have had any ill effects from Bombazine's tea; it obviously wasn't special enough, and now it was time to go home. She stood to leave and Bruiser led the way out of the cottage, followed by Bonny, but Tilly lingered. While Bombazine had been talking, she had found herself taking in every detail of the cottage: the old china plates; the horse brasses; the pots of herbs, all labelled; the hag stones that hung from the beams; the rusted horseshoes; and a rather fine collection of paintings. There was something very familiar about those, and, as she stood to leave, she realised what it was. 'Miss Bright,' she said, 'you have some lovely pictures. Do you know who painted them?'

'Bless you. That was me in another life,' said Bombazine. 'I always loved me paints. When I was a girl, I fell in love with the wrong cat – 'e was high born, and not for the likes of me. Before we parted, I painted a picture on 'is wall for 'im to remember me by, and 'e loved it so much that 'e gave me this cottage and the land around it. 'E married a beautiful cat and lived 'appy ever after, and I never saw 'im again, but 'is little girl used to visit me and dance for 'er stories.'

'Was that little girl Fluff Wither-Fork?'

Bombazine smiled. 'She was a lovely dancer, and Archie Wither-Fork was the love of my life, but Albertine Chop was my mother and that would never have done in them high circles. She was a bad'un, easily led by old Jenkin Cowdiddle. She cast me off as soon as she could, took 'erself off to the big 'ouse pretendin' to be a nanny – no mother at all, really. I lived in the old Folly for a time, doin' me paintin' till I got this place. Gave me a chance to explore them ice caves – very inspirin', they were, them and Albertine's book. That's all I have left of 'er – that, and the memory of 'er 'angin' from the Magic Tree. She got what she deserved for bein' so cruel to them Wither-Fork kittens. Just like Anthea Munch, really – no escapin' the day of judgement.'

Tilly left the cottage in the woods with her mind completely at rest. Something had been troubling her, and she now knew that it was the paintings she'd seen during their first visit to Bombazine. At last it all fitted into place, the Ice Maid's Tail was a completed jigsaw.

Chapter Twenty-Six

The late winter blossomed into a glorious spring. The No. 2 Feline Detective Agency had become a national news story after Hacky Redtop serialised the downfall of Preston and Anthea Munch in the *Daily Snout*. Bruiser was up for a national hero award, and Hettie and Tilly's phone hadn't stopped ringing with requests for interviews and a whole load of new cases for them to solve. Hettie was being picky about their next job, as Fluff Wither-Fork had paid them handsomely for the return of all the lost kittens, and she decided that they deserved a 'lazy spring'. It seemed that life in the town would take some time to get back to normal. When the story first broke, the townsfolk were besieged by journalists, all keen to put a different spin on the sensational case of Preston and Anthea Munch. Hettie, Tilly and Bruiser found it difficult to progress down the high street without being congratulated by the many grateful parents whose kittens had been safely returned to them, and the walls of their bedsitter were adorned with thank you cards and paintings which the kittens had created in their honour.

Lavender Stamp had been run ragged with the sheer volume of postcards and letters that she'd had to deliver to Hettie and Tilly from well-wishers, and Betty and Beryl were enlisted to help sort through them in case any required a reply. The invitation from Fluff Wither-Fork had almost been missed in the mountain of mail, but Beryl noticed it and passed it on.

'Fluff Wither-Fork's having a party!' said Tilly excitedly, abandoning her *Top Cat* jigsaw. 'We're all invited. It's on Friday at six o'clock in the Great Hall, and we've got to RSVP.'

'Is there going to be food?' asked Hettie, focusing on her priorities.

Tilly took a closer look at the invitation. 'It says there's going to be a running buffet.'

'Well, that's a date, then. I'll go and tell Bruiser. He's been stuck in his shed for days, up to something. All I know is that it includes a lot of hammering and banging about.'

'Maybe he's got a new hobby, or perhaps he's making something for Miss Scarlet?' Tilly suggested.

'It's a secret, whatever it is,' said Hettie. 'No doubt he'll tell us when he's ready.' She left Tilly to finish Officer Dibble's uniform, and struck out down the Butters' garden path.

****

Wither-Fork Hall looked resplendent in the spring sunshine as Bruiser drove Miss Scarlet through the Lodge gates. It was only a matter of weeks since the house and parkland had been wrapped in blizzards and ice; now, crocuses and daffodils lifted their heads in the sheer joy of their displays, and all of nature darted in and out of burrows and nests, celebrating the promise of warmer weather to come.

Poppa's van was parked outside the Hall when they arrived. He was sitting in it, reading a newspaper, and Bruiser shot off the bike to have a private word with him while Hettie and Tilly clambered out of the sidecar. 'Bruiser's being *very* secretive,' said Hettie. 'He's been like that for weeks.'

'Well, whatever he's up to, it's bound to be lovely,' said Tilly, lifting the giant knocker on the door to Wither-Fork Hall.

Blackberry Tibbs took her time in letting them in. Her kitchen had become an operational centre, primed and ready to feed over a hundred guests for Fluff's party, and Tilly's summons coincided with another batch of sausage rolls being rescued from the oven, while yet more miniature Cornish pasties took their place. 'Sorry I took so long,' Blackberry said, wiping her paws on an apron whose stains read like a rather agreeable menu, with hints of jam, flour, tomato sauce, beef gravy, custard and cream. 'Miss Wither-Fork will be over in a minute to do the meeting and greeting, but you're the first to arrive, so come in and make yourselves at home. Bonny was helping me, but she's gone off into the woods for some reason.'

The Great Hall looked magnificent. A fire roared in the grate, taking the chill out of the old walls, and the chandeliers sparkled and threw a magical light onto Bombazine's fresco, which seemed to have taken on a far less sinister appearance now that the legend of the Ice Maid's Tail had been finally laid to rest. Hettie marvelled at the trestle tables placed at the back of the hall, now groaning under the weight of Blackberry's labours: a giant joint of beef; several large chickens; decorated hams; and a whole salmon, all beautifully presented. The golden brown pastries were almost too perfect to be real, and the sweet table required closer inspection, so Tilly crossed over to do the honours. 'Oh look!' she cried. 'There's a swan made of meringue sitting on a nest of green jelly. And look at that tower of profiteroles! And a bowl of chocolate to dip them in. I love choux pastry!'

'You love any sort of pastry,' said Hettie, distracted from the food by a curious structure, covered with a blanket, that she recognised from Bruiser's shed. She was about to take a peep when the formidable sound of Fluff Wither-Fork's voice rang out across the hall. Fluff welcomed them, followed by Jaycloth and Windolene, who bore no resemblance now to the kittens rescued from the clutches of the Munches. The two young cats bounced across the hall, eager to greet

Hettie and Tilly and squealing with delight, then offering the same welcome to Bruiser as he arrived with Poppa.

'I see you still have Jaycloth and Windolene,' observed Hettie. 'No luck in finding their families?'

'It depends what you mean by luck,' said Fluff, looking slightly mischievous. 'We managed to return the rest of them – even Camay and Comfort, whose mother had died before they were abducted. They're now living happily with their aunt, and I hope they'll all be with us today.'

The guests began to arrive and Fluff went into perfect hostess mode, sharing a brief conversation with each newcomer as Blackberry – now changed out of her apron – took charge of a tray laden with glasses of sparkling wine, and orange juice for the younger guests. Hettie and Tilly recognised all the kittens from the Folly, done up in their Sunday best and clambering over each other in the joy of their reunion. Their grateful relatives looked on, thankful to Fluff and The No. 2 Feline Detective Agency for their deliverance from evil.

Hacky Redtop arrived with Prunella Snap to record the event for the *Snout's* society page, and Bruiser found himself under siege from the kittens, all desperate to have a picture taken with their hero. The residents from the allotments turned up *en masse*, mingling with Fluff's numerous acquaintances from the town – the Butter sisters and Lavender Stamp, and the entire volunteer fire brigade, who turned up in style on Lazarus Hambone's old fire engine.

When Fluff was satisfied that all her guests had arrived, she clapped her paws to attract everyone's attention. The chatter and clinking of glasses gradually died down as she made her way to the fireplace to address her audience. 'I'd like to take a few moments for some thank yous,' she began, 'but first I want to say how deeply sorry I am for trusting Preston and Anthea Munch, and allowing them onto my land to perform such cruelty. I was very fortunate to have The No. 2 Feline Detective Agency at my disposal throughout that terrible time, and I owe them a great debt of gratitude, which is impossible to repay.'

A cheer rose up from the guests as Hettie, Tilly, Bruiser and Poppa received a standing ovation; it was some time before Fluff was allowed to continue. 'I am indebted to Hacky Redtop's assistance in reuniting the lost kittens with their families, and to the residents here at the Hall for responding to my call to arms when it was most needed. A special thank you to Blackberry, who cooked and kept house, as well as becoming nurse and nanny during some of the most difficult days in Wither-Fork's history.'

A murmur of congratulations went round the crowd, and Blackberry stared shyly at her boots. 'The history of Wither-Fork Hall is a rich one, and, for me, a burden,' admitted Fluff. 'I look around the walls at my ancestors, knowing that I have failed to provide a future for the family line. Until a few weeks ago, I had accepted that Wither-Fork would have to pass out of the family after my death. I am delighted to say that this is no longer the case. Many of you here will know that I have been trying without success to trace the families of two of the abducted kittens. Jaycloth and Windolene, as they were formerly known, are genuine orphans. Today, I have had papers drawn up to adopt them both officially, and they will now be named Archie and Dulcie Wither-Fork. In the fullness of time, they will inherit the house and lands that have been in my family for generations.'

Archie and Dulcie beamed from behind the trestle table, where they'd each been nibbling on a sausage roll. They were too young to understand the enormity of what their benefactor had said, and were, for now, just happy to spend their days rattling around Wither-Fork in joyful contentment, knowing that the horrors of the Folly and all it conjured up were behind them. Archie had loved Dulcie from the moment he'd set eyes on her, and now their future would be together in all things.

'I just knew she was going to adopt them,' said Tilly joyfully.

'They've certainly landed on their paws,' said Hettie, 'and they deserve it after what they've been through. They'll thrive here at Wither-Fork. But why has Bruiser stepped forward? He's not going to give a speech, is he?'

Tilly giggled. Bruiser was a cat of very few words, especially in front of a crowd, and he made no attempt to speak, even though he was wearing his newly dry-cleaned waistcoat. It was Fluff Wither-Fork who continued with the announcements after calling Archie and Dulcie to come and stand beside her. 'I have commissioned a very special gift for my adopted kittens in the hope that they will learn to love this house and everything in it, just as I do. Mr Bruiser has spent many weeks on this, and he will now reveal it.'

Bruiser pulled his blanket off the structure that had so intrigued Hettie, and the crowd gasped as an identical dolls' house replica of Wither-Fork Hall was revealed. It was nothing like the sad, sinister little house that had played a large part in Hettie and Tilly's most recent case, and Archie and Dulcie squealed with delight as they and their friends from the Folly investigated Bruiser's work.

'So that's what he's been up to!' said Hettie. 'I suppose Poppa delivered it here in his van. We've been conspired against, but what a magnificent job he's made of it.'

Tilly's faith in dolls' houses was instantly restored as she marvelled at the detail, noting that all the tiny cats in the house seemed to be having fun, eating, drinking, reading and playing with the things that made growing up a joy.

With all the kittens occupied by Archie and Dulcie's new toy, Fluff nodded to Blackberry, who wheeled in her catering trolley, covered by a rather lovely piece of red velvet. In a moment of perfect timing, Bonny Grubb burst through the French windows with another cat who was clearly dressed for a party. Fluff beckoned them over to the fireplace, and waited for the attention of the room.

Tilly and Hettie stared open-mouthed at the latest arrival. 'I don't believe it! It can't be!' whispered Tilly.

'It is,' said Hettie, moving closer to the fireplace for a better view as Fluff clapped her paws again.

The room fell silent once more, curious to see what would happen next. With a flourish, Fluff removed the red velvet to reveal a stack of books. 'You will, I'm sure, be aware by now of *The Ice Maid's Tail*, a book written a long time ago at Wither-Fork by a former nanny here at the Hall. I have had the book reprinted and it will be sold throughout the tourist season, which starts tomorrow when we open our doors to the public once again. All proceeds will go to a new charity I've set up to help homeless cats and kittens, called The Archie and Dulcie Trust.'

The applause and cheering began again, but Fluff held up her paw, signalling that she hadn't quite finished. 'And now I come to a very special guest, a cat whose life has been bound to Wither-Fork out of love. Here, behind me, is her gift to my late father – a magnificent interpretation of *The Ice Maid's Tail*, now restored for all to see. I have taken the liberty of reproducing the fresco on the book jacket, and I now hope for the artist's approval. Let me introduce to you Miss Bombazine Bright.'

Bombazine shed many of her hundred years as she stared at the painting she'd created, remembering every brushstroke she'd made. To be back at Wither-Fork Hall, approved of and even revered, was more than enough magic for the cat who – as a young girl – had fallen hopelessly in love with the lord of the manor, and had had to live a solitary life, so close and yet so far away from the love she most desired.

Fluff Wither-Fork's guests erupted into unbridled merriment, clapping and cheering. Prunella Snap pushed through the crowd to capture Bombazine as she posed in front of her fresco, holding a copy of Albertine's book. An orderly queue formed at Blackberry's trolley, keen to snatch a copy before they went on general sale, and Bombazine was besieged by cats who wanted her to sign them.

'How strange that she's signing copies of her mother's book,' observed Hettie, joining the book queue with the intention of treating Tilly to a copy.

'I think it's a lovely ending,' said Tilly. 'Just like *The Ice Maid's Tail*, where everyone lives happily ever after.'

Postscript

For years to come, everyone would remember the party at Wither-Fork Hall. Fluff's guests ate, drank and were fantastically merry. Bombazine Bright had the time of her life and danced the night away, and was eventually escorted back to her cottage on Bruiser's arm. That night she died happily in her bed, knowing that her love letter to Archie Wither-Fork would be admired by the thousands of summer visitors who took afternoon tea in the Great Hall.

On Fluff's instructions, she was buried in the crypt of Wither-Fork Church, close to where Archie lay in his tomb. Her cottage became an added attraction to the visitors, and it is said that on frosty cold nights her ghost can be seen dancing round the Magic Tree.

THE END

Acknowledgements

As a child, fairy tales terrified me; as an adult, I can see why. In spite of all those well-known characters like Sleeping Beauty, Snow White and Little Red Riding Hood living happily ever after, it is the darker moments of their stories that have stayed with me, and we are repeatedly reminded that all the bad characters in those stories are just plain wicked. And so, in *The Ice Maid's Tail*, I wanted to create a story with a fairy tale at its heart, inhabited by witches, gypsies and a healthy dose of necromancy, all set against the backdrop of a land devoured by ice. I hope I've succeeded.

There was no shortage of inspiration for this book. There is an obvious nod to the work of Margaret Atwood, a brilliant writer who has created a terrifying world that is more truthful than fictional. I owe a great debt to my conversations with Lady Victoria Leatham for her insight into the running of a great English house at Burghley; Fluff Wither-Fork is a tribute to her. The grounds at Burghley provided me with an understanding of ice houses, and the magnificent kitchens, servants' quarters and nursery of Lanhydrock House in Cornwall offered me a wonderful step back in time, beyond the rope.

At the centre of this book is an anger aimed at those who take joy in the cruelty they inflict on animals; it is beyond my comprehension, and although my characters are all cats, the wicked ones also possess human traits that are perhaps less comfortable in this setting. Those who hide behind an air of benevolence may recognise themselves here, and those who seek to control the destiny of others may hopefully recognise their limitations before it is too late.

On a brighter note, it is always a joy to continue Hettie and Tilly's journey beyond the days when we had to say goodbye to them in life. They were, and still are, very fine cats, now joined by Bruiser and Molly Bloom. Wherever their spirits rest, Nicola and I know that they have never really left us. And finally to Nicola, who has laughed and cried in all the right places; without her love and encouragement, I doubt that Hettie and Tilly would ever have stirred from their fireside in the little room at the back of the bakery.

My thanks go to my editor Abbie Headon, Pete Duncan and all at Farrago; to Jason Anscomb for another fine book jacket; and to Jenny Funnell and all at W.F. Howes. 'Blessed be the fur!'

About the Author

Mandy Morton was born in Suffolk and after a short and successful music career in the 1970s as a singer-songwriter – during which time she recorded six albums and toured extensively throughout the UK and Scandinavia with her band – she joined the BBC, where she produced and presented arts-based programmes for local and national radio. She more recently presents The Eclectic Light Show on Cambridge 105 Radio. Mandy lives with her partner, who is also a crime writer, in Cambridge and Cornwall where there is always room for a long-haired tabby cat. She is the author of The No. 2 Feline Detective Agency series and also co-wrote *In Good Company* with Nicola Upson, which chronicles a year in the life of The Cambridge Arts Theatre.

Twitter: **@hettiebagshot** and **@icloudmandy**
Facebook: **HettieBagshotMysteries**

Also available

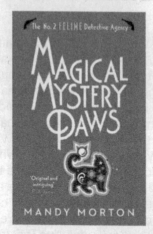

All aboard for the Summer of Fluff!

Meet **Hettie Bagshot**, a long-haired tabby cat whose whiskers twitch at the first sign of a mystery, and her best friend **Tilly Jenkins**. Together, they run **The No. 2 Feline Detective Agency**, and nothing will stop them from untangling each brain-teasing case that comes their way.

In scorching temperatures, Hettie Bagshot and her sidekick Tilly set out on a road trip to catch a killer cat amid a sea of entertainers. As Psycho Derek's bus lurches from one venue to the next, the killer strikes again. The big question for The No. 2 Feline Detective Agency is who will be next?

Will it be Patty Sniff, the ageing punk star? Or Kitty O'Shea from the Irish dance troupe? Or perhaps Belisha Beacon's days are numbered. As the fur flies and the animosity builds, Hettie and Tilly become embroiled in a world of music, mayhem and murder. As matters draw to a terrifying conclusion, will **Magical Mystery Paws** finally top the bill?

OUT NOW!

Also available

What mysteries lie beyond the gravy?

Psychic cat Irene Peggledrip is being visited by a band of malevolent spirits who all claim to be murderers. Not only is their message disturbing, but they cause chaos with indoor snowstorms, flying books and the untimely demise of a delicious Victoria sponge. Irene calls in Hettie and Tilly of The **No. 2 Feline Detective Agency** to help, but they're not sure how far their skills reach into the spirit realm.

Meanwhile, Lavender Stamp, the town's bad-tempered postmistress cat, has some good news to deliver to Tilly: she has won a competition to take afternoon tea with renowned mystery writer Agatha Crispy at her Devon home, Furaway House.

Will Hettie and Tilly finally lay the ghosts to rest? Can Molly Bloom's new café survive the seance? And will the moving claw give up its secrets before the gravy congeals? Find out in this latest adventure of **our favourite feline sleuths**.

OUT NOW!

Coming soon

A Pocket Full of Pie

The Town is preparing for The Great Easter Bake Off, but why are the contestants dropping like flies? As the pastry cutters come out, who will be next?

Hettie and Tilly are brought in to get to the bottom of this murky mixing bowl. Will the celebrity cook Fanny Haddock get her just desserts? And could the pigeon and partridge pie become a deadly game?

Join Hettie and Tilly, our feline sleuths, as they get to the crust of the matter and turn up the heat on this cat-a-strophic culinary disaster.

Note from the Publisher

To receive updates on new releases in The No. 2 Feline
Detective Agency series – plus special offers and news of
other humorous fiction series to make you smile – sign up
now to the Farrago mailing list at farragobooks.com/sign-up.